String Theory

Guitar Store Mysteries, vol. 2

Bing Turkby

First published in 2023 by

Guitarmerston North Books

Palmerston North

Aotearoa/New Zealand

Copyright © 2023 Bing Turkby

All rights reserved.

ISBN (Paperback): 978-0-473-68152-4

ISBN (ebook): 978-0-473-68153-1

Cover art and design by Jeroen ten Berge

The moral right of the author has been asserted.

String Theory

Chapter 1: Phosphor bronze

The sign above the Pick Me guitar shop swung in a gentle breeze, flashing strobes of reflected morning sunlight as if it was one of those fancy rack-mounted guitar tuners. Dana looked up at it and smiled as she unlocked the front door.

She loved her little shop. She was happy spending her days surrounded by nice guitars. Owning a guitar shop had always been her dream.

Her brother Ziggy would have loved it too, she thought, as she passed the giant tour poster on her way back to the counter. As always, she rested a hand on his picture for a second in acknowledgement. *I'm going to find out what happened to you, Zig,* she promised him, as she did every morning. Thanks to a friend with industry contacts, she now had some leads to follow in that regard. Soon she would meet with one of the last people to see her brother alive.

She couldn't dwell on that now. That was for later, and she had a shop to run. Dana placed a new guitar in the window, and it glowed in the morning sun like a stone that you pick up on the beach, that you can almost but not quite see through.

Don't worry, little guitar, she mentally apologised to it, I won't leave you in the sun for long. She knew how guitars didn't like that kind of thing, being predominantly nocturnal creatures. Also, their paint faded.

She went to the back room to unbox another instrument, and by the time she returned, her eager young shop assistant Brody was chatting with a customer. Dana smiled. Craig, the customer, basically lived in the shop. He must have been waiting nearby, ready to pop in as soon as the door was unlocked. He always had an oddball theory he wanted to expound. Dana was having trouble figuring out what today's topic was, so Brody brought her up to speed.

'Craig reckons that, since everything in the universe is made of matter, everything vibrates at a certain rate.'

'Frequency,' Craig interjected. 'Everything in the world has a certain resonant frequency. You know, like when you sit in a certain corner of a room and speak at just the right pitch, the whole room vibrates with it?'

Dana nodded. She had actually done this. If she

could be said to have such a thing as a party trick, this would be it. People were really freaked out by it, and they often took some persuading that she wasn't using a hidden amplifier.

'Right, so it's like that for everything in the whole world. In fact...' Craig started to swing his arms around wildly. Dana subtly moved some effect pedals and strings out of range. '...the whole actual planet has its own resonant frequency. All the land masses are in F.'

'Wow.' Brody looked fascinated. He loved this stuff. 'What about the ocean?' he asked.

'Oh, that's mostly in C.'

Dana groaned, and threw her hands up in disgust. 'I'm outta here. I didn't sign up for all the dad jokes.'

'What?' said Craig. 'It's true.' He was still pleading his innocence at Dana's back as she left the shop. 'C major for the oceans, C minor for the rivers!' he called out.

Dana's life had gotten a lot easier since Brody proved himself capable of looking after the Pick Me guitar shop all by himself. She didn't know how he'd cope with a busy crowd, but she really didn't have to worry about that, as one had never materialised. She absolutely trusted Brody to sit there and listen to Craig spout ridiculous musical theories, and sell the odd set of strings. Really, what more could she ask for?

It meant that she could now pop out to the supermarket or the hairdresser whenever she felt like it, which was an absolute luxury after years of being tied to the counter. She felt like a proper aristocrat. Not that there were many of those in Rockingham West. Dana's hometown was the epitome of small-town Aotearoa New Zealand, and that's what she liked about it. Still, a bit of daydreaming never hurt (no matter what her teachers had told her when she was a kid.)

Yes, she could see herself as the Duchess of Rockingham West, swanning around town, taking time to decide which type of cheese to buy, hardly a care in the world. Hmmm… what kind of cheese would a Duchess buy?

Dana chuckled to herself. As she drove to the supermarket in a falling-apart Volkswagen Beetle, she had to admit that glamorous wasn't really her style. She could do glam rock, in a pinch, but that was as close as she got.

Dana bought a few groceries, and then on her way out of the shop, she spotted Wade McNeish over in the far corner of the carpark. Well, this was awkward.

Wade was the policeman she'd worked with to track down the killer of local guitar teacher Gene Stevens a little while ago. OK, to be fair, it was actually her cat, Paws McCartney, who'd found the crucial clue, but Dana had done the legwork.

And, okay, to be even more truthful, she hadn't actually worked *with* the Police, so much as… hmmm… how would you say? Gone expressly against their wishes.

Constable McNeish and his boss DCI Mary Shaw had been intent on jailing a young guitar prodigy who was a student of Gene's, but Dana had a strong suspicion he wasn't the perpetrator, and she'd put her neck on the line to prove it.

After Dana and Brody vindicated themselves by bringing the real killer to justice by their own… idiosyncratic means, they'd been given the clear message to stay away from any police matters in future, and she hadn't seen Wade since.

Honestly, she was still a bit grumpy about the whole deal. Hadn't she solved the case, after all?

Now she thought about it, it was Detective Mary Shaw who had warned her off, not Wade. And he'd always been kind to her, so she gave him a cheery wave.

He caught sight of her, and instead of simply waving back, he walked over.

Crap, now Dana had to hurry to stuff her groceries in the car before Wade saw what she'd bought. She didn't want him thinking that the only things she planned to have for dinner tonight were two packets of instant noodles, two large tubs of cookie dough ice cream, and three mega packs of cat food. She assumed he'd realise the cat food was for Paws McCartney, but the rest was damning enough in itself.

Having reversed into the carpark, it meant that the front-facing luggage compartment of the Beetle was now in plain view, but she managed to slam it shut before Wade got too close.

'Hi, Dana,' he called out as he approached. 'How've you been? Haven't seen you in a while.'

'Well, yeah,' Dana straightened her blouse, 'if you recall, it's because I was banished by the high and mighty DCI Shaw.'

'Hah! True, she got her nose out of joint. But to be fair,' Wade wagged a finger at her, 'you did almost ruin the whole case.'

'Pfft! You lot were going to throw an innocent kid in jail, so I say it was worth it.'

'Hmmm.' Wade didn't look convinced. 'Anyway, Shaw might have cooled down a bit since then.'

'Oh,' said Dana. 'Does that mean you need my help on another case?'

'No, I just meant that she probably won't taser you on sight now.'

Dana sniffed. 'Great.'

'I mean, there probably aren't too many guitar-related cases on our books right now, anyway, Dana.' Wade laughed. 'I bet that was a bit of a one-off, you know?'

'I kind of hope so, Wade. I don't particularly enjoy thinking about death and killing very much. I'd far rather be playing guitar. Whereas you, I suppose, have to think about crimes all the time.'

Wade scratched his chin. 'Yep, it's the job, alright. Like, at the moment, we're working on a murder where the guy was garrotted.'

Dana was shocked. 'Oh no, that's horrible.'

'Yeah, it's a pretty rough way to go. And there are no fingerprints, or rather, too many. It was in a place where there were a whole lot of people coming and going. Anyway, we're hoping the residue on the victim's neck might be able to be identified. Seems like the killer didn't use just any old wire - it was some mixture of bronze and something else.'

'Phosphor bronze, maybe?'

Wade stared at Dana, his jaw slowly dropping, like a tired elevator. 'Yes, actually. It was phosphor bronze,' he finally said. 'Are you flipping kidding me? How did you know that?'

'Are you sure you want me to tell you? Or will you and Shaw just get mad at me again?'

'Oh, no.' Wade's shoulders sagged. 'You're going to say it's guitar-related, aren't you?'

'Quite possibly.' Dana shrugged, and turned to grab her trolley. 'But you know, the Police don't want me involved in this kind of thing any more,' she said breezily, 'so I guess that's the end of that.'

Wade's sighed a sigh as heavy as an Ozzy Osbourne album.

'Okay,' he said. 'I know I'm going to regret asking this, but I can't help myself. How did you know it was phosphor bronze?'

Dana turned back to Wade and crossed her arms. 'Well, I didn't know for sure. It's just that, you see, I sell a lot of guitar strings. A *lot*. And the most popular acoustic guitar strings I sell are phosphor bronze. So I see those two words in close proximity all the time. Which is why, as soon as you said bronze, my mind supplied the phosphor part. And, you know, I guess if a killer were looking for something handy to garrotte a person with, a guitar string would be perfect for the job.' Dana tilted her head to one side. 'I mean, I assume it would be. Not having a lot of experience in garrotting people, myself.' She shuddered.

Wade shook his head.

'Crikey. Ahhh, hell.' He scuffed a boot on the ground, then looked up at Dana. 'If, ah… hoo boy, here we go, I'm actually going to say this. If you were allowed to come and take a look, do you think you'd be able to tell for sure if it was a guitar string that did it?'

'Yeah, I think so. Wait.' Dana felt a chill down her back. 'Do you mean if I came to take a look at a dead body? Like, a person who's been strangled to death?'

'That's the idea, yep.' Wade puffed out his cheeks. 'Look, Shaw might not even go for it anyway, given your history. But if you can help us with the case, I'm of the opinion we should use your expertise. I think I can talk her round. And hey, listen. Yeah, you'd have to inspect a cadaver. It's never a lot of fun. But I'd be there with you the whole time. What do you say?'

Dana grabbed the shopping trolley and pushed past Wade. She hoped to run over his toes with it, but he had good reflexes, and stepped out of the way in time.

'Here's what I say,' she huffed. 'I say that the New Zealand Police send mixed messages. First it's all "stay away from this stuff". Next, it's "hey, actually, can you help us again?"' She slammed the trolley into the trolley park. It made a very satisfying clangour as the shockwaves rippled down the line from one trolley to the next. A small part of Dana's brain catalogued that sound as a potential percussion element for a song she was working on. (Draft title: *Found Sounds From Around Town*.)

Wade held up his hands in surrender.

'That is absolutely a fair thing to say. But, can I tell you something?'

Dana stuck her hands on her hips. 'Fire away.'

'I know that Shaw was unhappy about the way you blundered about in the last case we worked on together.'

'Blundered about? Me and Brody figured everything out for you, then handed you the killer on a plate!'

Wade bobbed his head. 'Yyyyeessss… Which is another way of saying that you and Brody broke into someone's house to obtain evidence illegally, and then almost got yourselves killed too.'

'Potato, tomato,' Dana replied.

'I think it's po-tay-to, po-tah-to.'

'This is more different than that.'

'Riiiiight.' Wade successfully suppressed ninety-five percent of a smile at this Dana-ism. 'Anyway, given all that palaver, I can understand why DCI Shaw said she didn't want you near any more cases in future.'

Dana sniffed. 'Your loss.'

'*Her* loss,' Wade replied. 'But maybe not mine.'

'What do you mean?'

'Well, I'm just spitballing here, but you see, the thing is, Dana. I thought you were a really valuable member of the team. I thought you brought some great insight, not to mention your local musical knowledge.'

'Bit of a moot point, if I'm not allowed to get involved any more.'

'Right, but bear with me.' Wade smiled at one hundred percent this time. 'Shaw knows how useful you were too, but she'd never admit she was wrong in banning you. However, I happen to have a wee bit of budget left for consultants this year. So I could hire you myself, and Shaw won't have to know about it.'

Dana narrowed her eyes. The money would certainly come in handy. She might even be able to replace the old sofa that Paws McCartney had been incrementally destroying for the last few years. Still, once bitten, twice shy and all that.

'Two questions,' said Dana eventually.

'Hit me.'

'One. How did you wind up with leftover money? Last time I was at the station I saw officers sweetening their coffee with packets of sugar they'd swiped from cafes.'

'Well, if you must know, I recently misplaced an informant who was on the payroll.'

'Careless. I usually find it helpful to think back to where I last saw the thing I lost. Where'd you last see the informant?'

'Out at the landfill.'

'He works at the landfill?'

'No, he was *in* the landfill.'

Dana grimaced. 'You really know how to sweet-talk a person into helping you.'

'Don't worry, this case won't be so dangerous.'

'How do you know that?'

Wade rubbed his chin. 'I dunno, it just seems less… gang-y.'

This did not fill Dana with confidence. But she was already halfway to saying yes to the gig. Not so much for the money, but more because she knew she could help out in a guitar-related case, something that not many other people could say they had experience with.

'Okay, question two. How will you keep my involvement secret from Shaw? Are you thinking you'll just claim all the local musical insights as your own? She's not an idiot, you know.'

'It's not like I'm going to lead you into the station

wearing a tiara and singing show tunes,' Wade protested. 'I just need the odd nudge in the right direction. And anyway, pursuant to that - '

'Pursuant. I like it.'

'Thanks, learned it at police school.' Wade cleared his throat. 'If I may proceed? Thank you. Pursuant to that point, Shaw is letting me take the reins on this one. She'll be doing the odd bit of oversight, but she's busy with a bigger case.'

'Bigger than murder?' Dana was taken aback.

'It's a multi-regional thing. Drug-running throughout the country, suspected Tajikistani gang involvement, horse conversion, you name it.'

Dana's brow furrowed. 'Is horse conversion a euphemism?'

'Not in this case, no.'

'Oh. Hence "take the reins". Got it.'

'Oof! No, that pun wasn't intended.'

'A likely *tail*.'

Wade knew when he was beaten, so he joined in. 'I can see you're champing at the bit to get involved, so what do you say? Are you in?'

Dana shrugged. 'Why not? I'm not one to look a gift horse in the mouth.'

'You really should, you know,' Wade replied. 'You can tell a lot about a horse's overall health from the condition of its gums, gift or no.'

Dana rolled her eyes. 'Alright, alright, enough horsing around.' She turned serious. 'When can I go and have a look at the victim?'

'Why the hurry?' asked Wade. 'Is your dinner melting, or something?' He gave her a wink and headed off.

Dana's ears burned, and she glared at Wade's receding form. Damn that cheeky, perceptive policeman.

'I'll text you later this afternoon,' Wade called out over his shoulder. 'Nice to be working with you again.'

Spatters of rain began to pelt Dana as she gave a rueful smile.

He'd keep.

Chapter 2: Mr Two the guitar tech

The Beetle's vintage wipers did valiant battle with the rain as Dana drove her grocery-hoard homeward. She felt like a Viking returning after a successful raid, except she was in a car rather than a boat, she was on a sealed road not a whale road, and nobody got injured or captured during her mission. Apart from all those things… yeah, Viking raid.

Dana could see sunshine on the ranges to the south of town, so she knew this rain would pass on by. She often tried to imagine what the land would have looked like a couple hundred years ago, before Pākehā – European people living in Aotearoa – built the town of Rockingham West.

It would have been a bugger of a place to try and drive a VW, that's for sure. Swampy and forest-y. But it would have been nice to have seen the area when it was still covered in trees, and resounding to the haunting calls of the native birds, many of which were now extinct.

The rain eased to a persistent mist, as if the sky was crying over the fate of its feathered children.

Dana actually liked the fact that it rained often in Rockingham West. It meant there was usually enough to keep the local water reservoir full. It wasn't the only weather-related bonus: there was more than enough wind to keep the town's wind turbines turning too. Whenever she was tempted to curse at the wind for blustering at her, she reminded herself that it helped keep the lights on.

With an eye on the road and a hand on the wheel, as per safety guidelines laid out by noted Health & Safety champion Jim Morrison, Dana used her spare hand to flick on the old steam-powered AM car radio. She smiled as she remembered how Brody had freaked out at finding an actual working radio in a car, last time he'd been a passenger. She had to remind herself that compact discs were museum pieces to his generation, and cassettes were a cool, new, completely irony-free phenomenon that older people just wouldn't understand.

She knew she was probably supposed to be frustrated by kids saying stuff like that, but she couldn't help herself: she loved it. She loved being just old enough for young people to think she was completely out of touch. Dana had never been especially cool as a young person, so it was a relief to finally be legitimately old enough for young people to sneer at. She'd grown into herself. The pressure of knowing all the right things to say and do was well and truly off her shoulders. Like a classic bass guitar line, Dana found herself sitting easily in the groove of her life now.

She loved the fact that the kids were moving on to cool new things, even if those cool new things were actually nothing more than crappy old things that had been outmoded several decades ago. She was genuinely happy that there were young people out there full of confidence in their awesomeness. Good for them! It was heartening to think that there were people in the world who seemed to know what was going on. Dana sure didn't. She knew guitars, and she knew cats, and she knew her old Beetle, and that was enough for her.

Although, being around Brody and his effortlessly cool bass-playing boyfriend Evan, Dana had started to notice a smidge of their confidence rub off on her. It was a most unusual feeling. She was thinking of getting purple streaks in her hair. To hell with it - why not? Who cares what anyone else thinks?

As she pulled into her driveway she was just starting to ponder whether all the confident people she had ever met had actually just been faking it, which would be both reassuring and at the same time immensely frustrating. If true, and had she known this secret earlier, her life would have been very different. Or at least, her hair would have been.

'Boss! Whassup?' Brody called out as she entered the shop, lugging her dolphin-friendly grocery bags. Dana approved of dolphins, and she hoped they would approve of her if they ever met.

'Really, Brody? Are we in a nineties high school sitcom now?'

'No ma'am, we are not. My apologies,' said Brody, in his best Forrest Gump.

'Crikey, this shop is like a box of chocolates,' Dana responded. 'You just never know which shop assistant's personality you're going to get.'

'Touché,' said Brody with a flourishy bow. For reasons unknown to the fashion agnostic people of Rockingham West, he was wearing a flowing purple silk scarf today, so the flourish factor was very high. His green flared trousers also wanted in on the act. 'Hey, you need a hand with those bags?'

'No, I'm good thanks, B. Just gonna stuff these things away and then, if you're okay holding the fort here for a bit longer I thought I might start to follow up on the names that Gordon gave us.'

'Oh, the people that used to be in Ziggy's road crew?'

'Yeah. I want to strike before the iron gets any colder. It's been a few years already and I'm only just finding out that one of Zig's roadies had his guitar this whole time.'

'Lucky that Gordon knows all the people who need knowing, huh?'

'Correct.' Dana made to head through to the back of the shop to lug her groceries upstairs. 'I can understand how someone who worked closely with Ziggy on his final tour might have ended up with his guitar, but I just can't believe that anyone in a crew that tight would have taken it while Ziggy was dying in a hotel room. And then never told me about it. I just have to find out what happened that day, Brodes.'

'I get it, boss. I'd like to know myself.' Brody cut open a box of guitar strings and began sorting them into piles of different size sets. 'Ziggy was just starting to make it big, and then – bam! The tragedy, and in mysterious circumstances too.'

'Agreed,' Dana huffed, as she passed through to the office.

As usual, Paws McCartney was sitting on her office chair like the world's fluffiest and least attentive store manager.

'Hey, Pawsy,' she called out to the dilapidated old cat. 'Keeping an eye on the accounts, are we?'

Paws raised his head a tiny fraction, regarding the room in resting feline mode without even making direct visual contact with Dana. His head began to slowly relax back towards the chair when suddenly his nostrils twitched. He leapt up and ran to Dana, purring loudly, and generally being the best cat anyone could ever hope to live with.

'Oh, you smelled the cat food did you, Paws?' said Dana. 'Or did you just remember that I brought you home from the SPCA and lavished love and attention on you for the last few years?'

Paws used the medium of purring, meowing and rubbing vigorously against Dana's shins to convey the phrase: Both those things, my favourite human!

Fortunately, Dana spoke Feline to a competent amateur level. She smiled, lugged the groceries upstairs and treated Paws to a little of his best-loved food.

While Paws hoovered up the grub and then set about giving himself a thorough cleaning, Dana changed into her 'interviewing a roadie' outfit.

This consisted of sneakers, ripped black jeans, and an old Motorhead t-shirt. She'd once had the good fortune to see Motorhead play live. If anyone asked her about the gig, she always said that they were louder than great. It was one of her top ten favourite gigs, in fact. Right up there with the time she went to see Billy Idol ironically, but then ended up genuinely enjoying herself as Idol and Steve Stevens tore up the stage.

She chuckled. When it comes to old rockers, you shouldn't underestimate them.

Standing in front of her mirror, she practiced some martial arts moves. Did she feel vaguely ridiculous doing this? Yes. But ever since she'd been attacked by a belligerent guitarist in her last investigation, she'd decided it couldn't hurt to learn to defend herself.

She was small, so she needed to learn something that utilised cunning rather than strength. After remembering that Ziggy used to have a poster of Bruce Lee in his bedroom, she'd done a bit of research and found out Lee had initially learned something called Wing Chun. Although Lee had later moved on and created his own art called Jeet Kune Do, Wing Chun was a great art for someone like Dana, as it favoured close contact, limiting the amount of force an opponent could deliver. Also, it was based on soft, relaxed movements, almost like tai chi. Dana had actually learned a bit of tai chi in the past, but didn't have the three decades or so it took to master it as a martial art, so had gone with Wing Chun instead.

Dana wasn't anticipating any trouble from the roadie she was about to visit, she just tried to fit in a few minutes' practice several times a day, with the intent of making the movements become second nature.

Like any martial arts student, she was aware that her best defence was to run away, but hopefully in a few years' time she might actually be of some use in a fight. Not that she wanted to hurt anyone, she just wanted to have a better chance of not getting hurt herself.

She gave her reflection a tight smile as she remembered how she'd neutralised her attacker in the alleyway behind a shabby pub. She'd been cunning that time, sure, but she'd also been incredibly lucky. She couldn't always count on a guy standing in front of her with legs apart while she held a hefty guitar stand that she could swing at his… ahem … middle tuning peg.

Dana scooted down the stairs, waved to Brody, and headed out.

A few minutes later she Beetled up to the house of one of Ziggy's old road crew. He lived in an older part of town that had been eaten up by gentrification and then ejected out the other end.

Many of the older houses in the area looked like drunken punters at a gig, almost leaning on each other to stay upright, but determined to make a go of it.

Dana was reminded of how fortunate she was to live in her cosy flat above the guitar store, with good insulation and a nice outlook over towards the ranges through the back window. The roadie was probably paying a fortune to live in this semi-ruin of a building. The way rent kept going up was criminal.

She knocked on the door, and heard muffled groans in response, then eventually there were slow footsteps up the hallway.

The door opened just a sliver, and a red-rimmed eye peered out.

Dana cleared her throat. 'Um, is Mr Two in?'

'This is he,' croaked the doorkeeper, in an accent that Dana classified as Off-Brand Jason Statham. 'Who's asking?'

A small cloud of smoke wafted out the door towards Dana's feet. Perhaps the guy was testing out a dry-ice machine for a stage show, or… no, there it was. Dry ice never smelled so sweet. It was a different kind of smoke being created inside the house, which explained the wariness of the occupant. Also the sluggishness.

'It's me, Dana,' said Dana, who was indeed Dana.

The red eye rolled hither and yon as its owner processed this information.

'Oh!' said the guy after a pause just long and awkward enough for Dana to nervously shift from foot to foot a few times, and think about scarpering. 'Ziggy's sister, right? Come in, come in!'

The door was thrown open, so that Dana could finally see the smoke-wreathed person in the hallway. Well, she could mostly see him, although he was somewhat obscured by the haze.

He was thin. Very thin. Dana got the distinct impression that the only things that ever passed this guy's lips were fluids and narcotic fug. His red hair was beginning to lose its colour, and there was the start of a bald patch that was threatening to morph into a monk's tonsure at a later date.

He was bedecked in something long and flowing – maybe a dressing gown? – in brilliant red, gold and green.

A smile was flashed towards Dana, although flashed was perhaps not quite the right term, since the teeth had lost their shine, and indeed some of them were lost altogether. The smile was brandished at her, perhaps?

Mr Two – for she assumed it was he – waved an arm towards an internal room. His gown floated behind him, echoing the gesture. Dana took a big breath of fresh air and entered. It was like venturing into the lair of a stoned dragon with a head cold. The humidity level immediately rocketed. She felt like a human hygrometer.

'Thanks for seeing me,' she went to say, except the thick atmosphere executed an assault on her open mouth and caused her to spend a minute or so hacking out coughs instead.

'Oh, sorry,' said Mr Two. 'Been trying out some new…' His wild eyes roamed the room for inspiration. 'Incense! That my… niece! Brought back from… ummm…' He trailed off, clicking his fingers, looking like he'd lost not just his train of thought but also his ticket of cogitation, his wallet of remembrance, and indeed the location of the nearest synapse station.

'No problem,' Dana wheezed. 'If I could just get a glass of water?'

'Hey, sure thing! Grab a seat and I'll be back in a tiddlywink.'

Dana spotted a window. She went and yanked it open then collapsed in a chair nearby, gulping in the clear air and trying to swat as much of the foggy stuff outside as possible.

A blessedly refreshing breeze puffed hesitantly at the window, then dipped its toe into the room, unsure of its surroundings. Dana surmised that Mr Two probably didn't usually allow such a thing in his house.

The breeze wandered through the room cautiously, wafting here and there. It caught a photograph that was propped on a nearby coffee table, and flipped it onto the floor as if testing its boundaries.

'Hey,' Dana scolded. 'Don't be messing the place up.' She cast her eyes about the room and reassessed her statement. 'Okay, don't be messing it up more than it already is, please.'

She bent and picked up the photo. In it, a young girl beamed a huge smile at the camera. She sat on top of a big old Fender Twin amplifier, and there was a drum kit in the background. It looked like she was on a stage somewhere. Happy amongst the chaos as grown-ups rushed around plugging things in.

Mr Two returned with a respectably clean glass of water and placed it on the coffee table.

'Here ya go.'

'Thanks.' She waved the photo at him. 'Who's the young lady?'

'Oh, that's umm…'

'Must be a musician's kid, I guess?'

Mr Two nodded slowly. 'Yeah. Yep. Musician's

kid from back in the day.' He cleared his throat. 'Here, let me pop that back.'

Dana got the feeling that she'd overstepped. She handed him the photo and he gently placed it on a bookshelf at the back of the room.

'Sorry,' said Dana. 'I wasn't poking through your stuff, it just fell on the floor and I picked it up.'

'All goods, all goods.' He shuffled back over and plonked himself down in a chair opposite Dana. 'Now. You're okay with the water? Sure you don't want something a bit more... you know?' He mimed tossing back a drink then crossed his eyes and stuck out his tongue.

Dana laughed. 'Thanks, but not right now. Important business, you see.'

'Yeah, yeah, man, yeah, of course.' Mr Two stroked his chin. 'You want to rap about the Zig?'

Dana had never rapped in her life. Not in the musical sense, not in the conversational sense, not in any sense that she could recall. She was sure that Christmas presents didn't count. But she nodded anyway, as if she were the rappingest of interlocutors. She was actually starting to enjoy the company of Mr Two – it reminded her of tagging along to gigs with Ziggy, and meeting all the interesting characters that coagulated around a band on the rise. Indeed, she had probably met Mr

Two way back when, but there'd been so many people swarming about Ziggy's successful band that she couldn't keep track.

'Before we start,' said Dana, 'do you mind if I ask you something?'

Mr Two spread his hands wide in magnanimity. 'I thought that's what you were here for, dude.'

Again, being called a dude was not something Dana was used to, but she thought she could pretend to be dude-adjacent for an hour or so.

'I just wondered why you're called Mr Two, if it's not too personal a question?'

'Oh, yeah, yeah, I forget that not everyone knows.' Mr Two settled back into his chair. 'Well, like, word started to get around that I could be done in two minutes, and people started calling me Mr Two Minutes, then it got shortened to just Mr Two.'

Dana blushed. Okay, yes, this was way too personal a question for her to be asking at the start of this conversation.

'Oh,' she stammered. 'Um, right…'

'I'm not just tooting my own tuba,' Mr Two continued, 'most guitar techs would take at least five minutes for a complete guitar string change, but I got it down to a fine art. Old strings gone, new ones installed, all stretched and tuned up - ' he clapped his hands together, 'two minutes flat!'

'Haha! Right, of course,' Dana laughed the relieved laugh of a person who had just successfully steered their ship away from a conversational iceberg. 'Yes, done in two minutes, a guitar string change is what you were talking about, that's cool. You must be very good at your job.'

'Sure, but there ain't a lot of call for it now, like. Most touring bands are cutting down on gear, which means they don't need so many people to look after it neither.'

'I'm sorry to hear that.'

'Yeah, well, the sound engineers are all happy because people are using smaller amps nowadays. Something to do with making it easier to mix the sound out front when the band isn't mucking it up by blasting walls of noise out of huge amp stacks.' Mr Two threw his hands in the air. 'Is that rock'n'roll, though?'

He stared at Dana.

'...' said Dana.

'Is it though?'

'Oh, you're actually asking me?'

'Yes! You tell me. Is it really rock'n'roll, when people gots tiny amps onstage, not making hardly any racket at all?'

'Well,' Dana rubbed her hands on the artfully ripped knees of her jeans, 'it must mean fewer problems with hearing loss, right?'

'Exactly!' Mr Two nearly launched himself right out of his chair. 'What kind of bullshit is that? If you want to be able to hear stuff, take up knitting.'

'To be fair,' said Dana, 'knitting needles are actually quite loud, especially if you're in a group of knitters.'

Mr Two paused for a second, nostrils flaring. 'Is that right?' He gave a nod of approval. 'I might look into that then. Rock'n'roll knitting group, nice one. Might make me a lovely woolly cover for me old guitar amp.'

'Sounds great!' said Dana. She would offer up a substantial chunk of coin to see Mr Two and his rock'n'roll knitting group in action. You know what? She might even join in.

'Anyway,' she said, picking up the fraying threads of the conversation, 'as you pointed out, I'm here to talk about Ziggy.'

'God rest 'im and keep 'im!' yelled Mr Two, his accent getting thicker in proportion to his emotional state. 'Our little 'endrix, he was. Played guitar like he had an 'ell'ound on his trail and a car battery wired to his scrotum.'

'Um, yeah. That was the general consensus,' Dana replied, surreptitiously checking the floor for dropped h's. 'You worked with him several times, is that right?'

'Oh yes! Oh good lord yes, I worked wiv 'im up and down the land.' Mr Two was starting to sound like a draft Monty Python sketch. Dana didn't know if he was becoming more or less authentic as he went on. Either way, it was terrific fun.

'I carried Zig's guitars and amps, I coiled his cables,' the cadaverous roadie continued. 'I stopped drunken punters from spilling their beer on his guitar effect pedals.' He grimaced. 'Well, I tried me best. It were difficult.' He shrugged. 'Specially with a pint in me 'and.'

'Right. I can imagine. It's just, I'm trying to piece together what happened on the day he...' Dana choked on the next word.

'Joined the great jam band in the sky?' suggested Mr Two, with a gentle smile.

Dana gave a small chuckle that definitely wasn't a stifled sob. 'Yes, I suppose you could say that.'

Mr Two got a faraway look in his eye. 'He'll be smoking weed with the baby Jesus right now, I 'spect.' His wistful smile faltered as he glanced back at Dana. 'Oh! Not that the Zig did that kind of fing, of course! Straight as a new car, he was. Subsisted on sunshine and shamrocks. Kind to animals, et cetera and all that.'

Dana laughed, and it was possibly the first time

in years that she'd laughed when talking to someone about her brother. 'It's okay, Mr Two, I know that Ziggy may have dabbled, but he was never into the hard stuff. Don't fret it.'

'As the guitarist said to the drummer,' Mr Two responded with a wink.

That was it. Either the residual airborne chemicals were having an effect on Dana, or she was simply enjoying this conversation immensely. Mr Two was quickly becoming one of her favourite people. Definitely in the top ten. Well, he'd have to be, with a name like that, wouldn't he?

'So anyway, I'd been trying for some time to track down Ziggy's guitar. It vanished on the day he… passed away.'

'I knows it,' the grizzled roadie muttered. 'I remember that day like it was tattooed on me. In fact, I'm pretty sure the date is tattooed on me somewhere. Let me just check, I think it was on me lower back.' He stood and Dana realised with horror that he was about to disrobe in front of her.

'That's fine!' she blurted. 'Honestly, no need. I know the date well.' She was relieved when he abandoned his ink-related quest and took his seat again. 'The guitar has recently surfaced again, and has been bought by Mikey Thunderbird.'

'That peacock! 'E's got more guitars than social

media's got arseholes. 'E better be playing all them bloody things. They needs attention!'

'I fully agree. A guitar's made to be played, right?'

'Amen, sister!'

'Well, you can relax. I met with Mikey and he actually does play all his guitars.'

Mr Two collapsed back into his chair. 'By John Bonham's sweaty jodhpurs, thank goodness for that.'

'Apparently he has so many guitars that he made up a roster to get round them all. But he loves those instruments, I can assure you. That's why I'm okay with him having Ziggy's guitar for now.'

'You'll get it back yourself though, won't you? Have it back where it belongs? Resting in the familial bosom, as it were?'

'I'd certainly like to. Don't know if I can afford it, though.'

'That Thunderbird fella should just give it yer. 'E can afford to. The cheek!'

'It's okay, honestly. For now, I'm focused on piecing together where the guitar went in the intervening years. Someone took that guitar as my brother lay dying, and I want to find that person so I can find out what actually happened. According to the person who sold the guitar to Mikey, it was a roadie who had it.'

Mr Two's face went red. His cheeks billowed out as if his tongue was in the America's Cup yacht race. His eyes bulged… well, his eyes were already quite bulged and red from his recent activity which Dana had interrupted, but if it were possible for them to bulge more, they would have.

'Whhhhaaaaaaat?!' hissed Mr Two, like an aggrieved gas leak. 'Someone is saying that one of me crew ripped off Ziggy's guitar, literally over 'is dead body?!'

'Well, we don't know the exact circumstances, that's why I'm trying to track everyone down and ask them if they know what happened.'

'They wouldn't! None of them would do such a fing.'

'They may not have stolen it, but one of them had it and I want to know why, and how. That person is probably the last one to see my brother alive, and I'd like to talk to them. Just to be clear, you hadn't seen the guitar since Ziggy… last played it?'

'No, miss Dana. I was on speaker pack-down that night. We was only half done when they came out and told us all to go home, there'd be no more tour because Ziggy was gone. Some of us went straight down the boozer and sank a few in his honour. Next thing I know it's a week later and I'm waking up in

Amsterdam, in someone's 'ouseboat.'

Dana raised an eyebrow. Mr Two shrugged, in a way that said these things happen to us all sometimes, don't they?

She'd love to hear the full story, but now was not the time.

'Right then, so who else was on the crew? Anyone in particular you think I should talk to first? I have a few more names from Gordon, at Meltdown Music, but maybe you can give me more details.'

'Yeah, well, me memory's a bit' he waggled a hand, 'wotsit… but I fink at that time we 'ad Eli of course.'

'I remember Eli. Lovely guy.'

'Yep, 'e is indeed. 'E's in the 'ostible now.'

'Oh, I didn't know that.'

'Aye, may his calluses rest in pieces. Cancer of the liver, poor sod.'

'I'm so sorry.'

'Yes, it'll be a much sadder world when he's buggered off, that's for sure.' Mr Two shook himself out of his reverie. 'Well, I think you and me both know Eli would never have taken Zig's guitar, and he never would have left him on his lonesome in that 'otel room, so let's cross 'im off the list, right?'

'Absolutely,' said Dana with conviction. She

knew that Ziggy had always regarded Eli almost like family. Trusted him with his life. More than that, he trusted him with his guitar.

'I'll go and visit him anyway though, to say hi.'

'Nice of yer. Now, who else was there? Right, we 'ad three blokes doing drums.'

Dana got out a notebook and pen. 'And what were their names?'

'No, no, love. It were a woman.'

'Sorry?'

'A woman. We called her Three Blokes.'

Dana sighed. She really didn't want to ask, but she could tell that Mr Two was about to explain the soubriquet anyway.

'If this is a lurid story, you really don't have to tell me it.'

'Oh, no, nuffink like that, Dana my dear! It's just that she worked as hard as three blokes. Put us lads to shame, she did.'

Another close call on the rocky road of the information superhighway. Dana was relieved.

'And, who else?' Mr Two gazed at the ceiling as if the names were written on it. 'Oh yeah, we 'ad Raisin Poop the sparky.' He winked. 'Always had currents running through 'im, you see.'

Dana put her head in her hands. That was an egregious one, for sure.

'Raisin's best mate Defib Dave was on general 'elf and safety oversight.'

For a second, Dana thought he was talking about a Dungeons and Dragons campaign.

'He also did a bit o' rigging. And Turps, Swiney and Tony Trauma was all there, just generally lugging shit about. Me and Eli were the specialists on guitars and bass, you see,' he said, with a proud lift of his chin. 'And Three Blokes looking after the drums, of course. The rest was doing the grunt work, putting shit where they was told and then loading it away again after.'

'Okay, thanks. Do you have contact details for any of them, by any chance?'

'I can get hold of 'em, sure. In fact, I did some work with Three Blokes just recently. Local gig, very small beer compared to the old glory days. Just a few tiny bloody amps, and three of us roadying. Couldn't get all the old crew together so we had to tap a local guy who knew a bit about instruments to help out. Andrew. He was handy, Andy, and very keen. You might have heard about it, the big Cranial Bypass reunion gig?'

Dana had indeed heard about the reunion gig, it being the biggest musical news in Rockingham West for, oh, about two hundred years. Dana had learned about the band through — who else? — her brother Ziggy, who'd been following the band since their early days, when a guitarist called Apocalypse BusLane (nickname: Pox, real name: Archie Evans) had met up with singer Horgen Greymantle (nickname: Horgs, real name: Hamish Green) while busking. Horgen had been doing doo-wop numbers to rake in the cash, but he hated singing that stuff. Once they got talking, they realised that the Venn diagram of their shared musical interests was basically just a circle, and that circle was full to the brim with psychedelic heavy rock.

When Pox showed Horgs some of the heavy riffs he'd been working on, the nucleus of the band Cranial Bypass was formed. Over the next few months they added a thunderous drummer, a nimble bass player, and as their music evolved into something more bombastic, they even threw in a keyboard player.

They'd played in pubs, then theatres, then arenas. They'd been on television, in films, and in jails. They grew their reputation, their prowess, and, most of all, their hair.

And then, like so many bands before them, they'd encountered "creative differences", and just like that they were over.

Until now.

There was intense excitement and interest from

all around the world when Cranial Bypass had announced their reunion gig. The residents of Rockingham West had their minds blown when they found out the band would be performing in their town. The reason given: "we really want to get back to our roots, you know?", according to the hitherto inaccessible Apocalypse BusLane.

Unfortunately, sadly, *tragically* for a guitar shop owner on the cusp of a major influx of guitar fans, Dana had recently heard bad news about the reunion gig.

'Didn't that get cancelled?' she asked.

'Spot on. But they didn't say why, right?'

'I assumed someone must have got sick.'

'Sick o' living, maybe.'

'What?'

'Listen.' Mr Two looked around, then scooted forward on his chair and waved at Dana to lean in, as if this secret was not safe between the two of them in a private living room. 'I stopped for a leak on me way out, and as I passed the green room I 'eard people talking. Then I saw a policeman coming out. And since I suddenly 'ad to do up me shoelace, I 'ad time to peer through the doorway, and I seen the singer from Cranial Bypass, Apocalypse BusLane, lying on the floor wiv 'is face all purple and 'is tongue hanging out.'

'That's horrible!'

'Yep.' The roadie's voice dropped so low it almost brushed the carpet. 'If I din't know any better, I'd say he'd been choked.'

Dana's hands went cold, and she almost dropped her glass of water. 'Oh my God,' she breathed.

'What, did he owe you money?'

'No, it's just…' Dana gulped. She raised her eyes to the ceiling as she worked through the implications, then she looked back at Mr Two. 'I think I might have an appointment with Apocalypse BusLane this afternoon.'

Chapter 3: Inspecting the victim

Dana thanked Mr Two for his time, and for offering to get in touch with the other roadies for her. She trundled her old VW back to the store, just in time for DC Wade McNeish to text her with an invitation to the city morgue. A gruesome proposal, but now she was intrigued to find out if it was indeed Apocalypse BusLane that Wade had been talking about earlier.

Brody bounded to meet her at the shop door, doing his best happy puppy impersonation. 'Hi, boss! Guess what?'

'What?'

'Seriously? You're not even going to guess?' Brody's purple scarf slowly wafted to the floor behind him as he came to rest.

'Sorry Brody, of course I'll guess.' Her eyes roved the store, taking in places where instruments had been moved to different hangers. Aha! She spotted a gap where…

'No!' she gasped. 'You haven't sold it, have you?'

'I sure have,' crowed Brody, striking a superhero pose with hands on hips, face lifted to the stars. 'I've only gone and done it.'

'Wow! You sold the double-neck.'

'The unsellable double-neck, isn't that what you called it?' Brody's self-satisfied smile threatened to blind passing drivers.

'I sure did. That thing has been an albatross around my neck for damn near four years now.' Dana dragged up a drum stool so she could sit and take it all in.

'An acoustic bass and banjo hybrid was always going to be a tricky sale,' Brody reflected.

'Thank you Brody, I am aware.' She tutted. 'And as you well know, I had to take it as a part trade for a much bigger sale, so I had no choice.' She looked over at the empty spot on the wall where the abomination had hung. It had been there for so long that the paint on the wall had faded around it, leaving the dank silhouette of one of the least-desirable instruments Dana had ever had the misfortune to deal in.

She slowly shook her head. Her disbelief was a pastoral melody, and her relief a ripping guitar solo.

'However did you do it, Brodes?'

'Remember that guy who bought a bulk lot of acoustic guitar strings a little while ago. Aaron someone?'

'Oh, yes, Aaron Swetters. He seemed like a nice guy. Little upset that we didn't have more acoustic instruments in-store, as I recall.'

'Yeah, he asked me to turn off the stereo while he was in. Said he couldn't stand synthetic noises.'

Dana chuckled. 'That'll be the one. Still, it takes all sorts, doesn't it?'

'Sure does! Anyway, I posted a photo of the double-neck on the local Folk Club site,' replied Brody, as he pretended to nonchalantly check his cuticles. 'I put a little message on there saying that the body was made from thousand-year-old swamp kauri – '

'Making it heavier than most peoples' cars.'

'I didn't mention that bit.'

'Good call.'

'And within about an hour, this guy turns up, plays it for a bit, and then just buys it!'

'Wow!'

'I know, right? We must've had it out the back last time he visited. He looked like he couldn't believe his luck when he laid eyes on it.'

Dana rose to her feet. 'Oh, Brody, I really want to

celebrate this sale but I have to go and meet Wade right now.'

Brody shrugged. 'It's okay.'

'No, it's not.' Dana thought for a second. This really was a big occasion. Not only had Brody shifted an item she was ecstatic to be rid of, it had also improved their cashflow situation. Even though she'd discounted it quite heavily, the bass/banjo still had a hefty price tag, since it was a custom-built monstrosity... errrr, instrument.

She clicked her fingers. 'If you're free tonight, maybe you and Evan would like to come round for dinner?'

Brody beamed. He loved showing off his boyfriend, and Dana knew it.

'Sounds great! Six thirty okay for you?'

Good Brody. He'd remembered that Dana was an early diner. He could be very thoughtful, when he thought about it...

'Perfect! I'll probably be back again before closing time, but just in case I don't...'

'Don't forget to lock up?'

'Well, that, but I was going to say, maybe you could sell that electric ukulele as well, since you're on a roll?'

'Awww, come on!' said Brody. 'Isn't one superhero sale per day enough for you?'

She smiled and patted him on the shoulder on her way out. The shop was in good hands. She was starting to miss it already, though. The shop was her happy place. But her mission to dig up information about Ziggy couldn't be ignored. Once that was all over, she looked forward to endless boring days at the counter.

Oh, unless DC McNeish kept finding guitar-related homicides to call her about, of course…

There was still a light, drizzly rain as she drove to the morgue. It would have been rather snuggly in the car, except her old Beetle had a few leaks in the roof. Still, at least there were holes in the floor to let the water out. Dana told herself that it was healthy to be closer to the elements. No need for a display on the dash to tell you the outside temperature when you could feel it on your toes.

She spotted Wade waiting for her in the carpark.

He gave her a cheery wave and called out to her. 'Hi! Dead on time, huh?'

'Seriously?' she said as she shut the Beetle's door. 'You're going with the gothic humour, are you?'

'It usually slays,' he replied. 'Aren't you going to lock your car?'

She shrugged. 'If you owned it, would you? At this point the only part of it worth any money is the fuel in the tank.'

'Sure, but if it gets stolen you'll have to walk home.'

Dana put a hand to her chest and fluttered her lashes in mock horror. 'Saints preserve me! If that were to happen, couldn't I rely on an officer of the constabulary to convey me homewards?'

'Only if you broke the law'. He led her to the door of the nondescript morgue building. 'Now come in out of the rain before you catch your death of a cold.'

'Uuurgh! I can't tell if you're being intentionally un-funny or not.'

Wade just smiled and led her into the labyrinthine complex.

After passing a few doors – some of which were open, and Dana very deliberately did not look into those – and navigating several twists and turns, Wade called a halt.

The door he was standing in front of looked like all the other doors they'd passed. It had a number on it, but nothing else marked it out. Dana supposed she'd been expecting to see a sign with *Scary Dead Bodies* written on it, or *Not For The Squeamish*.

But then, for the people who worked here, the bodies probably weren't scary, and those workers were very unlikely to be squeamish.

Unlike Dana. She was a quivering mass of squeam right now. She was like the world's biggest squeam pie. You could have filled a supertanker with her squeam and had some left over.

Shake it off, she told herself. You can do this.

'You don't have to do this, you know,' said Wade, as if her mind was a large print book, with illustrations.

Dana found an interesting piece of peeling paint to study. 'I kinda do,' she sighed.

'What do you mean?'

'It's just…' she looked Wade in the eye. 'I think I already know who the deceased person is. And if it's who I think it is, I really owe it to them.'

'Okay, wait a sec,' said Wade. 'First you reckon you know what was used to strangle the victim, and now you reckon you know who it is without even setting foot in the room to see them. So what gives? Have you been taking psychic pills or something?'

'Can you just trust me for now, please Wade? I promise I'll explain once I see the… the body.'

Wade held her eye for a long minute. Eventually he gave up, and shrugged.

'There better be a real good explanation for this,' he said as pulled the door open. 'And also, the explanation had better happen over a cold beer, and you'd better be buying.'

He waved her on into the room, where a lab-coated technician was fussing over a body which lay on a stainless steel table, covered by a sheet.

'Detective.' The technician nodded to Wade.

When Wade nodded back, the technician pulled away the sheet a little, exposing the corpse's head and shoulders.

Dana's heart sank. Straight away she recognised the deceased, even without their usual stage makeup, without the omnipresent guitar slung over their shoulder, without the larger-than-life swagger that had graced a thousand venues over the last several decades.

She'd know that facial profile anywhere. She was one of the guy's biggest fans.

Just as she'd feared, she was looking at the corpse of Apocalypse BusLane.

The once-powerful hands, which had pulled ethereal notes out of his guitar and rocked every stage worth rocking, would fret no more. Those gyrating hips, which had caused more fainting spells than a truck full of nitrous oxide, those very hips which had once been labelled a health hazard by the Surgeon General, lay still in front of her, on a cold steel bench.

'Oh, Wade,' she breathed.

Somehow time had passed. Somehow Wade was standing right next to her, and somehow she was holding onto his arm even though she didn't remember reaching for him.

'I'm sorry,' he said softly. 'You know who this guy is?'

'What?' Dana shook her head. The spell was broken. She swatted Wade's shoulder. 'Of course I do. Don't tell me you don't recognise Apocalypse BusLane? For goodness' sake, he's only one of the most famous guitarists ever to bend a string.'

Wade rubbed his shoulder and pretended to be grievously wounded.

'No, I haven't heard of him, actually.'

'Crikey, have you never listened to a rock song in your life?'

'Not really. More of a Madeleine Peyroux guy, me… What?'

Dana picked her jaw up off the floor and filed this information away for later investigation. The image of tough cop DC McNeish sitting in a comfy chair listening to mellow, sultry jazz stubbornly refused to get out of her brain.

'Okay, well, listen,' she said. 'Apocalypse BusLane is a big deal. Was a big deal. Still is a big deal, I'm sure.' She shook her head. 'I can't believe someone this famous can be dead without everyone knowing about it.'

'Oh, we've been told to keep this quiet. His manager wants us to find out what actually happened before making it public. Gotta contact the family too.'

'Family? Pox didn't have family. His parents passed away when he was quite young. No partner, no kids. It's well-known that he was all by himself.'

'Hmmm...' Wade fished out a notebook. 'Let's just say that he may not have had a partner, but he was party to several instances of... begetting.'

'Begetting? Really?' Dana raised an eyebrow.

'To be completely accurate, begetting and then buggering off. He had kids strewn around the country almost as if he was trying to populate the place single-handed.' Wade went red. 'Not single-handed. I didn't mean...'

'I got it, Wade.'

'Ahem. So, yeah, for now nobody knows about this, and you didn't see anything.'

'Hate to break it to you, but it's already on the musician's information superhighway.'

'The internet?'

'No, the roadies. If the guy I talked to knows about it, then it's safe to assume that every other roadie he ever met already knows too.'

'Shit.'

'Mind you, the roadie code might mean they'll keep it amongst themselves.'

'There's a roadie code?'

'Yes, definitely.' Dana thought about it. 'Most of it involves sleeping whenever you get the chance, and loading gear even when you're hungover, but they're fiercely loyal little creatures if you treat them well and don't feed them after midnight.'

'What? Why can't you feed them after midnight?'

'Oh Wade.' Dana's heart went out to the culturally clueless constable. 'Now I have to teach you about classic movies as well as classic rock, do I?'

Wade sniffed. 'Rock hasn't been around long enough to be called classic.'

'Rock has been there through all kinds of social change over the last few decades,' Dana bristled. 'You can't just dismiss that. What about three chords and the truth?'

'What about putting in some effort and learning a fourth chord?' He tut-tutted. 'I don't know, young people today.'

'Wade, we're the same age.'

He smiled, leaned in close and winked. 'I dye my hair,' he whispered. 'Now, if you're done disparaging the great spiritual art form that is jazz music, perhaps you're ready to have a look at the ligature marks on the victim?'

Dana had to admit that Wade's 'dumber than hell' act – if indeed it was an act – had successfully distracted her and lightened the mood, but now she had to get back to the business at hand. Was it suddenly colder in here? She shivered.

Wade escorted her to the table, giving a collegial nod to the morgue employee who discreetly went and headed out the door.

Dana had always dreamed of meeting Apocalypse BusLane. Now here she was, standing in the presence of greatness. Only, his greatness had fled; or rather, it had been cruelly taken from him.

Well, Dana was determined to help the Police figure out who did it, so that Pox's spirit could rest easy in the great green room in the sky.

Steeling herself, she leaned in to examine the body of the famous rocker.

Lying on the table, he could almost have been having a quick shut-eye between gigs. Except for the yellow-brown mark around his neck, which told a different tale.

Dana was grateful his eyes were closed too. They would probably be horribly bloodshot as an effect of being strangled - maybe worse. She didn't want to know. This was bad enough.

The line going around Pox's neck left a deep

groove, and had even broken the skin in several places. Dana wondered if Pox might have bled out even if the strangulation hadn't killed him.

Who would do something like this to a person? Put a wire around another human being's neck and squeeze the life out of them? She shuddered.

Wade cleared his throat in a very professional police manner. 'Well?' he said softly, 'what do you think? Can you tell if it was a guitar string that they used?'

Dana nodded. 'I think it was.'

'Can you seriously tell that just from looking?'

'Oh, I can't know for sure, but I can say that the spiralling groove marks here' – she showed Wade a particularly clear section of bruising – 'are consistent with a guitar string's construction.'

She leaned in to look closer again. 'I'd say it was an E or A string, somewhere around forty-five to fifty-five gauge.'

'Wait,' said Wade, 'you sound like you're talking about shotguns now. What's forty-five gauge?'

Dana had to stop and think about that for a second. Guitar strings had always been nine-to-forty-two gauge sets to her. Or twelve-to-fifty-two for acoustic guitars. But what did that actually measure?

She rummaged through the messy sock drawer

of her memory. Ah, that's it!

'It's a measurement of the diameter of the string, in inches. So, a forty-five gauge string is point zero four five of an inch.'

Wade raised a quizzical eyebrow. 'Why don't they say it in millimetres?'

'Probably the same reason you buy a forty-foot yacht and don't buy a… twelve point something metres one,' replied Dana with a small amount of mental contortion.

Wade gave her an even look and then jotted something in his notepad. 'There are a myriad of reasons why I don't buy an anything metres yacht.' He tapped his pencil on his pad. 'And the difficulty of converting units of measurement isn't one of them. Shall we?' He gestured to the door.

They exited the room, thanking the morgue employee who was waiting in the hallway, looking at his phone.

'Get what you need?' he asked

'Yes, thanks,' Wade replied. 'It should be easy to find the murderer now that we know they used a guitar string.'

'Are you kidding me?' said Dana. 'Do you have any idea how many sets of strings I sell each month? There are probably enough guitar strings laying around Rockingham West to twist them together and put up a new suspension bridge.'

'Oh. But you said they were acoustic strings, right? That must narrow things down a bit.'

'Sure, now we only have to talk to half the guitarists in town instead of the whole lot.'

'Okay,' said Wade as he led them back out to the carpark. 'Still, there can't be that many guitarists in town, can there? After all, there are only a dozen or so gig venues.'

Dana laughed. 'Right, and you think that each venue has an exclusive contract with a specific band, do you? You're also forgetting all the people who play guitar at home for their own enjoyment and never do a gig.'

'All right, I get it – '

'And on top of that you've got all the guitars played with Māori kapa haka cultural groups around the region. You don't often see those guitars onstage at open mic night at the Dog and Gristle.'

'Gotcha.'

'Plus the ones – '

'Oh, you're still going?'

' – that are bought to look nice on the wall of someone's flash house, or even the ones that are bought as investments, locked away and never played. Even those guitars get restrung sometimes, especially if a rich person wants to show the guitar off to guests.'

They walked over to Dana's VW and she took out her keys.

'Are you done?' said Wade. 'I think you've made your point.'

Dana stopped, keys halfway to the car door. 'Actually...' she murmured, half to herself, 'I recently sold a bulk lot of phosphor bronze acoustic guitar strings just like the one used to kill Apocalypse BusLane. But no, it couldn't be him...'

Wade already had his notepad out. 'Couldn't? Why not?'

Startled out of her thoughts, Dana looked up at Wade.

'Oh, he's a nice guy. A quiet guy. One of those mellow folkies you see at acoustic jam nights.'

'Takes all sorts,' said Wade with a shrug. 'Just give me his name, will you?'

Chapter 4: Dinner and a show

Dana Beetled home in low spirits, feeling bad about tattling on a customer. Still, the guy would surely be able to provide an alibi to clear his name, and then the police could move on to the next suspect. Dana hoped so, and not just because she was worried he'd try to return the bass/banjo hybrid instrument he'd recently bought.

No... No, it would turn out fine. She would have to put it out of her mind, especially since she was now headed home to host a celebratory dinner for Brody in honour of him selling the damn thing!

Paws McCartney greeted her in his usual manner. Namely by crying piteously and writhing around her feet, threatening to trip her with every step. Apparently he hadn't been fed for several years, and it was a straight-up miracle that he was still alive to complain about it.

Dana was pretty sure there should still be something in his bowl – yes, she checked and there was still a good amount of food left in there from earlier. Of course, it was over ten minutes old now, and therefore, under the Cat-Human Partnership Treaty of 1892, Paws had the right to refuse to eat it, and cry abuse.

Dana carefully tipped a tiny amount of new cat food on top of the older lot that was already in Paws' bowl, in the hope that he'd think he had a whole new fresh serving. Paws sat back on his haunches and stared at her. Did she really expect him to eat this rubbish?

No, of course that wasn't going to work.

She gave him a new bowl of food, and took the old one out the back to where birds could have a go at it, even though she knew that what would inevitably happen is that Paws would spot it later that evening and eat it anyway. Outside food and inside food were two completely different things, as far as Paws was concerned.

With her fussy feline sorted, Dana got stuck into preparing dinner for Brody and Evan.

She'd just removed a potato-topped bean casserole from the oven when her phone buzzed with a text from Brody saying they were at the door.

She went down to let them in, and found them with their heads together, having a whispered argument. Since they were both naturally introverted, it was like watching a kitten have a mild disagreement with a low-flying cloud.

'Oh, hi boss.' Brody swatted Evan's arm as he straightened up.

Evan's face went red. 'Hello, Dana. Thank you so much for having us over. May I say you're looking lovely tonight?'

'You certainly may,' said Dana, waving them in. 'Even though I don't think it's true, you're more than welcome to say it.'

They tramped upstairs to Dana's flat, and she watched them continue to bicker nonverbally as they went. It was all in the eyebrows and elbows. As far as modern dance went, it was pretty choreography, but as dinner company it left a lot to be desired.

'Are you two going to tell me what this is all about, or would you prefer to continue to act like two-year-olds all night?' she asked as they sat at the dinner table. 'Because I tell you what, as much as I was looking forward to your company, I also have a good book and half a bottle of leftover cooking wine as Option B, and that option is starting to look mighty appealing.'

Evan went to speak but caught a particularly forceful glare from Brody. Evan shrugged and mouthed 'what?' Brody mouthed back 'don't!'

Dana opened the door to the oven, where a feijoa and apple pie was baking. Sweet smells wafted out into the room and the boys' heads lifted in unison as they sniffed the air like hungry puppies.

'First person to tell me what's going on gets the biggest slice of pie,' Dana pronounced.

'Evan wants to jam with you!' Brody blurted.

Evan's jaw dropped open. 'You've been telling me for the last ten minutes how you didn't want me to ask her!'

'But...' Brody the puppy whined. 'You know...' he trailed off. 'Pie..!'

Dana shut the oven door and sat next to Evan at the table.

'Do you really want to jam with me?' she asked.

Evan shuffled in his seat, keeping his eyes on the table. 'Um, yeah, if... uh, if you don't mind? It's just that I've heard a lot about how good you are on guitar, and Brody's been getting pretty good on the drums now that we have an electronic kit set up at our place.'

'I told you,' Brody interrupted, 'Dana's way out of our league, music-wise. She can have her pick of band members. She won't want to jam with us.' He turned to Dana. 'Sorry boss, I told him you wouldn't be keen.'

'What are you talking about? Of course I'd be keen!'

'Really?' said Evan and Brody together.

'Yes, I think it sounds like fun. These days I'd rather have a jam with friends than join a serious band and have to commit to practices and late-night gigs. Let's do it!'

Evan beamed triumphantly. 'Yes! Thank you Dana. We could get together on the weekend maybe?'

'Oooh,' said Brody, 'that sounds cool. Sunday afternoon. Chips 'n' dip 'n' rock 'n' roll!'

'If we were a proper band,' said Dana, laughing, 'I'm sure that would be our name.'

There was a knock at the door.

'Oh,' said Dana, 'who could that be?'

'They must have smelled the pie too,' said Brody.

Dana went to answer the door, and returned with Detective Constable Wade McNeish.

'Hi all. Did I hear someone say pie just now?' said Wade, rubbing his hands together.

'Do you have the room bugged?' said Dana. 'Actually, we're having dinner to celebrate a big sale that Brody made.'

'Wonderful!' roared Wade, grabbing a seat at the table. 'This was good timing, eh lads?' He waggled his eyebrows at Brody. 'Now, don't let me interrupt. What were you all talking about?'

Dana brought the casserole to the table, then fished out an extra plate and cutlery for Wade. 'As a matter of fact, we were just organising a jam session for the weekend. What about you - what brings you here?' Dana fixed him with a look. 'Right at this moment?'

'Well, once again it seems my timing couldn't have been better.'

'You should try the drums then,' said Brody.

'What's that, son?'

'Sorry, nothing. Go on.'

'Right,' said Wade, as he served himself up an heroic portion of casserole. 'Yes, it's funny you should have just formed a band.'

'We didn't,' said Dana. 'We're just going to have a jam.'

Wade continued undeterred. 'Because our pool of suspects just expanded exponentially and we're going to have the devil of a time getting them all together to talk to.'

'Why's that?' Dana asked.

'You know the bloke you told me about?'

'Aaron Swetters, from the folk club?'

'That's the lad. Turns out he bought that bulk lot of guitar strings to dish out to anyone who needs them. Runs a program called…' he fished his notebook out of a pocket, while skilfully using his other hand to shovel a forkful of casserole into his mouth at the same time.

Brody winked at Evan, and whispered: 'Told you he'd be a good drummer – look at that limb independence.'

'Mmmm…' Wade went on. 'This is good. Ah yes, Swetters runs a program called Acoustic Youth. Trying to keep kids off the street and out of trouble by teaching them guitar.' He looked at the faces around the table. 'Seems to have worked out for you lot, but it doesn't sound like a winning employment strategy overall, does it?'

Dana rolled her eyes. 'It's not all about money, Wade. Playing music and being in a band helps your self-esteem, your literacy, numeracy, teamwork, even graphic design and management skills. Leaving all that aside, it's good for your soul. Isn't it, guys?'

Evan and Brody nodded enthusiastically.

'You need to worry about putting food on the table before you can worry about polishing up your soul, in my experience,' said Wade.

'Well, Wade,' said Dana, 'I can't do anything

about your lack of experience, so let's continue, shall we?'

Brody laughed and went for a high-five but immediately remembered that Dana didn't partake, so he switched to a thumbs-up instead.

'Oof,' said Evan. 'She got you there, mister policeman!'

Dana smiled at Wade to take the sting out of it, but the twinkle in his eye told her that she needn't have worried – he was obviously enjoying the banter immensely.

'That's me told,' he said. 'Right, so. Kids can help themselves to strings at this Acoustic Youth drop-in space.'

'Which is where?' asked Dana.

'I'm glad you asked,' said Wade, brandishing a triumphant finger. 'You know a place called The Riffery?'

Dana nodded. It was the best music venue in town, which wasn't saying much in a place the size of Rockingham West, but it was well-loved, and they often got touring bands through. It also happened to be where Evan and Brody had finally got together. Brody had dragged Dana along to see Evan's band This Plastic Happiness play. If she hadn't been there to pay Brody's door charge, they might not be having this lovely dinner right now. A lovely dinner which was still being interrupted by the police. She hoped Wade would navigate his way to the vicinity of his point soon.

'Yes,' said Dana. 'Weren't Cranial Bypass planning to do their reunion gig there?'

'Correctimundo. And now they're organising a tribute gig for our victim, yeah?'

'Wait,' said Brody, 'who's the victim?'

Dana quickly filled him in on the sad demise of one Apocalypse BusLane, erstwhile guitarist extraordinaire with Cranial Bypass.

Brody and Evan were both so shocked that Wade managed to get in a second helping while they processed the news.

'So anyway, as I said, they're organising a tribute gig for the guy, and there'll be several bands on the bill – all the acts who were lined up to play at Cranial Bypass' last gig. As well as that, many of the kids who attend the Acoustic Youth program will be there helping out. Basically, all the people we want to talk to will be there.'

Wade paused his monologue to look hopefully pieward.

Dana sighed and went back to the oven to see if the pie was ready yet.

'And...' Wade stopped to pat his tummy and emit a small burp. 'Excusez moi. Yeah, they're doing a tribute gig, and the main act is, tragically, short a guitarist.' He focused his attention on Dana. 'They need a guitar player. And we need someone on the inside, who can talk to the artists. And here you are, telling me that you're playing in bands again.' He smiled. 'What do you say? Are you in?'

It was a testament to Dana's dedication to the art of bakery that she didn't immediately drop the pie on the floor.

'But why don't you just go and talk to them all yourself?' Dana asked, after the pie had been carefully partitioned and swiftly devoured. 'As you've pointed out before, I'm not police.'

'Exactly that,' Wade replied. 'There was a certain… shall we say… reluctance on the part of Mr. Swetters to converse civilly with those of a police-like persuasion.'

Brody sniffed. 'He told you to piss off, did he?'

'That he did, young Brody. That he did. And he made it clear that many of the kids he worked with would feel the same. He then went on to pontificate on how many other musicians in the vicinity would share these sentiments. In fact, he expounded at length on the usefulness of the police force, the rights of citizens, and even at one point, memorably, the qualities of my ancestry, particularly the matrilineal aspect.'

Dana felt sorry for Wade, who was, after all, only trying to find out who'd killed a beloved musician. You'd think people would want to help one of their own.

'Do you really think they'll want to talk to me, though?' she asked.

'I know they will. I see them come to your shop, and all they do is talk to you.' Wade nodded. 'I bet you could stand outside for ten minutes on a fine day and learn more about what's going on in this town than I could in a dozen hour-long interviews.'

'He's not wrong,' said Brody.

'Thanks Brodes,' said Dana sarcastically.

'You're welcome, boss. Ouch!' He reached under the table to rub his shin where Evan had obviously just kicked him.

Wade grinned at Dana. 'He was a hero of yours, wasn't he? This bus driver chap? Wouldn't you like to pay tribute to him?'

'Apocalypse BusLane' said Dana, 'was indeed a formative influence on my guitar playing, but I think you could say the same for any number of guitarists around here. Cranial Bypass was huge. Everywhere. People will be falling over themselves to get that spot in the band. They'll be coming from miles around.'

'Oh yeah, people would kill for that opportunity,' said Brody, completely without guile.

In the awkward silence that followed this sentence, Dana could almost hear the gears turning in Brody's head as he worked his way through the implications.

'Oooohhhhhh…' he said eventually. 'You don't think…?'

Wade shrugged. "It's a possibility, I suppose.' He turned back to Dana. 'And there's only one way we're going to find out.'

'I told you, Wade, it's a moot point.' Dana got up to put the kettle on for a cup of tea. 'They'll already have someone in mind. They might even fly in a big-name guitarist from out of town for this.'

'Not gonna happen,' said Wade. 'The promoter's well out of pocket already, and he's billing it as a special event to give an unknown guitarist a chance. He said he'll pick a different guitarist from each town as they travel around.'

Dana almost dropped the teapot she'd just taken off a shelf. She made a mental note to stop picking up kitchenware just as Wade was about to say stuff. 'They're going to go on tour? After Pox has been killed?'

'I hate to break it to you, Ms Osborne, but people make a lot of money out of tragedy in the entertainment business.'

As if Dana didn't know this already. As if her own brother's death hadn't resulted in his record company releasing a lucrative box set of his band's recordings, and the remaining members all branching off into solo careers. So yes, she should have expected this, but somehow she was still surprised by the blatant cash-grab elicited by Pox's death. And yes, it hurt because it brought back memories of Ziggy's passing being turned into profits. Still, Wade wasn't to know about all that, and she wasn't about to lob that particular conversational hand grenade into her own dinner party. So she took the teapot over to the kitchen counter and busied herself with watching the kettle boil.

'I'm telling you,' Wade went on, 'I could smell the cash on the promoter's breath as he was telling me all this. He'll be raking it in, eventually, with the publicity over this whole affair.'

'Sounds like motive to me,' said Evan, whose crime-fighting expertise came from binge watching Ally McBeal episodes back-to-back for a whole weekend a few years ago while he was supposed to be studying for an exam.

'Could be,' said Wade. 'Would be great to find out, wouldn't it, Dana?'

She took her time putting tea bags into the pot, keeping her back to the room so she could wipe away a sneaky tear.

When she turned back around, she was all righteous determination.

'Okay, yes,' she said, simply.

Chapter 5: The plan

'I'm sorry, Brody,' said Dana, 'this was supposed to be a celebration dinner for you, and here we are planning some kind of…'

'Undercover mission!' yelled Brody. 'Yessss! Are you kidding? This is awesome. It's the best celebration ever. Thanks, boss.'

'The dinner was really nice, too, Dana,' said Evan. 'Even if Brody forgot to say so.' Daggers were glared, faces went red, as the rules of etiquette were enforced with extreme prejudice.

Evan was quickly becoming one of Dana's favourite people. For a boy she'd first seen when he was singing a song called Dead For Life, playing in a band whose style she'd labelled gloom-laden electro-plod, he really knew how to behave in polite company.

Dana and her visitors were relaxing with cups of

tea in Dana's lounge area, which was really just an alcove off the side of the dining area, which itself was really just an alcove off the kitchen, which was – in all honesty – simply an alcove off the hallway. Dana loved her little flat, but she wasn't used to having this many visitors all at once.

She wasn't used to having any visitors at all, truth be told. It wasn't usually her idea of a good time. She'd cleaned the bathroom obsessively earlier, worried that it wasn't tidy enough in case Brody or Evan had to use it, and she was worried even more now that there was an extra visitor here. Not that Wade was likely to arrest her for an untidy bathroom. She assumed.

Paws McCartney, on the other hand, was doing that thing cats can sometimes do, where they're immediately all over the visitors. Literally, in this case. He was rubbing against every limb on offer, leaving hairs on everyone's shins, laps and tummies. He was marking them, she supposed. They all belonged to Paws now. She imagined him giving a super-villain's laugh, rubbing his little toe-beans together and saying 'They're all miiiiine!'

'Dana?' said Wade.

'Hmmm?'

'Are you still with us?'

'Of course. Why?'

'You were quietly laughing to yourself, and staring into the distance. Was it something I said?'

'Ahem. No, sorry, I just… remembered a funny joke that a customer told.'

Wade looked unconvinced, but it was enough to start Brody laughing. 'Oh yeah - the ocean is in the key of C. Haha!'

Oops, Dana hadn't meant to hit shuffle on that particular playlist. Deflect!

'Anyway, Wade, you were saying there are several rehearsals organised?'

'That's right,' said Wade, as Paws McCartney attempted to insert his tail into Wade's mouth and/ or nose. 'So – mmphh – that means you'll have a few shots at talking to all the suspects.'

'Sure, but I'm not exactly trained in interrogation.'

'I'm not asking you to waterboard anyone, Dana.'

'I went waterboarding once,' Brody interjected. 'It was brilliant.'

Everybody frowned at Brody.

'Wakeboarding, Brody,' said Dana. 'You went wakeboarding. And you kept falling off.'

'Yeah, but it was brilliant fun!'

'Hmm,' said Dana, 'Wade, maybe we should continue this planning session later? By ourselves?'

'But then *I* won't be here,' Brody protested.

'Um, yeah.' Dana picked a few non-existent crumbs off her chair.

'But I'm an essential part of the mission, aren't I?' Brody was clearly hoping that audience votes would carry him through to the next round. 'I mean, I helped to solve that last case, didn't I?'

Dana had to admit this was true. If Brody hadn't accidentally recorded the confession on his phone, Gene Stevens' killer might still be roaming the streets. Or dive bars. Or wherever killers roamed.

Dana and Brody together made a team that wasn't so much good cop, bad cop, as competent person, distracting person. So far, they'd solved one hundred percent of the cases they'd worked on, and that was the kind of statistic you couldn't argue with.

However…

'I don't want to put you in harm's way, Brody,' Dana reasoned. 'The last case was a crime of passion, a one-off. We didn't think they would strike again. This time it could be a vicious serial killer for all we know. Could you do that to Evan?'

Oh yes, she was prepared to use the low blow, but only because she really did care about Brody, and would hate to see him get hurt. There would be a lot of people at these practices. A lot of moving parts, and they didn't know which parts were safe, and which were cutty and stabby. Or strangle-y, in this case.

Evan got up, collected Brody's teacup and went to the kitchen bench. Then he came back and collected Brody.

'She's right, B. I couldn't bear the thought of you going out and deliberately getting in the way of a killer.'

Brody's chin jutted out. 'I did it last time.'

Evan took Brody by the hand. 'Last time I wasn't here to stop you.'

'But it'll be safe!' Brody protested. 'Me and Dana will look out for each other. And we'll have earpieces, GPS tracking, and backup officers in a truck outside, right Wade?'

Wade noisily slurped the dregs of his tea before answering. 'You'll have a cellphone, your wits, and a meal allowance. However, you'll need to provide your own cellphone. And wits, of course. Oh, and make sure to keep receipts for your meals.'

'I've got tons of wits,' said Brody. 'And it was my cellphone that cracked the case last time.'

Wade waggled his head from side to side for a bit. 'True, it could be useful having two people on the inside instead of just one.'

Dana tsked. 'Don't be silly, Wade, I'm doing this on my own.' She stood up and made a show of stretching and yawning. 'Now, my goodness, is that the time? I have to be up early tomorrow, and I expect the rest of you do too.'

Subtle hint detected, Wade extracted himself from underneath Paws McCartney, and all the visitors went on their way.

'Well, Pawsy,' said Dana as she washed the chunky mugs that she used as teacups, 'looks like I'm joining a heavy metal band. What do you think of that?'

Paws stared intently at a patch of blank wall behind Dana's left ear, twitched his tail, and got ready to pounce at whatever imaginary beast he saw there.

Jumping at shadows, Dana thought. Hmmm…

Not especially buoyed by Paws' vote of confidence, Dana tossed the tea towel on the bench and went to bed.

Chapter 6: Dana ventures forth

Bright and early the next morning, Dana was up and practicing guitar before the shop opened. She had her headphones on while she played along with Cranial Bypass' seminal album *Amygdala Au Gratin*. The opening track was a dreamy soundscape that she could basically compose her own melodies over the top of, on the fly. This wouldn't be a problem for her, as she'd honed those skills on many a thorny jazz number, forcing herself to learn a lot of different styles of jazz over the years even though she wasn't a huge fan, because she was aware it progressed her as a player. So, with her huge melodic vocabulary, she was confident that she'd fit right in on track one: Neuroplastic Waste.

Track two, however – Synaptic Disconnect – was widely perceived to be one of Pox's pinnacle achievements on guitar. Its daring complexity was reflected in its popularity with die-hard fans.

Accordingly, audiences demanded it be played exactly as it sounded on the album, else they were wont to vent their displeasure in the comments section for weeks afterwards, and - worse - in the moshpit in realtime.

Never a huge fan of social media, Dana swore to never look at a comment section again in her life after this gig, and she'd just have to try to win the moshpit over – if she even got the job. Despite Wade's assurances, she knew that if she didn't nail Pox's guitar parts, Horgen Greymantle and the rest of the Cranial Bypass crew wouldn't let her within a mile of the stage, no matter what the promoter said.

Before any of that could happen, though, she wondered if she should contact Mr Two the roadie and let him know what she was doing.

Of course, she was aware that's not how undercover agents usually operated. Telling people you were going undercover did rather defeat the purpose. But if she just turned up without warning him, he might put two and two together and tell everyone she was there to smoke out the killer, since he already knew she'd been called to the morgue to examine Pox's body. Also, it might be useful to have someone else on her side. Unless he was the killer, of course…

No, he'd been onstage at the time of Pox's demise. He was in the clear. And besides, Dana liked him, and couldn't wait to hear more tall tales in his constantly mutating accent.

She tapped her lips with her guitar pick. Hmmm…what to do? In the end she decided discretion was the better part of valour. Hopefully, if Mr Two did see through her act, he'd play along, for Pox's sake.

Wait a minute. Hadn't Mr Two said that some of the old road crew were working on the Cranial Bypass gig before Pox was killed?

Dana seemed to recall the groan-inducing name Three Blokes being mentioned. And a ring-in, was it… Andy someone?

In that case, she would have two separate lines of enquiry to work on while at the venue. Crikey, this was all getting rather complicated. Dana felt like she'd need a whiteboard and a spreadsheet to keep track of things, but those were not items that rock musicians generally made use of at sweaty gig venues, so might be a bit of a giveaway. Luckily, as Wade had said, there'd be several rehearsals, so she could hopefully focus on just one or two people to talk to each time.

Dana puffed out her cheeks. The time for

planning was over. She needed to focus on what Wade had told her - just relax and be herself, and let people talk to her. She didn't need to orchestrate a formal interview, simply improvise like she usually did.

With that thought, she packed her guitar into its case and went off to persuade her old VW Beetle that today was a good day to drive.

The derelict old vehicle was, if not her pride and joy, then at least her stubborn defiance and mild amusement. It went through more oil than a chip shop on a Friday night, and could go from zero to one hundred km/hour. Eventually.

On the plus side, if anyone ever tried to steal it, she was confident it would be swiftly returned with an apology note taped to the bumper.

And anyway, Dana was not the kind of person who needed to race everywhere. She liked to drive at a slower pace. It gave her more time to look around and smell the sump oil.

She shook and rattled her way to the venue, which is where auditions, rehearsals, and eventually the gig itself would be held.

It was currently called The Riffery, but Dana always thought of it as Dave's Dive, which is what it was known as back when she started going to gigs. Before that it had been Jack's Shack, The

Three-Legged Dog, The Devil's Details and, way back in the seventies, Neil's Wholefood Bulk Bins. All of Neil's mates had hung around in the wholefood shop playing guitars, and eventually Neil realised he'd make more money turning it into a bar.

During the time when it had been known as Dave's Dive, Dana had seen a lot of great bands, a lot of not-very-good bands, and a lot of crappy bands that kept going until they turned into good bands. That's when Dana realised the key to success was the part where you persevere and keep learning.

She even knew of one act that was still not all that great musically, but had acquired legendary status simply by never stopping. Instead of trying to improve so that they gained fans, they just wore people down, creating fans by erosion.

There were so many different paths to success that a band could choose to tread, each requiring different footwear.

As she lugged her guitar into the loading bay at the back of the venue, she was almost bowled over by a guy carrying a huge box, hurrying out.

He only just spotted her in time, then overcorrected, and went arse over kite, scattering the contents of his box all over the carpark in the process.

'Awwww, jeez, come on!' he said, as he scrambled to his feet and dusted off his threadbare corduroy trousers. He ran one hand through his unkempt hair as the other one occupied itself with scratching his stomach. Dana would have preferred to be spared this sight, but as the guy had his shirt wide open, his gaunt frame was on public display.

If she hadn't already recognised him, his ragged attire and the dozens of packets of guitar strings now strewn across the carpark would have tipped her off. For this was none other than Aaron Swetters, folk musician, food-forager, part-time youth worker, and Rockingham West's premier protest singer.

'Hi, Aaron.' She gave an apologetic wave. 'Sorry about all your strings.'

'Oh, hi, Dana. It's okay, it's my fault. I wasn't looking where I was going. It was the universe telling me to slow down.'

'Gravity will do that,' said Dana with a smile.

'You feel it too?' Swetters looked at her intently. 'I know, right? Gravity, it's always trying to bring you down.'

'Yeah, but I mean, that's its job, right?'

He leaned back and nodded slowly. 'That's what they want you to think.'

Before Dana could think of a polite way to get the hell out of the conversation, Swetters spotted her guitar case.

'Oh no, don't tell me you're thinking of playing electric guitar. Don't you realise that electricity kills the soul of your music? Why don't you get a nice acoustic guitar? Come to one of my soul circle guitar jams one night, we've got a wicked vibe going.'

'Um, thanks for the offer, but I've got a lot on at the moment. In fact, I'm heading in to audition for Cranial Bypass. You're supporting them, right?'

Swetters sniffed. 'Salving their conscience, more like.'

Dana put down her case and leaned against the wall, settling in for a chat. 'What do you mean by that?'

Swetters waved a dismissive hand. 'Those rock stars, swanning around, spending their money on heroin and hand jobs while people are starving. I told him so once, that Apocalypse BusLane, at a festival we did at Ngahere Park.'

'Oh, I heard something about that. You spoke to him there?'

'Yes. Well…' Swetters brushed something off his knee. 'We exchanged some words after I switched off the main power to the PA system.'

Dana's mouth made an O.

'They were scaring the sheep!' Swetters proclaimed. 'Too bloody loud, that band. Always too loud.' He shook his head. 'Anyway, I was touring to promote my album Discardigan, the one about giving up on material wealth and fast fashion, you know the one?'

'Sure. Classic.' Dana was not lying. She knew of the album, and admired the fingerpicked guitar parts. And it was probably now old enough to legitimately be called classic, in truth.

'Cheers,' Swetters smiled at the compliment. 'So I had… a discussion with Pox about their stage volume, which turned into a conversation about conspicuous consumption, and ever since then they've often had me on the bill. I reckon it's just a bit of green-washing, making it look like they give a shit, you know?'

'If that's the case, I'm sure you turned them down, on principle, right?'

Swetters frowned. 'Well. No, I did the gigs. Got to get the message out there, I thought.'

'And the money was handy, too, I suspect.' Dana grinned.

'The money,' Swetters gestured to the carpark bestrewn with guitar string packets, 'went on youth programs and various charities, for the most part.'

'Oh,' said Dana, chastened. 'Good on you. So, um, when they asked you to do this latest gig, things were cool between you and Pox? I mean, you and the band? All of them, not just Pox?' Smooth, Dana, she told herself. Real smooth.

But Swetters didn't seem to notice the emphasis. 'Things were fine. Better than fine, really. Pox's attitude had changed recently. Maybe the alignment of the stars, or something…'

Dana raised an eyebrow.

'I mean, his personality seemed to have become more open, and creative. When he called me up for this gig, I told him I was working on a new album called Composterchild, about food security and unnecessary waste. And you know what he said?'

'Um, did he say, where do you get your album names from?'

'No,' said Swetters with a chuckle, 'he said he'd love to guest on the album. Maybe even help with the songwriting. Can you believe it?'

'I cannot,' said Dana, emphatically. 'That doesn't sound like the swaggering rock god Apocalypse BusLane that we've all read about in the court proceedings.'

'Exactly! But it's true. We were writing songs to make an album together, and I was kinda hoping we might tour it together. Imagine that!'

'Honestly,' said Dana, 'I'm really trying to imagine it, but I'm struggling. It just doesn't seem like the kind of thing he'd be into.'

Swetters shrugged. 'It's true though. Here, have a listen for yourself.' He pulled a flash drive from his pocket and handed it to her. 'There's half a dozen songs we wrote together on there. Like I said, he'd changed. Instead of being focused only on himself, and the current moment, he was actually talking about making things right for the coming generations.'

Dana frowned. It sounded like Apocalypse BusLane had had a complete personality replacement. Maybe he knew he was about to die? She pocketed the flash drive. There must be a clue in all of this, she thought. But it sure sounded like Aaron Swetters had no motive for murdering Pox. Quite the opposite, in fact.

Swetters turned towards the carpark. 'I'd better tidy up all these strings, anyway. Nice to see you again, Dana. Oh, and you can thank your assistant for me – that bass-banjo hybrid he sold me is an amazing instrument!'

'Oh yes, that. I'm so pleased it's gone to a good home,' said Dana, thankful that the home in question was not hers.

'I'm sure you're pleased,' said Swetters. 'Your

employee told me that you said it sounded like a herniated whale gargling a hacksaw blade.'

He winked at her, and sloped off to pick up his strings. Dana opened and closed her mouth, then realised anything she might say would only incriminate herself further, so she picked up her guitar and went inside.

The venue was bustling with energy, even though it wasn't open to the public yet. Word had gotten round that Cranial Bypass needed a stand-in guitarist, and every guitarist in town wanted to be the one standing, slouching or swaggering in that spot. Amongst the dozens of hopefuls wandering around chattering nervously like geese on a sugar high, she spotted a couple of her students, as well as a few people she knew from the shop, who quite possibly wouldn't even get picked for their own bands if they had to try out again, let alone perform with a top-flight act like Cranial Bypass.

But most guitarists were nothing if not self-deludedly hopeful. To them, it seemed there was always a chance that Horgen would detect in their under-developed fretboard skills the next breakout guitar hero, just waiting to be nurtured and tended, tied to the trellis of fame and cultivated into the correct shape.

Aha! Here, however, was a guitarist who absolutely deserved to be in the room. Nikau turned and noticed Dana looking at him, and immediately rushed over to her, a big grin on his face.

'Whaea Dana! Stoked to see you here!' he called out, and Dana surmised that he was using the Māori word for mother or auntie as a sign of respect, not a diss on her being older than him. She hoped. Well, at least he hadn't called her kuia – a female elder or grandparent!

He gave her a quick hug.

'I'm very pleased to see you here too, Nikau,' said Dana, and she meant it, even though it put a significant dent in her chances of getting the gig. Nikau was a prodigy on guitar.

'It's only thanks to you I'm here at all,' said Nikau. 'Gene gave me my start, but if it wasn't for you, I...'

He didn't have to finish his sentence. Dana knew that, if not for her and Brody sticking their noses into Wade's last case, this young man would probably be behind bars right now.

Nikau Daniels was the one who'd been found with a murdered man's expensive guitar, and all clues pointed to the scenario that Nikau had killed his mentor, Gene Stevens. Dana and Brody had refused to accept that this calm and dedicated young man could have done such a thing, so they kept digging until they uncovered the truth – it was Gene's son Devon who'd killed him, seemingly in a fit of pique at Gene showing more affection to Nikau than he did to Devon.

Before his passing, Gene was the top guitar teacher in town, and Nikau easily his star pupil. Dana was going to have to work extra hard to make the cut now.

'Well, I didn't even know you were into Cranial Bypass,' said Dana. 'Bit before your time, isn't it?'

He gave her a grin. 'Gotta respect the classics, right? You have to know where you came from to know where you're going, is what my koro always says.'

'How is your grandfather?'

Koro was the male equivalent of kuia, and Dana had often heard Nikau use it in context, so she knew who he was referring to. Dana kept in touch with Nikau to make sure he was doing okay, and she knew that Nikau loved his grandfather. The old man seemed to be a veritable font of wisdom, or at least wise sayings.

'He's fine, thanks,' said Nikau. 'He reckons I should start my own band and do something new, not hang around with these old geezers... no disrespect, whaea Dana, I don't mean you.'

'None taken,' she smiled.

Nikau shuffled his feet. 'So, yeah, whether I get this gig or not, I've got a couple of people in mind to maybe start up a new band with.'

Dana nodded. 'I'm sure that, no matter what happens here today, by this time next year everybody will know your name.'

'For the right reasons this time, hopefully.'

'Of course!' Dana laughed. 'I can tell you're going places, Nikau. You remind me so much of my brother.' Her voice broke a little on the last word, and Nikau gave her an empathetic smile.

'Get on with you,' Dana said, clapping him on the shoulder. 'You should be warming up, not listening to me banging on.'

'Good luck, whaea.'

'You too, Nikau.'

He turned back into the crowd and was soon enveloped in the press of bodies.

As Dana gazed around the venue's main room, wondering where to put her guitar, and if there was anything as mundane as a sign-up sheet, a roadie sauntered past. They were small but wiry, carrying a drum case in one hand and something that looked like it came from a budget droid repair shop in a film student's science fiction project in the other.

Dana knew this was a hi-hat stand, of course, but she often wondered what people must think when first confronted with the various apparatus you see at a rock gig. Leaving all that aside, could the person carrying this gear be the drum tech that Mr Two had spoken of? One of the people who'd been on Ziggy's last tour?

'Three Blokes!' Dana blurted out. And immediately realised her mistake.

More than three blokes turned to stare at her. Many blokes turned to stare. And to be clear, there were many blokes in attendance, and very few non-males. The majority of these blokes stopped what they were doing so that they could stare at Dana. From the look of it, fully half of them must have been thinking: surely this chick hasn't turned up to try out for Cranial Bypass, has she? But the rest of them obviously knew who she was, and she noted that many of the competent players were quietly putting their guitars back into cases, aware that there was no point trying out for the band if Dana was there.

Maybe Wade's plan was going to work out fine after all.

Unfortunately, the drum tech was long gone now, disappeared into the bowels of backstage. Dana would have to keep her eye out for her and try again later. The thought that the person who'd last seen Ziggy alive was potentially in the same room as her was bugging her like mad, but Dana was good at being patient and methodical, and she had to keep her mind on today's main objective. She needed to pass muster and join the band if she was to have a chance of following up any other leads.

'Dana!' roared a voice she'd been hoping to hear. Cleaving through the crowd like a rusty butter knife through a collection of small cheeses came her new friend Mr Two the roadie.

Dana smiled as the road-worn warrior enveloped her in a hug.

'Hi!' she replied. 'How's setup going?'

'Spiffing!' he yelled, as if everybody needed to hear this information from him right now and they should all shut up and listen. 'Couldn't be spiffing-ier.' He glanced at her guitar case and his eyes attempted to open even wider than they currently were. Quite a feat, on a man whose default expression was astonishment. 'Going to sling your six-string for us today, are yer? Bloody great! Can't wait to watch you tear some new holes in this old place.'

One of the less well-informed wannabe rock stars nearby gave a disdainful sniff. A small sound from such a big ego.

'I don't imagine some girl's gonna get the job,' he said, eyeing Dana with contempt, his excessively gelled hair bobbing about his head like a dirty halo. 'Cranial Bypass need a hard-rocking guy upfront, not some skirt. It's about talent, not eye candy.'

Dana just smiled. She was wearing jeans, anyway – it's not as though she'd donned a ball gown just to watch this loser try out. And if looks didn't count, she wondered why he'd obviously spent hours applying his makeup and squeezing into spandex.

Mr Two, however, felt compelled to defend her honour.

'Son, you better hope your guitar playing makes more sense than your stupid mouth. You're like a donkey teasing a dragon for having wings.'

Dana quite liked that line, mentally filing it away for her next songwriting session.

'Get back to your rocking chair, grandad!' the Day-Glo guitarist jeered, and walked off.

Mr Two blinked. He turned to Dana. 'How did he know about my rocking chair?'

Dana did a double-take. 'You have a rocking chair?'

Mr Two nodded, and hooked a thumb over his shoulder. 'Backstage. I always bring it wiv me. Calms me internals, you savvy? I take a wee breather in me rocker just after loading in, before everyfink gets busy. People been calling me a dirty old rocker for years now. I fort I might as well commit to it.'

Dana smiled at Mr Two's ever-changing accent, and his homespun wisdom.

'Oh hey,' she said, finally remembering the roadie she'd spotted just before Mr Two turned up, 'was that Three Blokes I saw earlier? Is she working this gig?'

'Right you are, young Dana. Haulin' tubs and tightenin' skins, is what she be doing. She'll be busy as all get-out right now, mind, if you're looking to initiate chin-waggery. But you'll be able to catch up with her while some of these drongos are trying and failing to join the band.' He gestured at the mass of hopeful guitarists. 'She'll be side-stage for the duration, in case somefing drum-related needs a drop of oil or a kick in the guts.' He gave her a wink, and swaggered off, in the manner of someone who's about to give some gear a good roadie-ing.

Dana cast about for a corner she could lurk in, but before she found one, a voice burst over the sound system.

'Okay, gentlemen...' there was a pause, and feedback to begin to swell, as is regulation in these scenarios. Dana looked up to the stage as one of the event personnel nudged the announcer, and pointed straight at her. The announcer cleared his throat, and continued: '...sorry, ladies and gentlemen. Welcome all, to the tryouts fooooor...'

Confused looks criss-crossed the room as everyone wondered if this second pause was for effect rather than a mistake. Finally the speakers leapt into action again as the announcer yelled: 'CRANIAL BYPASS!'

Chapter 7: The audition - part one

A few of the guitarists in the room cheered, but for others, the announcement was met with a combination of barely-contained nervousness and excitement, a few quick trips to the toilets, and a whole lot of people eyeing up their competition.

Helpers began circulating throughout the room, taking names and assigning numbers. Dana ended up with number five, thank goodness. By the size of the crowd, it was going to be a very long day, and she'd be pleased to have her turn and then get out of there.

'Don't lose track of this,' the person said as they handed her a slip of paper with the number on it. 'If you're not in the room when the number's called, you miss your shot. Good luck from all of us in the Hemisphere.' And then they were off to corral another guitarist, before Dana could say anything in reply.

Dana chuckled to herself. She used to be an official paid-up member of the Hemisphere herself. The Cranial Bypass fan club was huge, rabid and completely dedicated to all things Pox and Horgs. Oh, and the other band members too, of course, but everybody knew the show was all about the two stars out front; the superlative singer and the godlike guitarist – the golden larynx and the flaming frets.

Dana toyed absentmindedly with the slip of paper with her number on it as she once again scanned the room for somewhere to sit down and relax while she waited. Out of the corner of her eye she spotted a shabby couch that someone was just now rising out of. She made a beeline for it, trying not to look at it directly in case she tipped off anyone else and they beat her to it.

But just as she went to sink down into the seat, someone bumped her hip and sent her flying off to the side.

'Hey!' she said, just catching herself before she dropped her guitar, 'I'm sitting there.'

'Sorry boss!' said the offending hip-checker. 'Didn't see you. Crikey, it's busy here, isn't it?'

Dana turned right into the headlights of a

hundred-watt grin she knew only too well. It was, of course, her enthusiastic employee.

'Brody!' she exclaimed. 'What the hell are you doing here? We agreed you weren't going to come along to this.'

He stuck out his bottom lip. 'Actually, no. Everyone else agreed. I sure didn't. And anyway, I'm only here to try out.' He waved a battered guitar case in her face.

'Think about this,' Dana reasoned. 'What's Evan going to say when he finds out you came here?'

'Pretty sure he'll say "Damn, Brody, you look good fronting a famous rock band"'.

'That's – '

Dana's rebuttal was interrupted by someone yelling 'NUMBER ONE!' over the PA system.

Brody smiled again and waved his number at Dana. 'That's me. Wish me luck! Oh, and you can have the couch now, boss.'

Before Dana could tackle and hog-tie him, Brody was off towards the stage.

As Dana finally claimed her seat, she watched Brody hop up onto the stage, completely ignoring the stairs at the side. A roadie offered him a choice of amps to plug into. Dana nodded with satisfaction at the selection. There was a dilapidated Marshall amplifier head sat atop a matching speaker cabinet.

Both items looked like they'd travelled the world. On a budget. And there was a shiny Fender combo amp. A one-piece affair which, although smaller than the Marshall, was just as capable of moving serious air. Together these amps were the twin pillars of rock guitar.

Brody chose the Marshall – plugging straight in, with no effects pedals. It seemed a risky strategy to Dana, not having any electronic toys to cover potential mistakes. And she was certain there would be quite a few of those. Brody was incredibly keen, and he had the thing that experienced musicians called 'good feel'. But he was not what you'd call an advanced guitarist, and the Cranial Bypass material was definitely challenging.

Dana would be very surprised if Brody managed to impress a top-tier musician like Horgen Greymantle. Not that Horgs was present, anyway. Perhaps he was watching from the wings, or perhaps he was only going to show his face when the field had been whittled down a bit.

At least the actual Cranial Bypass drummer and bass player were there, so they'd be able to see how the hopeful guitarists would fit in with the rhythm section.

The bass player gave Brody a nod, and yelled out the name of a song. Immediately the drummer counted in, and by the time he'd done 'one and two' Brody just had time to adopt a look of immense panic. By 'three', he'd recovered enough to turn his guitar's volume knob up. On 'four' he rolled his shoulders, and then they were off.

Dana pre-emptively winced in sympathy, but then something odd happened.

Brody turned out to actually be quite good. Now, sure, he wasn't Jimi Hendrix incarnate. The spirit of Dimebag Darrell did not descend unto him and furnish him with an impressive array of arpeggiated runs for a solo. But he certainly appeared competent enough to earn his place in the room.

Dana found herself smiling, and nodding along with the groove of the song. This was delightfully unexpected. Had Brody actually been – deep breath – practicing?

The song finished, and the bass player made Brody's day – nay, his entire decade – by gracing him with a fist bump.

This was high praise indeed from the bassist - a famously taciturn individual. To the extent that, one time onstage, Pox had pointed out to him that his bass amp had caught fire. The bass player had just shrugged, and simply played faster so he could finish the set.

He was the kind of guy who didn't so much attend press interviews as torpedo them. Famously, at his wedding, his bride had to say 'he does'.

Brody looked ecstatic as he turned to leave the stage, but forgot he was still plugged in, and tripped over his guitar lead. He was still smiling as a roadie rushed over to help him up from where he'd face-planted onto the vocal monitor.

Dana left him to his performance high and abandoned her seat in search of Three Blokes, the drum tech.

Chapter 8: Talking to Three Blokes

Wending her way through the crowd, Dana spotted a door leading to the backstage area, off to the left of the huge main PA speakers. Being an audition day, there was no need for the door to be locked, or for any security presence, as everyone in the room now either had a number identifying them, or else they were working there.

Dana went up a small flight of stairs and found herself right at the side of the stage, just as guitar-god hopeful number two was plugging in. As predicted, Three Blokes the drum roadie was there, watching the proceedings with a relaxed stance but an air of readiness. Dana knew that no matter how well prepped the stage was, there's always a chance that accidents can happen, and the roadie's professional pride would require them to fix anything that broke within seconds, using nothing but gaffer tape and determination if need be.

She went to clear her throat to get Three Blokes' attention, but she'd already been spotted. A roadie learned to develop a sixth sense which told them when someone else was backstage, even if they were approaching from behind. Somehow, through all the noise and commotion, they had a superpower which told them to look out in case someone was carrying something heavy nearby and was about to drop it on them.

The roadie turned to see who it was, and they gave Dana a quick chin-lift in greeting, then turned back to their vigilant surveillance of the stage.

'Um,' Dana ventured, 'Hi. You're Three Blokes, right?'

The roadie belted out a laugh in response, still watching the stage as she replied. 'Oh my god. You've been talking to Gerry, haven't you?'

'Gerry?'

This brought forth another laugh. 'Yes. He calls himself Mister Two. Wants everyone to have a nickname for some bloody reason. His real name's Gerald Twomey.'

'Ooohhhhh…'

Finally the roadie turned to give Dana her full attention.

'I'm Cass, by the way. Cassandra Trippel.' She

extended a hand for Dana to shake.

'Aha,' said Dana, 'Trippel. Three Blokes. I think I'm starting to see a pattern here.'

Cass winked. 'Yep, you got it. Gerry's about as subtle as a soft drink marketing campaign.'

Dana shrugged. 'True, but I'm already kind of missing the idea of calling him Mister Two, if I'm honest.'

'Yes, to be fair, it does engender a certain feeling of camaraderie, so I suppose I get why he does it. I don't know, though. I find that working in close proximity with people over time grows that feeling naturally anyway. The road crew, the sound engineer, the band members, you all get to know each other really well when you're on tour, so you don't have to force it.'

'You knew my brother well, then,' Dana said.

Dana was watching Cass closely, so she spotted a shadow flit across her face before she looked away, fixing her gaze back on the stage. She muttered something that Dana didn't catch. It was buried under the roar from the band.

Dana shifted her weight on her feet, steeled herself, and forged on. 'I wondered if you knew who I was.'

Cass paused, then sighed before answering. 'I can see it now. Obviously you're Zig's sister.' She turned and studied Dana. 'You might not look exactly like him, but there's definitely a lot of him in you. You carry yourself the same way. And your smile...' She broke off, and looked back at the stage.

Dana took a deep breath and asked the question she dreaded hearing the answer to.

'Were you there when..? Do you know what happened to Ziggy? At the end?'

Cass froze. The only movement in her body was her nostrils flaring. Even her eyes stayed fixed on one spot.

'I have to know,' Dana continued, her voice breaking. 'Please. Can you tell me what happened?'

Cass' mouth worked soundlessly for a second. 'I...'

A crash came from the stage. Dana looked over and saw that one of the drummer's cymbal stands was lying on its side, the cymbal bent and useless.

By the time Dana turned back, Cass the roadie had disappeared. She shot out onto the stage with a replacement cymbal in her hand, swapped it with the broken one, and reinstalled the stand where it was supposed to be. Then, instead of returning to Dana, she slipped off the other side of the stage, and vanished into the darkness.

As the music rose in volume again, Dana let out a wordless yell of frustration.

Chapter 9: Dana's first audition

Dana went around to the other side of the stage but Cass was nowhere to be found. In desperation she fruitlessly traversed the bowels of the backstage area, but it was starting to look as though Three Blokes – aka Cassandra Trippel – had copied the King, and left the building. Given the way that her and Mr Two had described their devotion to duty, this was a shocking turn of events. Surely she'd still be around somewhere, watching from a dark corner?

As Dana prepared for yet another round of searching, she heard the whine of a hungry puppy. Or maybe it was a distressed gazelle? No, wait, it sounded like... ah, it was Brody, calling her name.

What the heck did he want now? Didn't he know she was doing important stuff?

With a huff, Dana set off towards the source of

the noise. As she emerged near the front of the stage, Brody finally spotted her.

'Ah! There… you are… boss!' He gasped as he raced over to her. 'Five!'

'What?' said Dana. 'You have to use your words, Brody. Numbers aren't helping much.'

'It's you!' he puffed. 'Number… five!' Brody grabbed her arm. 'You! Five… guitar…shred… Cranial…'

Oh shit. Dana suddenly realised what he was on about. She was number five, of course, in the tryouts for the replacement guitarist for Cranial Bypass!

Thank goodness her guitar case was still in her hand. She raced onto the stage, just as the announcer was about to step back up to the microphone with a big number six in his paws.

'Wait!' she cried. 'I'm here! Number five, reporting for duty.'

He gave her a sour look, and tapped his watch. Dana really hoped this guy wasn't one of the judges. She pulled her guitar from its case, along with two cables and a small booster effect pedal, and plugged into the same Marshall that Brody had used.

She looked around to see the bass player and drummer waiting for her with arms crossed.

'Sorry, you two… um, family emergency.'

The bass player sniffed at this news. 'Brains come before blood, if you want to be in the Cranial Bypass crew.'

Dana took this to be an oblique reference to the name of the band, and not some gruesome threat.

'Oh,' the bassist continued with a smirk as he spotted her effect pedal, 'and I see you're using a talent booster. Best of luck, chica.'

Wow, it turned out that the bass player's reputation for never saying a word was completely unfounded. Not only that, when he did speak, it turned out he was, well, a bit of dick.

Dana simply smiled in response.

The bass player called out the name of a song.

The drummer counted it in.

And they were off.

'Far out, Wade!' yelled Brody later that night. 'You should have seen her tear the place apart! She was on fire! It was like Cory Wong and Kerry King crammed into one pair of jeans!'

'Don't know either of those names, but it sounds impressive,' said Wade, around a mouthful of stir-fried fridge remnants.

Dana's place was once again the venue for a meeting of what was starting to become known as the Mysterious Undercover Guitarist Society. Dana still had reservations about the whole thing, so she thought it was an appropriate acronym. They had to be a bunch of mugs to get involved in a guitar-related murder case. Again.

Wade, Brody and Evan were back in her lounge, but at least this time they had brought food with them.

'No, Pawsy!' Dana shooed her cat away as he was just about to jump up on Evan's lap to try and steal his dinner. Paws had the decency to look guilty as he slunk away, but Dana could swear he looked back to plan his next mission. Then again, even if Paws McCartney had been allowed to sit at the table he still would still have had trouble fighting off Wade for any leftovers.

Brody was the one who had stir-fried whatever vegetables he found in his fridge, and biffed it on top of some noodles. Evan had provided some gorgeous miniature puff-pastry pizza-type things, the vast majority of which had disappeared into Wade's gaping maw at pretty much the same time as he was saying hello to everyone.

Dana was both impressed and shocked at how much Wade could eat, and the velocity at which he did it. He also somehow managed to stay trim, which Dana thought should be a jailable offence.

Wade spotted Dana's raised eyebrow. 'Gotta eat fast when you grow up with five brothers,' he mumbled as he began to demolish the dessert that he'd brought along to share.

Dana frowned. 'I thought you only had three brothers?'

'Yeah,' Wade shrugged, 'but I'm just saying, if you had five brothers you'd learn to eat fast.'

It's a truth well-known to anyone who watches crime shows that a police officer in want of a snack is a terrifying thing, and presumably at baby police school they are taught to ingest calories at every opportunity, lest they be caught short on a stake-out, or some other assignment far from the deli aisle.

So Dana considered her rapidly diminishing pantry stocks as simply the price one paid for law and order.

'Back to the audition though,' said Wade as he licked his spoon and eyed Dana's plate wistfully. 'So you did well, then?'

'I think I fluffed the bridge a bit,' Dana replied, 'but I did okay.'

'Did okay?' Brody roared. 'Doing okay is dipping your toes in the ocean. But you were swimming with dolphins, boss.'

Dana smiled at Brody's aquatic compliment.

Though the audition had been nerve-wracking, she had to admit once she'd actually started playing, it had been fun. And given the talent of the rhythm section, it made playing the guitar so much easier. To be immersed in a group of people simultaneously playing their asses off while also listening intently to each other was indeed like swimming with dolphins, or flying with eagles, or... well, you could choose your favourite ecstatic animal-based imagery, and it would probably fit the bill.

Knowing that the groove was solid, she had no fear the song would fall apart, as they so often do with less proficient musicians. And knowing that people were there to hear what she could do when she really let rip was... well, initially it was daunting. But the drummer flashed her a smile as soon as Dana competently navigated the tricky intro to the song, and even the bass player came around well before the solo section, so she could feel them both egging her on, pouring their energy into the song in order that she was free to take flight.

And so she did.

Having missed some of the other contestants while she was looking for the runaway roadie Cass, Dana still didn't know how she ranked in the auditions, but at least she knew she hadn't embarrassed herself. There were one or two other guitarists there that she knew would have acquitted themselves well, one of them being the precociously talented Nikau Daniels.

She didn't possess any laurels, but even if she did, she wouldn't be resting on them right now.

'So, our plan progresses,' said Wade, with more confidence than Dana felt. 'As I knew it would.'

'Don't enumerate your roosters just yet, Wade,' said Dana. 'There's a fair bit of competition. Like Brody, for example. He also played really well.'

'Thanks, boss!' Brody beamed, until Evan caught his eye and gave him a look that said: there is a discussion waiting to happen when we get home.

Dana saw and correctly interpreted this look, so she quickly changed the subject.

'I spoke to Aaron Swetters, by the way.'

Wade gave her a blank look.

'He's the guy I told you about,' she reminded him. 'He bought a whole lot of phosphor bronze guitar strings a little while back.'

'Oh yeah, that guy,' said Wade. 'And did you shake any clues out of him? Or a confession, maybe?'

'Quite the opposite, I'm afraid. I don't think he's got an evil bone in his body.'

'I dunno about that,' Brody interjected. 'He does

own a double-neck bass banjo hybrid, after all. He's obviously comfortable with inflicting pain on others.'

Dana laughed. 'Well, get used to it Brody, because Swetters is planning a new album, and he was intending to write some songs with Apocalypse BusLane. Once word of that gets around, you won't be able to move without hearing the bass-jo.'

'What?' said Brody. 'Swetters and Pox, collaborating? I don't believe it. I thought you said they hated each other?'

Dana got up to put the kettle on. 'Turns out they made up recently. Swetters said Pox seemed to have had a change of heart, and wanted to do something to help leave the world a better place after he'd gone.'

'Hmmm…' said Wade. 'A marked behavioural change just before he turns up dead? Could well be related. That was good work, Dana. Did he say anything else?'

'No, but since we now know that he gives away all those strings to at-risk youth, and uses the profits from his support slots with Cranial Bypass to fund charitable works, it very much paints the picture of man who wouldn't want to bite the hand that feeds, you know? Especially if him and Pox were working on an album together.'

'To be fair,' said Evan, 'we only have his word for that.'

Wade nodded. 'You're not wrong. Dana will have to get us more indisputable evidence than that if she wants to clear this sweaty guy's name.'

'Swetters,' Dana called out over the sound of the kettle boiling. 'His name is Swetters, not sweaty.'

'I'd be sweating if I was him,' said Wade. 'You're doing good work, Dana, but this bloke is still a suspect, okay?'

'How about this then?' said Dana. 'I've heard the demos.' She poured the boiling water into the teapot and paused for a second to inhale the rich aroma.

'Demos of him and Apocalypse BusLane?' Evan burst out, his voice rising with excitement. 'You're telling us that you've heard unreleased demos of new BusLane material? With Aaron bloody Swetters?!'

Dana smiled. 'That's right.'

There was a moment of silence as the musicians took time to mull over the significance of this… and while Wade contemplated wrestling Paws McCartney for a scrap of pastry that had fallen onto the floor.

'And?!!!' Brody broke the silence. 'Don't keep me in suspenders. What was the music like?'

'I guess you'll just have to wait for the album to come out, won't you?' said Dana. She laughed at the look on Brody's face. 'I'm sorry, Brodes, he swore me to secrecy. And it was only a demo anyway, it might sound quite different once it's been recorded properly. Although I kind of hope Aaron puts it out as is, so we get to hear Pox's last recording exactly the way he heard it.'

Brody looked like he was about to cry foul on Dana's decision not to divulge more information, but Wade inserted himself back into the conversation before he could do so.

'Okay then, so it seems like Swetters isn't a good fit for the murder then.'

'Oh, Wade,' Dana groaned, 'Swetters isn't a good fit? How long have you been sitting on that remark?'

Wade chuckled. 'You got me - I actually prepped that one before I came over here this evening. But, moving on. Who are you going to talk to next?'

Dana deposited cups of tea in front of everyone and offered a packet of biscuits around. She surreptitiously palmed a few biscuits before the packet reached Wade, since they would probably not survive an encounter with him.

'How about this?' she said as she plopped into her chair. 'How about we wait to hear if I even get past the first audition before we plan any more little chats, shall we?'

'Failing to plan is planning to fail,' Wade intoned. 'They said so at the last professional development day I was sent to. I'm still not sure who I annoyed, that got me punished with that.' He shrugged ruefully.

'Well, don't worry, I'm planning alright. I'm planning on having a nice hot bath and then reading my book.' Dana popped a biscuit in her mouth and waggled her eyebrows at Wade. She wasn't about to take on any extra pressure from him. If she made the cut, she would simply approach people as they became available. It's not as though she could schedule visits with them anyway, without tipping her hand.

So Wade would just have to chill out.

Actually, he looked more dozy than chilled. The sheer quantity of food he'd consumed tonight was obviously having a soporific effect on him.

She swallowed the remains of her biscuit and cleared her throat. 'Speaking of plans, maybe it's time you popped home, officer? Let your stomach have a rest for a bit, hmm? While you plan what to have for breakfast.'

Chapter 10: The call-back

Next morning, true to form, Dana was woken by Paws McCartney batting at her nose and kneading her chest.

'Ow! Paws, you're a menace.' She decanted him from the bed and put her slippers on. Oh well, she needed to be up early today anyway. It was the weekend, which was the busiest time for the shop. Not so much in terms of sales, more in terms of people coming in to play classic rock riffs for thirty minutes through amps they couldn't afford while their partner was in another shop.

'C'mon, you furry fiend,' she called to Paws as she went to top up his food bowl. He leapt up, and executed some truly impressive Empire Strikes Back-style zig-zags between Dana's legs as she walked to the kitchen. Paws seemed unconcerned that if he tripped Dana and she broke her neck, she wouldn't be able to feed him.

One of these days Dana was going to have to have a talk with him about consequences.

When she got downstairs to prepare the shop for opening, Brody was already waiting at the back door. Dana did a double-take, and then checked her watch. No, she wasn't late.

She unlocked the door and let him in. 'Brody, what's going on? Is everything okay?' More softly: 'Oh, hon. Did Evan kick you out?'

'What?' squawked Brody. 'No! Of course not. Why would you say that?'

'Sorry!' Dana winced. 'It's just, you know, it's… early for you.'

'I couldn't wait to get over here after I got that text message, to find out if you got in or not.'

Brody threw his coat in a corner and rounded on Dana, his eyes as wide as a gatefold vinyl LP. 'So?'

'What text?' Dana fished her phone out of her jeans pocket. 'I haven't even looked at this thing yet today.'

'It's only a text from the Cranial Bypass management!' Brody was thrumming with excitement.

'Oh wow,' said Dana. 'So, you made the cut?'
'Hell no!'
'Then why are you so excited?'
'Because surely you did. Come on,' Brody made

hurry-up gestures with his hands. 'Tell me!'

Dana breathed deeply: in - two - three, out - two - three. Then checked her messages.

By now, Brody was hopping from foot to foot like the floor was on fire.

Dana froze in shock, then looked up at him.

'I'm in,' she whispered. 'Brody, they want me to come back. I'm in the final five.' She felt like she was floating off the floor. Her brain had gone all fuzzy.

'Yes!!!' Brody yelled. 'This is so cool! My boss is going to be in Cranial Bypass! We're going to have such a great time!'

Dana shook herself out of her surprise. 'What do you mean we?'

'Well, I'll come with you, right? Tune up your guitar and stuff.' Brody hunched over and looked out the corner of his eyes. 'And then while you're playing guitar, I'll sneak around and find the killer.'

'No,' said Dana emphatically. 'Someone has to stay here to run the shop. In case you haven't noticed, it's down to either you or Paws McCartney.'

Paws chose that moment to strut into the middle of the room, flop himself down and vigorously clean his privates.

Dana glanced from the cat back to Brody. 'And as

much I admire Paws' body-positive confidence, that kind of display isn't going to sell many guitars. So you're in charge while I'm out, Brodes.'

'Awwww.'

She had a brainwave. 'Hey, maybe Evan would like to come and help out? Keep you company and earn a few dollars while he's here.'

'Seriously? That would be cool!' Brody's happy-puppy face warmed Dana's heart. It was nice to be able to cheer him up like that. The bonus for her was that Evan was sensible, stable and polite. Brody could be nominally in charge, but Dana knew she could rely on Evan in case of emergencies.

'Right then, you give Evan a call and I'll go and get ready.'

Brody stopped mid-happy dance. 'You're going now?'

'Yep,' Dana waved her phone at him. 'Apparently they want to make the final decision today, so the five finalists are supposed to be back at The Riffery in...' she checked the message. 'Wow, in just under an hour.'

Her heart immediately took this opportunity to double-time the beat, as if building up to a bombastic chorus in a metal band. Dana's palms went clammy. This was a big deal - she was trying out for a spot in a legendary band. And on top of that, she was supposed to stay cool and investigate a murder at the same time? Why the hell had she agreed to this insane plan? Oh, that's right. Wade had forced her into it.

She did her breathing again. Nothing else for it. She needed to forget everything else, and just focus on playing guitar. Lucky for Dana, playing guitar was her happy place.

She forced herself to slowly look around at all the guitars hanging on the shop walls. That always calmed her down. Guitars were so cool. They looked awesome, and were always there for you, ready to convey whatever emotion you were having trouble saying with words. She gave Brody a smile and headed back upstairs to prepare.

'Want me to contact Wade too? Tell him the good news?' Brody called out.

She paused. 'No,' she called back. 'don't bother him on a weekend. Wait till we know one way or the other.'

'Okay, boss. Good luck, and don't worry about the shop. I'll look after the place.' Dana heard a thump, a stifled curse, and a twanging sound as if someone had dropped a guitar and then got their hand caught in the strings and then tried to extricate it without letting anyone else know, but made a meal of it.

She sighed. 'Thanks, Brody.' Evan was going to have his work cut out for him.

For phase two of the Mysterious Undercover Guitar Society project, Dana decided to take her own amplifier. At the first audition, backline amplifiers had been provided, but now it was time to step up the professionalism, and Dana wanted them to know she was serious, which meant demonstrating that she had her own gear that was up to the job. It also meant she could take an amplifier that she knew well. It was like being a race-car driver. They wouldn't turn up to a race and ask to borrow whatever car was laying around. You had to know your equipment inside out, and know how it would handle in the tight corners, just like with guitars. Dana had been using the same guitar, amp and pedal combination for years now, so she knew exactly how she would sound in any room. She knew that the amp would respond to her guitar's volume control in a certain way, becoming clean and jangly when she turned down, and roaring with overdrive when she turned up. You really couldn't afford surprises when performing with a top-level act in front of hundreds of people. Stuff-ups would not be appreciated.

Her humbucker-equipped Telecaster could belt

out a rock riff along with the best of them, and there was a special switching arrangement which made it sound more like a traditional Tele – quieter and more spanky – when she needed it. Her amplifier was based on the classic Marshall Plexi design, but in a custom 1 x 12 combo that was easy to carry. It had also been modified with an extra boost that she could switch on or off with a footswitch.

She loved all these little details that made her job so much easier, and allowed her to fit into any musical situation. She knew that her audience wouldn't know or care about any of the subtle mods on her equipment, and that's how she liked it. They shouldn't notice her gear - only her playing.

Of course, there would always be other gear nerds in the audience, the ones who would have an opinion on Telecasters versus Les Pauls for this or that application. But if the majority of the listening public went home happy, that's all that mattered.

There were some guitars that got noticed by almost everyone, even non-players. Guitars such as an over-the-top dream guitar like a vintage Draydon Weka, for example. Like the one that Gene Stevens had owned before his untimely demise, and which was now on loan to Nikau Daniels. Dana smiled. She was pretty sure she'd be seeing that guitar again today. Nikau was such a great player, she knew he would've made the cut too.

When she arrived at The Riffery, her suspicion was confirmed. Nikau was waiting at the back door, along with three others. Dana waved at him and she got a cheery smile in return.

She puffed out her cheeks. Whew. This was it, then.

The other day they'd been amongst the multitudinous ranks of the Possibles, and now it was down to the final five Probables. If she wanted to unearth the killer of Apocalypse BusLane, and get more leads on what happened to her brother, Dana was going to have to perform a blinder today.

The venue's door creaked open, and some peeling paint drifted away into the carpark as a man's head poked out.

'Hi all!' he chirped. 'Right on time – that's what I like to see.' He beckoned them inside. His smile was perpetually set to stun, it seemed. Dana could easily navigate the dim corridor just from the glare of his pearly white teeth.

The guitarists were gently corralled into the green room backstage. Dana noted that the decor and furniture looked sad and abused in the harsh light of day. It wasn't being fair to the room, really, letting people in before dark. It felt like they were intruding on the room's private time.

One thing which really stuck out was a big old rocking chair. Mr Two's seat of choice, she presumed. On an impulse, she sat in it. Then immediately regretted it, as she couldn't stop bobbing back and forth while their handler briefed them.

'Okay,' said Mister Smiley. 'First things first, my name is Trent Grainger and I'm the manager of Cranial Bypass. Well, specifically I'm Horgen Greymantle's manager, but for the purposes of this project I'm running the whole thing, alright?'

Everyone nodded. Message received. Do not make this man's day any more difficult than it needs to be.

While he went on to tell them how the audition process worked, Dana subconsciously fidgeted with the arms of the chair. They were carved, rather magnificently really. Someone very skilled had put a lot of time into this piece of furniture. She could see why Mr Two – Gerald, as Cass had informed her – would lug it around with him. It certainly was very calming to sit in. Hmmm. It felt like the little raised area at the end might lift up on a hidden hinge. Maybe there was a small compartment under there?

'Dana, is it?'

Dana's head snapped up. She stared directly into

Trent's wall of shiny white teeth. Shit. What had she missed?

'Um… yes?'

'You got all that, did you, darling?'

'I'm not your darling, but I think I have the general gist.'

Well, damn. What had she just told herself not two minutes ago about staying on this guy's good side? Still, sexist comments were best nipped in the bud, she usually found. A bit of tough love at the start of a relationship could save a lot of heartache later.

She chanced a grin.

Trent stared at her for what felt like an eternity, before finally chuckling. 'Fair call. Sorry. Did you get everything I said, though?'

She cleared her throat. A small group of butterflies attempted to make a break for it, out of her stomach and into her larynx. Seriously? she mentally scolded them. Now is not the time, please.

'Ah, yes, I believe I heard everything.' She ticked points off on her fingers. 'First, we have a five-minute chat with the drummer and the bass player, and sort out what we'll be playing. Secondly,' the butterflies fluttered at her throat again, 'ahem… Horgen joins us and we then play two songs with the full band. Thirdly, the band goes off to compare notes for fifteen minutes, and then it's the next person's turn.'

If she hadn't been staring him right in the teeth she might not have noticed when Mr Smiley's smile faltered for half a second.

'You missed the bit about being asked back for a one-on-one with Horgs after everyone has auditioned. Did you not think that was important?'

Dana's face caught fire, and she self-immolated into a small pile of ashes which floated out the door on a gust of wind. Metaphorically speaking.

'Sorry,' she squeaked.

'That's quite alright,' he leaned closer, 'darling.' He straightened up again and shone his five-hundred-watt smile around the shabby room, flashing across the slouching forms of five guitarists, most of whom weren't used to being up this early and communicating with other humans. 'So let's kick off, shall we? You.' He pointed at Dana. 'Are you ready?'

'Absolutely,' she stammered, feeling like her lips had gone numb.

'I doubt it,' he sneered, 'but try and convince me, huh?' He jerked his head towards the door.

Dana rocked herself forwards out of the chair, and picked up her guitar case and amplifier.

The reassuring weight of the guitar against one

leg and the amp resting against the other grounded her. Now she was home. Wherever her guitar was, she could be comfortable.

Sure, she'd prefer to be at her actual home, relaxing on her sofa, or chatting with Brody in the shop, but once she had her guitar in hand, she knew who she was and what she could do.

She felt calm, relaxed, and ready to face the next challenge.

Confidently, she strode through the door.

And bumped straight into Detective Chief Inspector Mary Shaw.

Oh no!

Dana froze. Damn, she'd been found out. Maybe Wade had blabbed about what they were up to. Or DCI Shaw had put two and two together and assumed Dana would stick her nose into a music-related case. Or maybe Shaw had been having Dana covertly tailed ever since the last case, just to make sure she stayed out of the way?

A tiny part of her brain was yelling at her, trying to tell her something was wrong with DCI Shaw today, but her panic wasn't having any of that, and refused to listen.

This was not good. Dana hoped she wouldn't end up in jail. She hadn't even liked sharing a room at sleepovers when she was a kid – how would she handle sharing a cell? What if her cellmate Shotgun Sharlene didn't like reading?!

Oh my goodness, who'd look after Paws McCartney?

Dana started to hyperventilate.

'Miss Osborne?' said Shaw.

'Ms.' Dana gasped, hauling in a breath.

Shaw rolled her eyes. 'Sorry, Ms Osborne. How I've missed our delightful conversations. What are you…?' Shaw cut herself off as realisation dawned. 'Oh, of course. You're trying out to replace Apocalypse BusLane in Cranial Bypass, am I right?'

Dana sent a message to her neck, telling it to nod her head. It managed a reasonable facsimile of a normal person nod. When would the handcuffs come out? Why was Shaw toying with her?

'Yes,' Dana wheezed, 'just playing guitar. I play guitar, you know, so it's perfectly normal for me to be here. In this situation.'

DCI Shaw gave her a long, slow look that could have cooked a steamed pudding to perfection.

'I understand that,' she replied slowly. 'I do remember that you play guitar, Dana. Are you feeling okay?'

'Sure, good, happy, good,' said Dana. 'Okay. Anyway, gotta shoot, scoot, shoot off. Playing guitar, you know.'

Shaw pursed her lips. 'Right. Off you go, then. Nice to see you again.'

The fist that had been clenched around Dana's heart started to loosen. Maybe she wasn't going to be spending her nights playing bridge on a smuggled deck of cards with Shotgun Sharlene after all.

Her feet went to race out of there, but now that her panic was receding, her brain finally engaged, and she stopped in her tracks. Shaw looked different because Dana had never seen her like this - out of uniform. This detail was glaringly obvious now that Dana could breathe properly again. So, if Shaw wasn't here on official business...

'DCI Shaw?'

'Yes?'

'May I ask what are you doing here?'

Shaw smiled. 'Why? Are you worried I'll steal your spot?'

This thought was so far from occurring to Dana that it could not be seen with the strongest telescope on Earth. For a second she thought Shaw might actually be serious. Could it be true that Shaw played guitar? So she hadn't needed her for the earlier case after all? What the hell was going on?

'Don't worry, Dana, I'm only here visiting

someone.'

Well, okay, that made more sense. Except…

'Visiting?' said Dana. 'You have a friend at a seedy music venue?'

'Hey!' said a voice behind her. 'That was uncalled for.' Sione, the owner of The Riffery lurched past carrying a tray of semi-clean pint glasses.

'Sorry!' Dana called after him. 'You know I love this place, right?'

He turned back and winked at her and then disappeared around the corner into the bar.

Dana turned her attention back to DCI Shaw, and was surprised to see that it was now Shaw who looked uncomfortable.

The Inspector scratched the back of her neck. 'Ah, look, I'm trying to keep it quiet, okay?'

'Keep what quiet?' said Dana, instinctively lowering her voice.

Shaw sighed. 'I'm here to see my wife, Hinemoa. She's in one of the support acts.'

'Hinemoa..?' said Dana. 'Oh!' she cried. 'Your wife is *that* Hinemoa - the one from the band Giant Penguins?'

'Yes,' hissed Shaw. 'But keep it down, would you? We don't want people to know.'

'Know what? That you're…' whispered Dana, glancing left and right before continuing.

'Lesbians?'

Shaw snorted. 'What? No! Why would anyone care about that?' She lowered her voice to a whisper again. 'No, she just doesn't want too many people to know that she's married to a police officer. Some of the other band members have had… interactions with the force from time to time in the past, and she just wants them to all get to know each other a bit better before she tells them.'

'Oh.' said Dana awkwardly. 'Yeah, no, I mean why would anyone care about the… the other thing, right? Hah! Okay, really gotta go now. Bye!'

Dana scuttled off towards the stage while Shaw scuttled off the other way, further into the warren of corridors, neither of them keen to prolong the embarrassing encounter.

At the stairs to the stage she found that Trent Grainger had gone a different way and somehow scurried ahead of her, and now stood tapping his foot and checking his watch, pointedly.

'You've got two minutes left of your five-minute chat with the rhythm section, Osborne.' He jerked a thumb towards the stage. 'Best get on with it, huh?'

Dana loved to rock but she knew better than to rock the boat any further with the unpleasant band manager. She almost hoped she wouldn't get the gig, so she didn't have to share airspace with him again. That wouldn't help bring Pox's killer to justice though, so she gave Grainger a businesslike nod, and went to meet the band.

Lugging her amp and guitar onto the hallowed boards of The Riffery's main stage, she caught the eye of the bass player who'd been dismissive of her at the previous audition.

This time round, thank goodness, he greeted her with a smile.

'Hi,' he said, reaching out to help her with her amplifier. 'I'm Oliver Chen. Sorry about giving you a hard time in the first round.'

'I'm sorry I was late for my call-up. How about we say we're even, and start again with a clean slate?'

'Well, to be fair, you're late again this time, so you're down two to one, I'm afraid.'

Dana's heart sank. He was right. She was hardly in any danger of impressing them with her professionalism. Trying to do two jobs at once was not paying dividends for her so far. She'd have to try harder from now on. At least Oliver was still smiling — that was a good sign.

'I'm sorry, Oliver, it won't happen again. I mean it, I really enjoyed playing with you last time. You have such a solid groove.'

'Thanks! Well, half of that is due to old Tubs here,' he hooked a thumb toward the drum kit, behind which lurked the imposing figure of Cranial Bypass' drummer.

'Call me that again and I'll have your head on a hi-hat stand, Abyss,' the drummer grumbled as he adjusted his cymbals.

'I thought his stage name was Wulfric Foehammer?' Dana whispered. 'Just like you're called Plangent Abyss.'

'Oh, sure,' Oliver laughed, 'but way back when we were coming up with stage names, Spooky Tubs was one of the options we brainstormed, and I just always preferred that one.'

'Oi!' Wulfric bellowed. 'Do you want me to tell the nice lady what name I suggested for you?'

Oliver blanched. 'No need, mate. Really.'

Wulfric got up and walked over to shake Dana's hand. 'Hi. I'm Marty Bianchi. You don't have to use our stage names today. Unless it helps you get in the vibe. Isn't that right, Anti Spewmante?' He directed this last comment to Oliver.

'Oh shut up, you dick,' Oliver retorted as he went to get his bass off its stand.

Dana sensed the push and pull of the in-jokes, tensions and camaraderie of a long-established band at work, so she did not pry further into the origin of these nicknames, and instead set up her amp and tuned her guitar.

Thanks to the previous audition, Marty and Oliver had a good idea of how Dana played guitar, so it was easy for them to decide on the two songs to play today.

As she put her guitar on a stand near her amp, someone tapped her shoulder.

'Oh, are we ready to…' she turned around and found herself looking directly at one of Ziggy's old music posters. Except no, this was for real. It was actually Horgen Greymantle in front of her! He looked exactly as he had when his visage hung on Ziggy's wall all those years ago, except there was perhaps a bit more spackle holding the drywall of his features together these days, underneath the blacked-out eye makeup and long shaggy hair of his stage persona. Or, who knows, maybe that's what he always looked like?

Oh, she wished Ziggy could have been here for this. He would have been so excited to meet one of his musical heroes. He would have been even more excited to have met Apocalypse BusLane, but tragically, fate decreed that they had both passed beyond the veil by this time.

'Hi, Dana is it?' said the mysterious master of metal music.

'Yes, h-hi,' Dana stammered. 'So nice to meet you, Mr. Greymantle.'

A gregarious smile cracked his ragged features. 'Please, call me Hamish.'

Dana suppressed an urge to curtsey. 'It doesn't seem proper, somehow, Mr. Greymantle,' she said with an attempt at an Elizabeth Bennett-style accent.

He guffawed. 'Right you are, ma'am. Horgs it is.' He inclined his head towards where the rhythm section leaned against a bass amp, chatting. 'My boys tell me you aced the first audition. Looking forward to seeing what you can do this time round.'

'I'll do my best, sir.'

He leaned in conspiratorially. 'Don't hold back, young lady. I work best when Archie is pushing me with his guitar playing... Was pushing me, I mean.' A look of sadness and raw grief crossed the parts of his face that weren't buried under makeup. 'When Archie really got into it, he amped me up and I sang better. So I want you to get into it, and get in my face if you need to. Okay?'

Dana took a second to realise that Archie meant Apocalypse BusLane. She was still adjusting to the idea that these were real people, not superhuman characters from some alternate reality.

But now she got it. These were just musicians,

like all the other people she'd played with over the years. They wanted her to do well. They wanted her to push them, in the same way they would push her to greater heights. This audition wasn't a chance for them to put people down, it was a chance for them to find the right person to lift them up.

She smiled. 'Yes sir.'

With that in mind, the band members took their positions, and cranked into it. Once again, the time passed in a whirl, as Dana was enveloped by the superb musicianship of the top-tier band. This time, however, she reminded herself to make eye contact with the others in turn, expressing herself with nothing more than the movement of her body and the sound of her guitar. Greymantle, Foehammer and Abyss caught her enthusiasm, and rocked all the harder for it. At one point she really did swagger over to Horgen and play an ad-libbed, syncopated version of the riff right at him. To her delight, he caught the rhythm and sent it back her way with his own twist on it, and a high falsetto wail to cap it off.

She was having a blast, and was caught completely off-guard when, halfway through the second song, she spotted a shadowy figure at the side of the stage. She recognised that black-clad form. She knew from the easy familiarity with the stage, and the way they fixated on the drums. It was Cassandra Trippel, the roadie who held the key to the truth of Ziggy's demise. Damn it, why did she have to appear right now, when Dana couldn't talk to her?

Dana almost fumbled the next chord change, and had to force herself to put Cass out of her mind. She couldn't allow herself to be distracted right now, it would only ruin her chances of catching up with the roadie at a later date. Focus, Dana!

She eased herself back into the zone by following Wulfric Foehammer's kick drum and hi-hat pattern, and after a few bars she was deep in the groove again.

She had so much fun, it was devastating when the song finally ended, dropping her back to reality.

Still, she consoled herself with the knowledge that even if she didn't get the job, she could always say with pride that she'd played with Cranial Bypass, and held her own.

She packed away her guitar, and with smiles and nods all round, she lugged her gear offstage.

Her good mood was almost shattered by the sight of grumpy band manager Trent Grainger lurking in the corridor. And tantalisingly, just beyond him she could see the swift-retreating back of… darn it, Cass the roadie! Dana really wanted to talk to her, but she knew better than to rudely push past Greasy Grainger while carrying her guitar and amp. If she wanted to land the job with the band, she needed to ingratiate herself with Grainger. She knew how these things worked. The band manager usually had final say, no matter how big the artist they worked for.

So instead of pursuing Cass, she pasted a smile on her face and said 'Hi, Trent. That went really well, I thought.'

'Okay, cool, I wasn't really listening.'

'Seriously?' said Dana before she could stop herself. 'I kinda thought that was the point of today.'

'Is it though, darl… Dana?'

Chalk up one small win to Dana. Either he'd taken on board her feedback about being called darling, or else he thought he might open himself up to an expensive lawsuit if he didn't stop it. She was happy no matter what the reason. But still, what was up with his attitude now?

'I'm sorry,' said Dana, 'what do you mean, exactly? I came here to play guitar with Cranial Bypass, and today is all about showing that I'm good enough.'

'Sure,' said Grainger, checking his phone. 'You'd

think that would be what today is about, and yet I've just had a conversation with a backstage chick...' okay, thought Dana, he might not have completely learned his lesson yet. He hooked a thumb over his shoulder in the direction Cass had disappeared. '...and she reckons you've been harassing her.'

'What?! I have not. I just wanted to talk to her.'

'Well, guess what?' Grainger jabbed his finger at Dana. 'She doesn't want to talk to you. And she has asked me to remove you from the running because she doesn't want to work with you.'

'Wha...?' Dana's mouth opened and closed like an offended goldfish. 'You can't do that.'

'I absolutely can,' Grainger stated, as he fished through his pockets and produced a cigarette. 'I can do whatever I like. Pretty much.' He sighed. 'Except that Horgs has already said that he likes your playing, so if I chuck you out now I'd just be asking for a rock star-sized tantrum.'

Dana relaxed. Thank goodness!

'But I'll be trying my best to make sure you don't make the cut,' Grainger continued, shooting down Dana's hopes all over again. 'And even if you do,' he continued, 'you will be forbidden from going anywhere near that roadie chick, you understand?'

Dana swallowed her pride and nodded. 'Yes, I

understand. Now, if you don't mind, I'd really like to put this amp down.'

'All good by me.' Grainger sniffed. 'You might as well head home. We'll give you a call when it's time to do the debrief.' His attention had already turned back to his cigarette. The clicking of a lighter followed her down the hallway.

She hefted her guitar and amp, put her head down and trudged along the warren of corridors, keen to put some distance between herself and the odious man.

Unfortunately, in her haste, she rounded a corner and bumped into someone else. Thank goodness her music shop instincts kicked in - she gripped her equipment tight, sunk her weight into the soles of her feet, and managed to stay upright without dropping any of her precious cargo.

The same could not be said of her bumpee.

The slight young man toppled backwards, and the bass guitar case he'd been holding went crashing to the floor.

'Oh, hell! No!' he cried, as he crawled over to the case and then hovered fretfully around it like it was a dying penguin, and the last penguin doctor had left the area to go on vacation two days ago.

Dana sighed. Was she ever going to make her way out of this building?

'It's okay,' she said in her best horse-calming voice. She put her gear down and knelt by the stricken youngster, putting a hand on his shoulder. 'The case looks fine. Maybe a wee scuff on the bottom, but that might even give it a bit more rock'n'roll street cred, actually.'

'It's not the case I'm bloody well worried about,' he moaned, 'it's what's inside.'

Dana gave the case a professional glance. 'Late seventies or early eighties Music Man StingRay bass, I'm guessing?'

'Wha..? How did you know that?'

Dana tapped the logo riveted to the top of the tweed-covered case. 'This is the early Music Man logo. Music Man was bought out by Ernie Ball in around 1984. So this logo tells me it was from before that date. The case is the right size for a bass, and Music Man became famous for their StingRay basses around that time. The Bongo didn't come out till much later. So I'm thinking early StingRay.'

The young man now looked close to tears. 'You're right. You're absolutely right. But don't you see? It's a flipping classic. It belongs to Plangent Abyss. And I just dropped it! What if I've broken it? I'm too scared to open the case and check.'

Dana gave his shoulder another pat. 'I wouldn't be too worried if I was you. The bass is probably much more durable than the case that's wrapped around it. I've known people who used a StingRay to hammer in fence posts on the farm.'

'Really?' The guy's eyes went wide.

'Well, no, not really. I'm just saying, they are pretty sturdy. A wee drop like that is very unlikely to have harmed it. Let's have a look, shall we?'

With Dana's encouraging smile urging him on, the young man undid the latches and slowly lifted the lid. He kept his eyes half-averted, as if he was opening the trunk of the old Chevy Malibu in the film Repo Man, expecting radioactive aliens to turn him to ash.

To his great relief, and Dana's nod of satisfaction, the bass looked fine, and he remained un-immolated. Dana reached toward the instrument, glancing at the guy for permission to inspect it.

'Go for it,' he said, sitting back on his heels and puffing his cheeks out.

'I'm Dana, by the way.'

'Hi Dana. I'm Andrew. You can call me Andy.' He finally had the mental bandwidth to tear his focus from the bass. He looked around at Dana and her gear. 'Oh, are you one of the Inklings?'

Dana looked up from the bass. 'Inklings?'

Andy looked embarrassed. 'Oh, uh…that's what the band are calling the people trying out for Pox's spot.'

At Dana's confused look, he went on. 'You aren't fully-formed thoughts in the Cranial crew yet, so you're all just inklings at this point. You see?' He shrugged. 'They really like their brain metaphors in this band.'

Dana chuckled. 'Gotcha. And yes, I'm trying out… I'm an Inkling, as you say. Just had my audition now, actually. Hey, this is a really nice bass, by the way.' She handed it to him. 'And you'll be pleased to know it looks absolutely fine. I run a music shop. Done a million repairs. So I do know what I'm talking about when I say that.'

'Ohhh!' said Andy. 'You're Dana Osborne.'

Here it comes, thought Dana.

'Ziggy's sister!'

…aaaand there it is.

'Yes,' she said, 'Ziggy's sister. And I assume you're part of the backstage crew? Or were you in the process of stealing this rather valuable bass when I bumped into you?'

Andy looked completely shocked, and Dana chuckled. 'Don't worry, I saw that you have a crew lanyard, and by the stricken look on your face when you dropped the bass, I can tell you're just doing your job. Also, I have a friend who mentioned there was an Andy working this gig.'

'A friend mentioned me? What did they say?' Andy turned away, to reverently lay the bass back in its case and gently latch it shut.

'Just that you'd been called in to make up numbers.' Dana decided to discreetly leave out the bit where Mr Two had said that Andy seemed obsessed with Cranial Bypass and would have done the roadie work for free. 'And that you knew a bit about guitars.'

'Right. Well. I just got let go from my last job and needed some cash, and this turned up at just the right time.' He hung his head.

'You must have been upset when Pox passed away then.'

Andy lifted his head and gave her a strange look. Kind of… startled. 'Why do you say that?'

'Well,' said Dana, thinking it rather bleeding obvious. 'You just said you needed money, and you got offered this job. And then the whole thing imploded before it even got going.'

'Oh. Yeah. No, you're right. It was a bummer.' He got up and brushed the knees of his jeans, then grabbed the bass case.

'Still, at least you got to meet the great Apocalypse BusLane before he died. Did you get to talk to him much?'

'What? No, not as much as I'd have liked. I have

to go, sorry.' He hefted the case and stormed off.

'Okay,' said Dana, left by herself on the floor. 'Bye, then.' She stared after the strange young man. Then she sighed, stood up, grabbed her gear, and made one more attempt to get out of there.

To her great relief, she finally made it out of the venue without anyone else either running into her or running away from her. It was, frankly, almost a let-down after the last few action-packed minutes. But she took the win, and finally let the weight relax off her shoulders as she slumped into the stiffly-sprung interior of her old Volkswagen. She'd done her best at the audition, and now all she could do was wait to hear what Horgen and the rest of the Cranial Bypass team said.

Chapter 11: Back to the shop

After parking her Beetle at the shop, Dana entered through the back door, and froze.

Something was off. Evan was standing behind the counter, and Brody was faking nonchalance over by the bass amps. For some reason Evan's shirt was torn and he had a plaster on the back of his hand.

Neither of them said a word, but Evan was grinning like a dating show compere and Brody was kind of… squirming with excitement.

'What are you two up to?' she said slowly, as she took a step into the showroom.

'Ta da!' yelled Brody, thrusting his hands towards a display over in the electric guitar section.

Dana turned slowly, in the best horror movie fashion. In her mind, the violins shrieked towards a crescendo. Aaargh! What was that?

Oh no…it was her. She flinched away.

Someone had blown up a photo of her and made a life-size cut-out display out of it, along with a huge banner which read: The new guitarist in Cranial Bypass shops at Pick Me Guitar Shop!

'Well, what do you think?' Brody jiggled with excitement at her side.

'So, so…' she breathed.

'So…?'

'So many things wrong with this.'

'What? This will be great for business. We've already had a few new people come in since this was in the window.'

Dana's shoulders slumped. 'But, Brody, I'm not even in Cranial Bypass yet. It might not happen.' She thought back to what Trent Grainger had said. 'In fact, it almost definitely won't happen.'

'Oh, come on, you've got to be more positive,' said Brody, and he patted her on the shoulder in a semi-encouraging manner.

'Says the guy who won't order pizza online in case the pizza mafia steal his credit card details.'

'What's this now?' said Evan, hurrying over as he sensed an embarrassing story.

'Never mind that,' said Brody quickly. 'We're talking about Dana. And we're celebrating how awesome you are. You're at the top of your game!'

'Well if that's true,' she retorted, 'why did you say "shops at Pick Me" and not "owns Pick Me"? You do remember that I own this whole shop, don't you?'

'Actually, we did brainstorm that, but we felt that "shops" made you more relatable, you know, to the general public. As a… you know… as a woman about town.' Brody petered out.

Dana levelled a stare at him which could have powered all the bass amplifiers of John Entwistle of The Who.

'Just to be clear,' she enunciated slowly, 'you're saying that a woman who runs a successful business isn't relatable?'

'Successful? Would we call the shop successful? Oof!' Brody clutched his shin as Evan moved in to salvage the situation.

Ever the diplomat, Evan chimed in with: 'What my potentially ex-boyfriend means to say is, if we said you own the shop, then people will say oh well, you have to say you buy from here anyway. But if we say the guitarist from Cranial Bypass chooses to shop here, well, it's more of an endorsement, you see?'

Dana raised an eyebrow at him. Wow, Evan was good at this. He didn't crack, not even a little bit. He simply kept a calm smile on his face.

Dammit, he obviously knew that Dana had a soft spot for him. It wasn't just because he kept Brody organised. Evan was kind, and polite, and not noisy like the other young men who came into the shop. As much as Dana liked to play guitar loud, being noisy in a musical way was quite different to being just generally a noisy person. Evan had the same quiet soul and competent musicianship as Dana, so she felt a kinship. And the way he rounded out Brody's worst instincts made her want to keep him around.

'Okay, fine, but just take it down, will you, guys? I've had a very strange day and I don't feel like looking at...' she waved a hand in the direction of the display, '*me.*'

Brody opened his mouth to object but Evan beat him to it.

'Of course, Dana. Is it okay if we keep it out the back until they make the announcement?'

Dana laughed. 'Sure, Evan.' She was certain that Cranial Bypass wouldn't be announcing her as the replacement guitarist. She'd sneak back down tonight and chuck her doppelgänger in the bin. Or maybe even burn it. That would be cathartic.

'So, how has the day been here at the shop?' She plopped herself onto a drum throne and took a deep breath of the guitar-laden air.

'Good!' Brody replied. 'We finally persuaded Matiu to buy that bass amp he's been looking at for the last six months.'

'Oh, nice one. He's been in here most days trying it out, so it's pretty obvious he loves it. He'll have to think of something else to try out, so he has another excuse to visit the shop and chat.'

'And Evan did some tidying up.'

Dana was suddenly alarmed at the thought of the immaculate Evan tidying up her ramshackle wee shop. What horrors had he encountered?

He must have understood the look on her face.

'Oh, I just did some dusting and stuff, you know.'

'And you cleaned up the back room,' said Brody.

'Wait, you didn't go near my office chair, did you?' said Dana. 'Because Paws McCartney would have had something to say about that.'

Evan raised his bandaged hand, and gestured at his torn shirt. 'Yeah, he did make his feelings pretty clear on that point, actually. I was only trying to give him a nice blanket to curl up on, but he thought he was being evicted.'

Dana couldn't help a small laugh escaping her lips. 'Oh, I'm sorry Evan, but you should have known better than to try to move Pawsy once he's settled.'

'I do now. And FYI, I think you should rename him Claws McCartney.'

'He took off upstairs,' Brody added. 'We chucked some fresh cat food in his bowl and left him to calm down.'

'But enough about me being lacerated by your attack cat,' said Evan. 'Tell us all about the audition. Did you get to meet Horgen? What are the other band members like? We need details!'

Dana opened her mouth to answer but Brody cut in.

'No, we'd better wait for Wade.'

'Wade's coming round?' Dana wouldn't have minded some more time to herself. She'd had quite enough human interaction for the day, thank you very much.

'Yeah, he'll be here soon. Then we can go over the day's events and make our next plan.' Brody rubbed his hands together. That boy loved a good planning session.

Dana levered herself up off the stool. 'Oh alright, but just give me a few minutes to relax with a cup of tea, will you?'

'Sounds great!' yelled Brody. 'Black with two sugars, thanks. Ow!'

Dana turned to see him clutching his other shin. Evan gave her a wink and shooed her out of the room.

Yes, she would happily adopt that boy. Brody could visit sometimes, if he behaved.

Dana did get time to have a nice cuppa, but all too soon it was time for another meeting of Team Whatever The Heck They'd Named This Operation – honestly she could no longer remember.

She was finding the challenge of auditioning for Cranial Bypass both daunting and invigorating. She enjoyed hanging out with Mr Two whenever she got the chance. She was determined to catch Pox's killer and bring them to justice. Heck, she even felt pretty good about the way she didn't let creeps like Trent Grainger get under her skin.

It had been a guitar-nerd highlight jamming with Ollie, Marty and Horgen (she still couldn't imagine calling him Hamish).

But knowing there was a murderer out there somewhere – and a slippery roadie who wouldn't talk to her – was proving immensely frustrating.

Dana was fully committed now, and felt like she was up to the task... well, tasks plural, really. She even kinda enjoyed these sessions, talking everything over with Brody, Evan and Wade each time she came home. And she could hardly deny them their vicarious thrills, could she? Could she?

No, she supposed she couldn't.

She just needed a little more alone time to recharge her batteries, is all. Brody was all over her like an excitable puppy, and Wade always threw her such tricky questions while demolishing the supplies in her pantry.

Still, she knew this was all part of the deal with this project.

It all seemed such a long time ago, but it was only a matter of days since Wade had volunteered her to go undercover and attempt to out-fret every other guitar-slinger in the vicinity while uncovering a murderer, but she was already surrounded by several likely suspects. Too many, really. She hoped Wade had some insight that would help her.

Mind you, it was a moot point now that she knew Grainger wasn't going to let her in the band no matter how well she played.

'Wade's here!' Brody called from downstairs. Dana levered herself out of her chair and went to break the news to the others, and endure their questioning.

Uncharacteristically, Wade had brought food. Even more surprising, he'd brought enough to share.

Dana had skipped lunch, what with her busy

morning, so she was ravenous.

Wade held aloft bags of goodies from the bakery next door.

'What do you have in there?' asked Dana.

'To be honest, I'm not too sure,' said Wade, placing the bags on the counter. 'Half the stuff in there I've never heard of. I reckon they're just making it up. I mean, tell me, what the heck is a paneeney? Or a brooshetty?'

'Oooh - you brought bruschetta?' Brody pounced on the bags like a starving, skinny, guitar-playing lion. 'It's great! It's an antipasto.'

Wade leaned over Brody's shoulder. 'Looks like chopped tomatoes on small toast to me.'

'Oh, so don't you want any?'

Wade hip-checked Brody out of the way, almost causing him to drop the bruschetta he was clutching. 'I didn't say that, did I?' He de-bagged some paper plates and, as a belated attempt to prove he had good manners, passed them out to everyone before loading up his own plate.

'Thanks Wade,' said Dana. 'This is very thoughtful of you.'

'No worries,' said Wade, eyeing a panini dubiously. 'What's this red stuff in here?'

'Oh, that's sun-dried tomatoes,' Evan informed him. 'They're sun-dried, then seasoned and stored in oil. Very tasty.'

'Wait, so they take tomatoes – one of nature's wettest creations – and dry them?'

'Yeah. helps preserve them.'

'Okay, but then they put them in a liquid?'

'Sure. Again, for flavouring but also to make them last.'

Wade shook his head. 'Thought I'd heard it all. They take the liquid out of the tomatoes, to make them last longer. Then, obviously realising their mistake, they put them back in a liquid, to make them last longer. What a bloody waste of time. Could have just left them wet.'

'So, don't you want that then?' asked Brody, lurking nearby.

'Jeez! Once again, I did not say that.' Wade hastily took a large bite of the panini. His eyes closed in ecstasy. 'Oh my god,' he mumbled around a mouthful of food. 'Okay I get it now. This is delicious.'

Dana laughed as Wade went back to pile his plate with more food he couldn't pronounce.

'I thought you guys were poor,' Wade said over his shoulder. 'How come you know so much about rich people food?'

'Poor?!' Brody squawked.

'Rich people food?' Evan objected.

'Guys?' Dana growled.

'Whoah, whoah, chill out.' Wade laughed. 'You're easier to wind up than the Professional Conduct Review Board.'

Dana waited for Wade to look up so she could raise an inquisitive eyebrow at him.

Wade waved her off. 'Oh come on – I'm joking!'

Dana decided to take him at his word on that, and moved on.

'Hey,' she said, 'I have a bone to pick with you, mister police officer.'

'Please, we're all friends here. Call me Detective Inspector.'

'Ha ha,' Dana fake-laughed at him. 'But seriously. How could you not tell me that Shaw would be at the venue?'

'Shaw?' Wade scrunched up his face. 'Why would she be there?'

'Her wife is in one of the support bands.'

'Hinemoa's in a band?'

'Yes! Didn't you know? You work with Shaw every day. Don't you talk about personal stuff?'

Wade recoiled. 'God no! Why would we do that?'

Dana threw her hands in the air. 'Oh, I don't know, maybe to show an interest in them as a human being?'

Wade shook his head. 'No. Acceptable topics of

conversation at work are as follows.' He ticked them off on his greasy fingers. 'One: the weather. Always either too hot or too cold. No other variations allowed, except for heavy rain. Two: they should pay us more for doing some of this stuff. Three: it's acceptable to ask how a colleague's weekend was, but the only appropriate response is: could have been longer. Honestly Dana, how can you not know this?'

'I give up,' she replied. 'I completely failed to account for the social mores of the average Kiwi male.'

'Hey! I'm not average.'

'That's true,' she smiled, 'you'd have to really push to make average.'

Wade took a mock arrow to the heart, and made a show of staggering backwards.

'Wait,' said Evan, 'did Shaw twig what you were up to then? With regard to the whole covertly scoping out a murderer situation?'

'No, thank goodness. She was a bit on the back foot herself, trying to keep things on the down-low as she visited Hinemoa. So I got away with it, I think.'

Dana knew that Shaw would undoubtedly rumble her if they talked for longer than two minutes. She was no dummy. So if Dana was to get the job with Cranial Bypass, things could get tricky. But hey, it must be time to rip that particular band-aid off.

'Um, guys, I need to tell you something.' Deep breath. 'I won't be getting the Cranial Bypass gig.'

'Oh wow,' said Brody, 'did you really mess up your playing today? Is it on YouTube?' He was quick to move his leg out of Evan's kicking range this time. Brody might not be the shiniest guitar in the showroom, but he learned eventually.

'Actually, Brodes,' said Dana, 'I think I played really well today. It felt like the top-class rhythm section really pushed me higher than ever, and Horgen was sweet. He told me to get in there and bring some energy, so I did.' Dana allowed herself a proud wee smile. She would savour that memory forever.

'What's the problem then, boss?'

'It's just…' she tossed the remainder of her ciabatta back onto her plate, 'one of the roadies told the band manager she didn't want me there.' Dana left out the part about it being the one roadie she really wanted to talk to about Ziggy. That was her business, whereas this meeting was about finding Pox's murderer. 'Not only that, the manager himself was a bit of a creep and I got on the wrong side of him right from the start, unfortunately.'

Wade held up a finger to indicate that he would speak as soon as he'd swallowed, python-like, a good quarter of the items on his plate.

The others watched, fascinated and horrified in equal measure, as he completed this procedure.

'Ahem. Now, surely it's not all up to the roadie or the manager though, right? If Horgen likes you, that's all that matters, I'd say.'

'Wade, with all due respect – '

'Which means none,' Brody sniggered.

'Thank you, Brody,' Dana continued. 'To be fair, Wade, you don't know how these things work in the musical world. Sometimes a manager can be like a facilitator, getting the paperwork done and coordinating the schedules. But other times, they are the be all and end all, in charge of every detail. What they say goes. I don't know which type of relationship Horgen had with this Grainger guy, and I guess we won't know until the call-back.'

'Ooh yeah,' said Evan. 'When do you have to go back? Did you get to talk to Horgs much? Was he an okay guy or a dick? What kind of bass did Plangent Abyss bring to the session? These, and many other questions, beg to be answered.'

Dana chuckled. 'All shall be revealed, young one. Oh, and funny you should mention the bass guitar. I actually bumped into the guitar tech who was carrying one of Ollie's basses.'

'Well, well, well. Ollie is it?' said Brody. 'On a first-name basis now, are we? Sounds like things did go pretty good today, after all. Nudge, nudge.'

'You don't have to say nudge if you're actually nudging me, B,' Evan complained, rubbing his ribs. 'But you're not wrong. Dana, we're going to need details if you were getting cosy with the bass player. Wait, isn't he married?'

'Not any more.'

'Did he let you tune his G string?' said Brody, waggling his eyebrows.

'Oh, Brody!' Dana groaned. 'That's the oldest line in the book, and it's just cringy.'

'Cringe.'

'What?'

'We just say cringe now,' Brody explained. 'Not cringey.'

Dana frowned. 'Do we, though? Sounds a bit… cringey to just say cringe. Anyway, can we get back to the topic at hand, please?'

'Sure. You were telling us about – ' Brody batted his eyelashes, 'Ollie.'

'Yes,' said Dana, ploughing on through this conversation and pretending the others weren't teasing her. 'I was telling you that I bumped into this kid who was carrying Oll… Plangent Abyss' bass guitar, and he dropped it.'

'No!' Brody jumped to his feet.

Evan covered his mouth with his hands, shocked.

'By Tony Iommi's band-sawed fingertip!' Brody incanted in a whisper, crossing himself in a complicated runic pattern. 'May the Master of Sick Riffs protect us and guide us.'

'It's okay,' said Dana, lifting her hands and attempting to calm the spooked horses. 'All is well. The Riff Master must have intervened. The bass is fine.'

'Oh, thank the woods and the wires. I think my stomach had a heart attack just then.'

Dana smiled. She had definitely found her tribe. People who cared that much about a musical instrument were her kind of people.

'But yeah, I talked to the guy for a minute. His name's Andrew. I'd been told earlier by Mr. Two… mey,' she caught herself just in time and used Gerald's full name rather than his self-imposed nickname, 'that they took on Andrew because they needed an extra roadie.'

'And you think that's suspicious?' asked Wade, pointing at her with a breadstick.

'Not that part,' said Dana, 'but the part where Andrew took off like a spooked poodle certainly was.'

'And what exactly spooked this particular poodle, do you think?'

'Well, I don't know if it was just a coincidence – '

'No such thing,' said Brody confidently.

'In that case,' Dana continued, avoiding a ten-minute tangential conversation about coincidence, 'it was definitely when I mentioned Pox.'

'Oooooh,' said Brody, slapping a hand on his knee. 'He did it. Case closed.'

'Thanks, Brody,' said Wade. 'Crikey, you're good at this.'

'Really?'

'No, you dingbat! Now, let Dana tell us the full story, please.'

Dana suppressed a smile. 'Okay, so I just asked Andrew if he'd talked to Pox much before he was killed. You know, thinking that a young guy getting a chance to work with a big-name band, it would have been pretty exciting, right?'

'I'd have thought,' said Evan.

'Yeah, but the guy spooked – '

'Like a poodle,' said Brody.

Dana grudgingly, graciously agreed. 'Yes, I did say like a poodle, didn't I? And it happened as soon as I mentioned Pox's name. He grabbed the bass and took off without another word.'

'So, shall we bring him in, Wade?' Brody asked.

'Who's we, and why are we bringing him somewhere?' Wade leaned back in his seat. 'Honestly, Brody, if you wanted me to arrest every single person who rushes while doing their job, I'd have to arrest everybody...' he paused for effect, 'except maybe you.'

'Hey!' Brody protested, but Evan was in stitches, and it was catching. Soon they were all laughing, while Brody good-naturedly tried to strike a pose as a diligent and energetic employee.

'Seriously though, Brody,' Wade continued eventually, 'there could be any number of reasons why this Andrew guy rushed away, and there are plenty more suspects for Dana to check out before we make any accusations, okay?'

'You're right about that,' said Dana. 'I know it's horrible for me to say this, but I'd kind of like it to be the manager if it has to be anyone. Such a creep. And we've crossed Aaron Swetters off the list but there are still plenty of people in support acts that I want to talk to, plus more backstage crew.'

Chapter 12: The hire

While everyone was processing this, Dana's phone rang. She went to her bedroom to take the call.

'What now, boys?' said Wade as she left the room. 'Do we have to talk about women, so we don't fail the Bechdel test?'

'I think you're getting that around the wrong way,' said Evan. 'And anyway, you're barking up the wrong tree with us, mate.'

Brody shifted in his seat. 'This conversation just got real weird. Can we go back to the murder stuff please?'

'Sure, hon, if it'll make you happy.' Evan patted Brody's arm, then turned to Wade. 'I hope you won't take this the wrong way, mister policeman, but it kinda seems like you're just sitting around waiting for Dana to solve this case for you.'

'Hey', said Brody, 'that's not completely fair.'

'Thanks, Brody!' said Wade.

'He's not just sitting around, he's also doing a lot of eating.'

'Oi!' Wade wiped some garlic butter from the corner of his mouth. 'Take it easy, kid. It might not look like I'm doing much, but you don't hear about everything I get up to, okay? And might I just remind you, this is all part of my plan, and so far it's coming together nicely.'

'What's coming together nicely?' asked Dana as she came back into the room. 'Has someone put the kettle on?'

Embarrassed looks criss-crossed the room as the boys all realised they probably should have thought of that.

'Ahem, sorry, no,' said Wade. 'I was just telling the young ones that my plan was coming together.'

'Well, I suppose you're right actually,' said Dana. 'That was Creepy McCreeperson on the phone, the manager of Cranial Bypass. He asked me to come back in for my chat with Horgen in half an hour.'

'That's great! See, it progresses just as I expected.'

'Cool your chevrons, officer,' Dana replied, 'it doesn't mean anything, it's literally just the last part of the selection process. They have to do it, to give the appearance of following all the rules.'

She went to get the tea underway since nobody

else was making a move to get out of their chair.

Quarter of an hour later, Dana was driving alongside the river. She knew of a good parking spot only a two-minute walk from the venue and it was a nice night to look out over the gently flowing water. Dana locked her old VW and strode off towards The Riffery.

As the venue came into view, the sun glanced off the corrugated iron roof like a drumstick ricocheting off a ride cymbal.

It was too light, too bright. The place really only felt like a rock venue once the sunlight retreated. Darkness hid the dishevelled appearance it projected during the daytime, and it could almost have been any hip venue in a town like New York, if it weren't for the sandal- and walk-shorts-wearing office crowd that materialised for after-work drinkies from 5 till 7pm most weekdays.

Today being a Saturday, there was none of that crew in evidence, and it was too early for the serious weekend party people to be out. There was an eerie crepuscular vibe where The Riffery was still just a boring old building like any other, and not quite the pied-à-terre for gods of the rock'n'roll pantheon just yet.

That was fine by Dana, right now. She was

already intimidated enough without the thought of intruding upon the abode of musical deities.

She made her way through the back door and into the bowels of the backstage area, passing storage rooms, the artists' green room, and then… what was that sound?

Behind the door to some random room, she could hear… oh shit! It sounded like someone being strangled!

The murderer was striking again!

Dana's heart pounded. She couldn't breathe properly.

What should she do? Call Wade? No, it would take too long for him to get here. Heck, even if she ran to get Sione from his office it would be too late for the poor victim on the other side of the door.

Dana was going to have to take care of this herself.

She grabbed her keys and put them between her fingers just like the internet told her to do, took three sharp breaths, then flung the door open.

What she saw chilled her to the bone.

Mr Two lay askew on his rocking chair, his tongue lolling out.

A stringy strand of saliva hung disturbingly from his mouth down to his shoulder.

His body jerked once… twice…

Then he gave a huge snore, scratched himself in the privates, and turned over in his chair.

Oh. Snoring, not strangling.

Dana tried in vain to tell her adrenal glands that everything was fine, but they wouldn't listen. They thought she was still in mortal danger.

She collapsed to the floor, puffing out short breaths as she tried to calm down. Her keys slipped from her fingers, clattering onto the concrete.

This small tinkling sound, of all things, is what woke up the sleeping roadie.

'Oh, Dana, hello me old china.' Still half-asleep, his ever-mutating accent had a soft rasp. 'I's just sitting 'ere uh… going over the stage plot for the next show, you understand.'

Dana wiped the corners of her eyes, pulled up a beer crate, and sat next to the old roadie. She put a hand on his gently rocking forearm.

'You gave me a hell of a fright,' she said.

'How could I give yer a fright? I was asl… I mean, I were just sitting 'ere finking quietly.'

Dana chuckled and rolled her eyes. 'Right, of course. I was just being silly.'

'Wot're you in for now, girl? You got the job yet?'

'Not yet,' Dana shook her head. 'Not ever, probably, but I'm here to have my chat with Horgen.'

'You met all the others already, I 'spect? They's good people, all in all.'

'Yeah, I thought so too. Even bumped into the young roadie you told me about. The one you hired on for this event.'

'Ah, wee Andrew,' quoth Mr. Two.

'Do you know him very well?' asked Dana, deciding it would be worth being a little bit late to her meeting if she could unearth some new information.

'Not well enough, milady, but I know he be a good lad. 'Always 'elping people with their work, always using his manners. Wouldn't say boo to a mallard, that boy.'

Dana nodded in agreement with this waterfowl-based assessment. 'I only spoke to him once – literally bumped into him – and he seemed gentle and caring. Well, he certainly cared about the bass guitar he was carrying, and that says a lot about a person, as far as I'm concerned. It's just...'

'Wot, love?'

Dana let out a long, slow breath. 'I don't know. He seemed to go all cagey when I mentioned Pox.' She glanced sidelong at Mr Two. 'You don't think he had anything to do with Pox's death, do you?'

Mr Two stared at her for a second, and then burst out laughing. 'Andy?! Kill Pox?! 'Ave you been foraging the funny fungi, my girl? You're out of yer wotsit if you think that boy could off ol' Poxy.'

Dana blushed. 'Right, right. Sorry. Of course, that slightly-built guy wouldn't have the strength to strangle someone as strong as Pox. He looked really timid, too.'

'Oh, that's not what I meant, guitar girl.'

'Huh? Then what did you mean?'

Mr Two froze. 'Ahhh, well, no, now I fink about it, you're right, he is a dinky wee geezer. He'd never be strong enough to kill a bear of a man like Pox.'

Dana frowned. 'But you were about to say something else, right?'

Mr Two mimed confusion. 'Were I? I don't fink so, my dear.'

Dana was about to press the point when a harried-looking guy with a headset rushed into the room, spotted her and grabbed her by the arm. 'Dana Osborne? You're late! Horgen is waiting for you – come on!'

The assistant hauled her off the beer crate and out of the room. She looked back just before she was yanked out of the doorway, and saw Mr Two, who was still staring at her, suddenly look down at his hands, and begin picking at the arm of his rocking chair, avoiding her gaze.

Dana was dragged bodily to a meeting room behind The Riffery's bar area. As a long-term denizen of the establishment, she knew for a fact that up until a month ago this meeting room had actually been the place where they kept the spare bar towels and pint glasses. With the announcement that Cranial Bypass would be playing a reunion show at the venue, Sione the owner had obviously done his best to undertake some refurbishments which better reflected the status of the visiting musicians.

He'd cleared out the detritus, and crammed in an old formica-topped table and an assortment of skip-bin salvage chairs.

Actually, Dana quite liked the look of that table. She knew that some of the mid-previous-century pieces (oh my goodness how old did that make her sound?) were becoming collectable now. What was once a scuffed old table that your gran would have thrown out might now be a hipster treasure you'd find at a micro-brewery, propping up beards and beers.

She made a mental note to ask Sione if he'd part with this one, after this... this whole situation with the gig and the murderer-catching and everything, was over.

'Alright, Dana?'

The person who'd addressed her was sitting on a rickety chair at the table she'd been staring at for an uncomfortably long time now. Oh crikey, it was Horgen. She'd been standing here looking at a formica table while Horgen Greymantle of Cranial Bypass waited to talk to her. Well, this really couldn't have gone any better, could it?

'Ah, hi, Horgen, Mr. Greymantle I mean,' she stammered. 'I'm sorry, it's been a bit of a whirlwind day and it appears I haven't had enough cups of tea to function correctly.'

'We'll soon fix that, Dana.' He smiled, and gave a nod to the assistant who'd led her there. They scuttled off, presumably in search of a teapot.

'Please sit,' said Horgen, indicating one of the charity-shop reject chairs. 'Let's talk.'

Dana gave him a small bow because wow, it turned out she really didn't know how to behave when talking to famous people at all. If only she could channel the feeling she'd had while playing guitar with Horgen's band. The confidence, the camaraderie, the ease. But for some reason, talking to him with actual words and sentences completely messed with her head.

'Now, Dana, let's get this out of the way right at the start — you've got the job.'

Dana floated upwards. She could see her body

still sitting in the chair, but she was rising above it. She noticed that Horgen was looking at her physical form, expecting a response, but she was no longer there; she was coming apart, splitting into individual atoms and being blown away on the air currents.

Was she still breathing? How could one tell from this distance? There was a ringing in her ears, and a numbness in her arms.

All of a sudden, there was a click, and she slammed back into her body. Horgen's hand was in front of her face, and he was snapping his fingers at her, and giving her a concerned look.

'Are you okay, Dana?'

Her mouth moved soundlessly for a minute, like a bad backup singer miming when they forget the words. Eventually she found her voice.

'String winders on special this week,' she croaked.

'What's that, love?'

'String winders. They're on special. At my shop. This week.' She shook her head to clear the lingering fuzziness. 'Sorry. Not relevant. Did you actually say I got the job?'

'I did.'

'...'

'Well,' he continued, since Dana had ceased to

function again, 'you could say thank you, if you want.'

'Thank you, if you want.' Dana's brain finally switched back on and she corrected herself. 'I mean, thank you! Thank you so much for this opportunity. Oh my goodness, I can't wait to tell my brother about this!'

'Ah, your brother? Um, isn't he…?'

'Oh, he's dead, yes, but I talk to his poster each night before I go to bed.' Crap. Did she just say that out loud? Dana's face immediately felt like it had caught fire. She really hoped she didn't cry in front of the nice rock god fellow. 'I, um… I like to tell him how my day went, and anything guitar-related, you know.' She coughed. 'I can't believe I'm telling you all this. I can't believe I'm still talking. Would you mind terribly if I slapped myself a little bit right now? I think I'm having a stroke.'

Oh, how Ziggy would have loved to be here for this news. Not the embarrassing revelation of personal details which Dana had just blurted out, but to be there to witness her elevation to rock royalty. Ziggy had always been one to celebrate the success of others. There's enough love to go round, he often said. It's not a zero-sum thing. The more love you give, the more love there is.

So, while many musicians would be jealous of

Dana, thinking she'd stolen their chance at making it big, Ziggy would have been confident enough to know that another opportunity would arise as long as you're good enough.

The fact that Dana could no longer have an actual conversation with a real live Ziggy now made her heart ache. She missed him so much. Like a guitar without a tuner. Like a singer without a microphone. Like a musical heart without a beat.

Thus it was that she sat there like a sack of spuds while one of the world's most famous musicians tried to console her over winning a spot in a top band.

Eventually cups of tea arrived and normality was restored.

Horgen assured her that he completely understood her reaction. 'This is big news, I get it. You freaked out for a while, it's to be expected.' He raised his cup in salute to her. 'Cheers. You've earned it.'

Dana smiled shyly. 'Thanks. I'm surprised you didn't go with Nikau, though. Fresh young talent, and all that.'

She remembered watching the young guitarist not so long ago at a gig and being very impressed with him.

'Oh, he was good, no doubt about it,' said

Horgen. 'But you were better.'

Dana blushed. Again. Maybe even harder this time. She mumbled a few self-deprecatory words, but Horgen waved them away.

'No, sincerely, you were the best of the lot, and that's why you're here now. You had the musical vocabulary that we're looking for, and when I asked you to push me along a bit, you did. Nikau was good, but he doesn't have your experience. He thought I was asking him to show off for the crowd, but you knew that I was asking for someone to push the band to be better. There's a difference, and you got it.'

Dana was smiling. She could almost get used to being praised like this. It felt mortifying and rewarding in equal measure. But wait…

'Um, do you mind if I ask you something, Mr. Greymantle?'

'Of course. And please, call me Horgen at least if you won't call me Hamish.'

'Thank you, Horgen. It's just that your manager… intimated…' discreet euphemism, 'that I wasn't in the running. Why the change of heart?'

'Oh, there's no change there, I'm afraid, Dana.' Horgen stared at his teacup with a rueful look. 'I don't know why he took against you, but he doesn't want you in the band.' Horgen looked up and caught Dana's eye. 'Sadly for him, though, I told him he could shove it, because you're the one I want. Ollie and Marty backed me up, but I would have pushed for you even if they hadn't. Frankly, you're the best guitarist I've ever played with.'

'Hah! Except for Pox, of course.'

He pursed his lips and shrugged. 'Out of respect for the dearly departed, I'll agree with you on that point. But frankly it would be a close run thing. I would have loved to see you and him go head to head.' A shadow crossed his face, and he looked back down into his cup, as if expecting the tea leaves to provide him with some consolation.

Dana knew this feeling well. She wished she could tell him that she was here to find Pox's killer, maybe it would help ease his pain a little. Instead, all she could say was: 'It hurts, right?'

Horgen glanced up at her under his brows. For a second he looked fierce, angry even. Then his features softened back into sorrow. 'Yes. It should never have happened.'

He cleared his throat. 'But hey, we're here to celebrate today. Let's not dwell on the sad things, okay?'

Dana assayed a tentative smile. 'Okay. Let's both put away our ghosts for a little while. Maybe another cup of tea will help?'

'Tell you what,' Horgen replied, fishing under his chair and conjuring forth a bottle and two small glasses, 'how about a tipple of something else?' he said as he brandished the water of life.

'Oooh,' said Dana, 'is that a Talisker? I could sample a dram.'

'You'll need it,' he said as he poured two generous measures.

'Why's that?'

He raised his glass to her. 'Because in two minutes, Trent Grainger is going to come in and go over your contract.' He winked at Dana's shocked expression. 'Cheers.'

Chapter 13: Giant penguins and an evening swim

Thankfully Horgen stayed in the room while his odious manager went through Dana's contract clause by clause. She really didn't want to be alone with Grainger Danger.

Eventually they reached the end and she realised that Trent expected her to sign right away. She mustered the courage to tell him she'd get the contract back to him once her lawyer had looked it over.

Grainger snorted. 'As if. You'll sign it now or you don't get the gig.'

Horgen intervened. 'Now, now, Trent, play nice. I chose Dana and I want her to feel comfortable. If she wants her lawyer to look the contract over then that's what will happen.' He looked at Dana and raised an eyebrow in query.

'Yes, I never sign anything unless my lawyer has

checked it out first. It won't take long, I promise. But I'm not signing right now. That's not negotiable.' She crossed her arms.

Grainger glared at her for a bit, then turned his gaze on Horgen. It was some small comfort to Dana that he was an equal-opportunity glarer. She didn't feel quite so singled out.

Horgen matched his manager stare for stare, until Grainger gave up, tossed the contract onto the pinkish formica tabletop and stormed out.

'Suit your goddamn self,' he grumbled as he lurched into the hallway.

'Don't mind if I do,' said Horgen, as he topped up his glass and then waved the bottle in Dana's direction.

She sighed. 'I'd better not, I have to drive. But thank you.'

'You're very welcome. So, we'll see you on Monday at the crack of afternoon, yeah?'

Dana was impressed. That was an earlier start than she'd expected. She made a mental note to ask Evan if he'd like some more hours at the shop. Presumably he'd jump at the chance to get paid to hang out with his boyfriend a bit more.

'Right you are, boss. See you then!' She gave Horgen a crisp salute, which felt like progress compared to her haphazard bow from earlier.

When she left, her step had a spring in it. Like a well-adjusted whammy bar on a Stratocaster, she mused.

Dana fairly skipped out of the back room and into the main venue area, where she spotted the owner tidying up one of the booths.

'Sione,' she called out, 'I like what you've done with that room.'

He straightened from his task and stretched his back. 'Cheers,' he grunted, 'I'm trying to uplift my professionalism in the infrastructure space.'

Dana stared at him with her mouth open. 'What the hell was that about? Are you feeling okay?'

Sione laughed. 'Sorry. I've been at council hearings all week for our liquor licence renewal. Some of the jargon has lodged in my head and I can't seem to flush it out. What I meant to say was I'm trying to spruce the place up a bit.' He sighed. 'I feel like I'm pivoting proactively into wordsmithing.' He shook himself. 'Damn. Happened again.'

Dana laughed, and went to turn for the exit. But before she did, she noticed movement on the stage out of the corner of her eye.

'Oh cool,' said Sione, following her gaze. 'Looks like giant penguins.'

For a second Dana got her hopes up. Then she

remembered there was a band called Giant Penguins, so it wasn't going to be the long-extinct real-life variety.

Still, she was quite excited to see the band. She'd been hearing good things about them but hadn't made it to a gig to see them herself. How fortunate to catch them at a rehearsal.

Dana loved seeing bands at rehearsals, when they were sharing banter and showing off for each other, without having to worry about pleasing a crowd. Some bands were at their best like that, making music for their musical friends, sharing a joke by playing phrases of different tunes to each other in the middle of their songs and so on.

On the other hand, many bands weren't like that at all, and only really came alive when they had a big, enthusiastic audience in front of them.

Dana loved being present at these occasions so she got to find out for herself which kind of band they were.

She raised her eyebrows in query to Sione, inclining her head towards a booth. In reply, he made a be my guest gesture, and carried on with his work as she settled in.

The band members started setting themselves up onstage, but one of them broke ranks and came out into the main room. Spotting Dana in her booth, they came over.

'Hi, you're Dana, right?'

'Hi! Yes, that's me.'

'You might not remember me. I'm – '

'Classic Seventies Mustang short-scale bass, with original racing stripe.' Dana smiled. 'We ordered some short-scale flatwound strings for you to try out. Also, I recently found out you're married to Detective Chief Inspector Mary Shaw. Hello, Hinemoa Bennett.' Dana put out her hand to shake.

Dumbfounded, Hinemoa did so. 'How the heck did you remember that about my bass? You must sell hundreds of sets of strings.'

'Sure, but it's not often I have to make a special order like that. Usually it's off-the-shelf 45-105 gauge, long-scale roundwounds for bass players. The only thing that differs is the brand preference. Nice to get something different for a change.' She gestured for Hinemoa to take a seat.

'Thanks. Want a beer?' Hinemoa held up a bottle.

'No, I'm good, ta. But you go ahead'

She watched as Hinemoa realised it wasn't a twist-top bottle and she couldn't get the cap off. Dana pulled a wee gizmo out of her jeans pocket.

'Combination string winder, string cutter, and bottle opener. I always carry one.' She thought back to her meeting with Horgen, and how she'd embarrassed herself by babbling about string winders. To be fair, though, they *were* on special, and it was always a good idea to carry one with you. She was proving it right now.

Hinemoa took it with a nod of thanks, opened the bottle and passed the opener back. 'Cheers!'

'You're welcome. Hey, so those flatwound strings must sound amazing on the Mustang. How are you liking them?'

Hinemoa's eyes lit up and she leaned in. 'Oh my god, they're so good! Through a nice big amp like that beast – ' she pointed to the immense house bass amplifier up on the stage ' – it's magical. Like communing with mountains or something.'

Dana laughed. She couldn't imagine Mary Shaw talking about magic. Heck, she couldn't even imagine Shaw listening to someone else talk like that. It must be quite an eclectic household at the Shaw-Bennett residence.

'What the short-scale basses lack in sustain they sure make up for in funky low-end thump, that's for sure.'

'I'll say,' Hinemoa enthused. 'I mean, I still use my 5-string Jazz bass at a lot of gigs, but for what we're doing in Giant Penguins, the Mustang is perfect.'

'Speaking of which, what are you doing out here

— shouldn't you be onstage with the others?' Dana held up a placatory hand. 'Not that I'm kicking you out of the booth! I just wondered why you're not sound-checking with the rest of the group.'

Hinemoa gave her a warm smile. 'It's okay, Dana, I'm not offended. I know what you mean. Most bands wouldn't do it like this, but I usually come out here first to make sure everything else is in balance before I join in with my bass. It's sometimes tricky to balance rock'n'roll instruments like drums and electric guitar with the taonga puoro, the traditional Māori instruments. So I sit out a song or two to make sure it sounds right out front. Once they're sorted I join in. It's usually fairly straightforward to add the bass in at that point, since I'm not stepping on anyone else's toes, frequency-wise.'

This comment reminded Dana of her customer Craig's ridiculous assertions about the fundamental frequency of the ocean being in C, and she had to stop herself from snorting out a laugh.

The band started up a song, helping her to shunt that silly train of thought off to a different station.

It began with Miriama Tipene-Dawes, the taonga puoro player, making a tapping sound. Dana was too far away to see but she thought Miriama was tapping two stones together perhaps.

The sound reverberated in the mostly empty room, bouncing from one wall to the other.

Dana leaned towards Hinemoa. 'What's happening in this part? I confess I don't really understand this.'

Hinemoa chuckled. 'Ah, we get that comment quite often. There's a lot going on here but it's not really my place to explain. You need to talk to Miri. But for now, stop trying to understand it, and just experience it.'

'Oh, okay.' Dana leaned back in her seat, not completely sure what to do with that advice. But after a minute, just focusing on the sound and the space, she felt… a change in the air. Something she couldn't explain, but a shift in the atmosphere, which somehow sharpened her senses at the same time as unmooring her. As a synthesiser joined in with a low drone, the hairs on her arms stood up. She turned to share her amazement, but Hinemoa was sitting up straight with her eyes closed and a look of intense concentration. Dana thought it best not to disturb her as she was obviously listening for subtleties in the balance of sounds, ready to report back to the band. So Dana settled back in and just soaked in the performance. It continued to build to a crescendo as the drums came in, followed by electric guitar.

After a few minutes, or maybe a few hours, things gently wound down, and Dana resurfaced, a bit surprised to find herself back in the usual humdrum existence again.

Hinemoa drew a breath in through her nose, opened her eyes, and said: 'It's good.'

'I sure thought so,' said Dana softly. 'I wonder if that's what it feels like when you take psychedelics?'

'Couldn't say,' said Hinemoa, with a studiously blank face.

Dana laughed. 'You all must be such chilled out people.'

Now it was Hinemoa's turn to laugh. 'You'd think so, right? But no, we're just normal people. In fact, Miri's probably the feistiest one out of all of us.'

'Really?'

'Oh yeah.' Hinemoa got up to head over to the stage. 'You should have seen her have a go at Apocalypse BusLane a few months back.'

'Wait, what?' Suddenly Dana was at full attention. 'What was she angry about?'

'Oh, it's water under the bridge now, but I think it was something like... umm...oh yeah, Miri had got it into her head that some of the Cranial Bypass lyrics were white supremacist, so when she ran into

Pox backstage one time, she bailed him up about it. She was well riled up. I thought she was going to go for him right there.' Hinemoa glanced back at the stage. 'Listen, sorry, I've got to go, they're waiting for me.' She hurried off.

Dana was left sitting there with her mouth open. Damn! Another suspect, and still no clearer picture of what had happened to Pox.

As she tried to fit the puzzle pieces together in her head, she watched Hinemoa join her bandmates onstage. Everyone was smiling at each other, and they launched into another one of their consciousness-enhancing songs, but Dana was no longer in the mood for it.

Dana took a leisurely stroll, thankful that she'd parked by the river, as it gave her time to let the observations and information from the day settle in her mind. She picked her way along the darkening riverbank, careful not to get too close and fall in. Like a good dub reggae song, the river appeared calm but had a strong flow.

She was almost back at her car when she heard a muffled yell and a loud splash upstream.

The light was waning but she could swear she saw a person-shaped shadow lope off through the riparian plantings further up the river. A horrible thought occurred. Maybe someone had thrown a stray kitten in a sack into the river to drown. People did that sometimes, didn't they?

Dana knew she might be accused of having an overactive imagination. But even so, she'd never forgive herself if she didn't at least go and have a closer look.

She hurried along up the bank, and peered out into the water. Was that bubbles she could see, just a little way out into the river?

Dana knew the riverbed dropped away quickly, so even though the bubbles weren't far in, the water could be quite deep.

She dithered for a second, but then something popped up downstream. Was that a shoe? A person's shoe? Shit, was there a person in there, drowning?!

The bubbles were still rising to the surface but there weren't so many of them now. If it was a person down there, they might not have much time left.

Dana raced back to her car, yanked open the front storage compartment of the old VW Beetle, and pulled out a rope. Rushing back to the bank, she tied one end of the rope around a tree and the other around her waist, then jumped into the river.

The freezing cold of the water shocked the air out

of her lungs. She bobbed to the surface and forced herself to take a deep breath, then dove back down. For the first time in her entire life Dana was glad of that Year 5 trip to Okoia School pool, which had been so cold it was like wearing ice cream underwear. When she and her classmates had been forced to jump into the pool by their sadistic headmaster, Dana's limbic system had shut down for a few seconds that had felt like an eternity. She'd been sure she would involuntarily take in a lungful of water, and an image had flashed through her mind: her headmaster pretending to be sorry while informing her parents that Dana had never surfaced.

The memory of that terrifying inter-school visit had stayed with her, so she was able to override the irrational part of her mind that was screaming at her: you'll never breathe again and you'll die down here.

The current tried to drag her downstream, but her rope held tight. Dana thrust her head underwater and blinked, trying to make out shapes in the dimness. Weeds, roots and a startled eel were all she could see to her right. But to her left - was that a submerged log? No, it could be a person. But why weren't they trying to swim?

She half-walked, half-swam her way towards the

submerged figure, and plunged down to the riverbed. When she got close enough she could see that they weren't swimming because their arms and legs were tied. And they weren't rising to the surface because there was a weight attached to their ankles. What the hell?

Now that she was almost right next to them, she could clearly see their eyes, wide open with fear. The bubbles were leaking out of their nose. Even in the dark, underwater, she thought she recognised the person.

Could it be? Was that Andrew, the young roadie? Why had someone trussed him up, weighted him down, and thrown him in the river?

No time to think about that now. She was running out of breath herself. She had to go back up to the surface or she'd be no use at all. Luckily the surface was not very far away. She was in maybe twice her own height of water. Certainly it was enough for someone to drown in, but thankfully it was still easy for her to push herself off the riverbed to go back up. The look on Andrew's face as she swam up, away from him – it was pure terror. She knew straight away she'd never forget that.

Dana broke the surface, gasped a lungful of fresh air, and dove right back down. First things first, she needed to cut the weight off Andrew.

She'd like to say he looked relieved to see her back, but frankly he mostly looked scared and purple in the face. She needed to be quick!

She grabbed his shirt and pulled herself down towards his feet. What was weighing him down? Was it…? Yes, it was an old guitar amplifier. Dana would never admit it, but a teensy, tiny part of her brain took half a millisecond to stop and think: that's a waste of a good amplifier. She mentally shook herself. Focus, Dana! What was it tied to him with?

She grabbed the rope. But it wasn't a rope. With a shock, she realised it was a guitar string. Was it possible there was another guitar string murderer? No, it might well be the same person who killed Pox. But there was no time to think about that. What was she going to do? A guitar string was too strong for her to snap, and too tough to bite through.

Wait! Dana shoved a hand into her pocket.

Thank goodness, it was still there. She pulled out her combination string winder, string cutter, and bottle opener. (On special at Pick Me Guitar Shop this week.) Haha, saved by the reasonably-priced guitar accessory!

As Andrew ceased to struggle and his body started to go limp, Dana manoeuvred the string cutter into place, and gave a firm snip!

The string cutter pinged out of her hand and was washed away down the river, ending up buried in some silt. Dana managed to keep her mouth shut even though she wanted to cry out in frustration.

Her heart quailed. The river buffeted her, poking its cold fingers up her nostrils.

Dana looked at Andrew's splotchy face, and saw his shoulders spasm with the effort not to inhale water.

She was not going to let him die like this. Not on her watch.

Without stopping to think too much about it, she untied the rope from her waist, and was immediately shunted downstream by the current.

She tumbled along the riverbed, and as she went, her hands raked the silt at the bottom. Please, please, please let her find it – aha! The guitar gods were obviously watching over them both, because she felt the familiar plastic shape of the string cutter, and latched onto it, shoving it back into her pocket.

By digging her fingers into the muddy riverbed, she crawled her way back to where Andrew was bobbing in the water like a sad balloon, the river pushing back against her the whole time.

Once again she put the cutter to the guitar string. Once again she gave a determined snip, and this time, thank goodness, the string was cut, and Andrew came free… only to barrel into her and carry the both of them off down the river.

In Dana's mind there wasn't much going on now except a wordless shriek of despair, but as she flew along, out of the corner of her eye she spied the end of her rope.

Her limbs thought faster than her brain: one arm went around Andrew's waist, the other arm shot out to grab the rope.

With an almighty tug, the rope went taut, and she almost lost her grip on the flailing, unconscious roadie. Through sheer determination she held on, and as the rope pulled straight, the river current finally started to help by pushing them towards the bank.

It seemed like hours had passed, but maybe it had only been a few seconds. Dana's head broke the surface and she breathed deeply, then she dragged Andrew up out of the water, onto the rough dirt of the riverbank.

She quickly untied her rope, and snipped Andrew's hands and feet free, then rushed to check if he was breathing.

He lay there, pale and limp in the moonlight, and Dana's heart sank as she realised maybe she'd taken too long.

She gave him a thump on the back. No response.

Another. Was it her imagination, or did he gag a little that time?

She started pumping his chest, and giving him mouth-to-mouth, completely winging it as she'd forgotten how many beats to the bar it was, and hadn't they updated the tempo from Staying Alive to some other song now? She had no idea, but surely anything she did was better than nothing.

Her arms had all the strength of microwaved jelly now, but she kept going even though she started to get winded herself, and there was a ringing in her ears, until finally – finally – with a cough and a splutter, a lungful of river water jetted out of Andrew's mouth and he took a gasping breath of fresh air.

Dana collapsed next to him and closed her eyes.

Chapter 14: Who tried to kill Andrew?

'For the hero!' cried Evan the next day. 'I've made you a big plate of pancakes, drowning in maple syrup. Oh, dammit! I'm an idiot.' He looked crestfallen. 'I didn't mean to say *drowning*. I've made you pancakes with lots of syrup. Sorry.'

'It's fine, Evan, now gimme those pancakes before they get cold.' Dana was salivating. She knew that Evan was great in the kitchen, and she could really get used to being waited on.

Dana had been checked over by an ambulance crew after she'd crawled out of the river the previous night. The medics had let her go home on condition that she take it easy the next day, and now that the next day had arrived and Evan was doting on her, she planned on taking it very easy indeed.

It was an added bonus that Evan's pancakes were… well, she didn't want to say *to die for*, so she settled on divine instead.

Last night was already a bit of a blur in her memory. Everything had happened so fast. She didn't even remember calling the emergency services. Yet somehow, after the ambulance crew had seen to her, and carted Andrew away, Wade had turned up.

Wade had taken her home, and had told Brody what happened, and Brody told Evan, and next thing you know, Dana had a personal chef and home care assistant at the door.

Paws McCartney was still upset with Evan about the whole 'cleaning up' fiasco from the day before, but with the judicious application of kitty treats, Evan was winning Paws over, and there were no more claws on display.

The old fur-ball now had Dana at home for the day, and prone on the sofa, which meant she was basically a big cat pillow. Or at least, that's how Paws was treating her. He helped out in his own way, giving Dana the odd full-body massage whenever he got up to reposition himself.

She was looking forward to lying there quietly all day. After her pancakes she would ask Evan to cart a few books through from her bedroom, and then hopefully he'd take the hint and leave her be till the next mealtime.

The first forkful of pancake was almost at her mouth when there was a knock at the door.

No.

No, no, no.

No visitors today. Hadn't she earned some time alone with her cat, her books, and her on-call personal attendant?

'Just leave it, Evan,' she called out, but he already had his hand on the doorknob.

'This will be Brody and Wade,' he called back.

'They can leave their tributes at the door.' She waved him off. 'Flowers will keep till I've finished these pancakes. Chocolate will last too.'

Actually, this was nothing more than a hopeful bluff on Dana's part. She had no idea how long chocolate would last in the wild. Whenever she brought some home it never lasted more than a day, so the natural life of a bar had never been scientifically tested, as far as she knew.

'Oh, Dana,' Evan tutted, 'they're here to discuss the case. I'm letting them in.'

And he did.

'Hi, Dana!' Wade chirped, 'how's the rescuer feeling today? Are those pancakes? Mmm… I'll grab a fork.' He made a beeline for the cutlery drawer, and then buzzed happily over to the sofa, nudging her legs out of the way so he could sit and attack the plate from close range.

Dana sighed, and tried to stake her claim to at least half the plate before Wade took it all into custody.

'I'm fine, thanks, Wade. Just a bit shaken. It's really only hitting home for me now, actually. Last night I just did what needed to be done, but today it all feels so surreal, you know?'

'Oh yeah, I understand that for sure. After your first year of policing you get used to the dramatic situations, but to start with it's pretty confronting, right? Don't worry, you'll become accustomed to it soon enough.' He speared another gorgeous fluffy pancake as Dana wasted precious eating time wondering if she even wanted to become accustomed to dangerous situations and attempted murders.

Brody pulled up a kitchen chair, turned it backwards and straddled it, then stood back up, adjusted his trousers and tried again. There was a slightly pained look on his face which told Dana that he was regretting this bold strategy. When he spoke, his voice was maybe a couple of tones higher than normal.

'Handy for you that DCI Shaw was walking along the river around the same time, huh?'

'Shaw? What do you mean?' asked Dana.

'She's the one who found you and Andrew, and called it in.'

'Shaw did? What was she doing there?'

'Going for a walk, is what she said. Right, Wade?'

'Mmmph.' Wade was concentrating on mopping up the remaining drops of syrup. 'Yeah,' he shrugged. 'She'd dropped her missus off at the venue for sound trials or something.'

'Singer Games,' said Brody.

'Soundcheck,' said Dana, with a raised eyebrow directed at Brody, acknowledging his wordplay. 'I was there, but I didn't see Shaw.'

'Seashore,' Brody pumped his fist in celebration of his linguistic repartee. Evan grabbed his arm and gently lowered it, shaking his head.

'I dunno,' said Wade. 'Jeez. All I know is, she told me that she dropped Hinemoa off and went for a walk. Do you want me to track her GPS coordinates or something?'

It wasn't like Wade to get annoyed so quickly, Dana reflected. She wondered if there was some tension between him and Shaw at the moment. That would be a shame — they were a good team.

'Sorry Wade, I was just saying.'

'Well, as Brody said, lucky for you she wasn't far away. She got the ambos on the scene right quick, which is just as well for Andrew.'

'Wait, what's an ambo?'

'Ambulance driver.'

'I thought they were called Zambucks.'

'Nope,' Brody interjected, 'that's a South African antelope isn't it?'

'No, you're thinking of springbok.'

Brody shook his head and produced a condescending chuckle. 'Dana, Dana. Of course not, the Springboks are a rugby team.'

Dana let out a sigh that sounded like an aggrieved kettle, and decided to steer the conversation back to the person who almost died the night before.

'How's Andrew doing?' she asked Wade. 'Have you found out who tried to drown him yet?'

In a show of contrition, Wade actually took the pancake plate to the sink. 'No, he's not talking yet. He's taking a while to recover. Took in a good lungful of river water before you managed to get him free, unfortunately. So we don't have any clues to go on yet.'

'Well, we do have some clues,' said Dana. 'All these guitar strings that keep popping up.'

'True,' said Wade, plopping himself into an armchair. 'But if we start looking at who has access to lots of guitar strings, that puts you at the top of the suspect list, doesn't it?'

'Shut up, Wade.'

He spread his hands. 'Hey, my point stands. So, do you have any other ideas?'

Dana thought back to the previous night, trying to sift her memory for anything else that might be useful in identifying the perpetrator.

She ran through the events in her mind, thinking it was indeed lucky for her that Shaw had turned up on the scene so soon. That made her think of her conversation with Hinemoa, and… oh!

'Actually, I have a new suspect. For Pox's murder anyway. Hinemoa's bandmate, Miriama. Apparently she was seen having a huge row with Pox not so long ago.'

'And you think she might have a grudge against young Andrew too?'

'Who knows, but it's a start, right?'

Wade stuck out his bottom lip as he considered it. 'Yeah, I guess so. If you can have a chat with her, she might reveal some connection we don't know about yet.'

'It's just so scary that someone tried to kill the guy in such a horrible way,' said Evan.

'Unless he was the person who killed Pox, and somebody tried to kill him in retaliation,' Brody rebutted. 'In which case, good riddance.'

'Well, that kinda leads into my next thing, which

is to ask Wade: what do you think this means? Is it more likely it's the same person who killed Pox that tried to kill Andrew, or do you think this is unconnected?'

Wade breathed out through his nose and looked at the ceiling for inspiration. 'Two scenarios spring to mind. One, and most likely, it's the same person both times. Or, option two. This Andrew kid killed Pox and then someone else tried to kill him. Oh, I guess option three could be that someone else killed Pox and then a completely different person went for the roadie.'

'Well,' said Evan, putting his hands on his knees, 'thanks, officer. That really clears things up.'

'You're very welcome, young one. Your tax dollars at work.' He raised an imaginary glass and toasted Evan.

Evan was having none of this. 'Does anyone else think it's starting to get too dangerous?' he said, looking to the others for backup. 'People are still trying to do murders out there.'

'Not Dana though,' said Wade. 'Who'd want to murder Dana?'

'Um… thanks?' said Dana.

Evan wasn't going to give up that easily. 'Some psychotic serial killer, maybe?'

'No way,' said Wade, 'not gonna happen. There's

no connection between Dana and the other victims. Honestly you guys, in my professional opinion there's nothing to worry about.'

'Would you mind if I continue to worry in my capacity as a private individual?'

'You're welcome to do so in your own time, young Evan. Pro bono worrying isn't covered in the police operations manual.'

'That's good to know.'

Dana, lying on her couch with half a serving of pancakes in her tummy and a cat wedged behind her knees, suddenly felt very tired and not really in the mood for more detecting and puzzle-solving.

Evan noticed her eyelids drooping. 'Maybe we can think about that tomorrow, huh guys? Let Dana have a nap. I think she's earned it.'

Chapter 15: The 'ostible

Dana napped throughout the day, in a very decadent manner, with Evan bringing her hot chocolate and other treats on demand. She felt like the fictional Cleopatra, Queen of Egypt, from the old soap ads. But probably not real-life Cleopatra, Queen of Egypt, as there were no niggling administrative tasks to preside over, warring factions to reconcile, or royal submissions to hear.

She could very much get used to throwing herself into a river if it meant getting this kind of treatment afterwards.

Actually that wasn't quite true. She knew exactly how lucky she'd been to survive at all. Many people drowned in rivers around Aotearoa every year, not realising how dangerous they could get, even when they weren't in high flow. In fact, the more she thought about it, the more scared she retrospectively got. Thank goodness she hadn't had time to stop and think about it before jumping in.

Still, she was very glad she'd done so. Saving Andrew from a horrible fate was well worth it.

She shivered. Whoever was out there killing people – or trying to – must be especially evil to do something so callous, cold and calculated.

Dana assumed it was the same person who'd killed Pox that tossed Andrew in the river, but perhaps she only assumed so because she couldn't stand the thought there might be two evil bastards out there at the same time.

She could do with something to take her mind off it. And, since Cass had turned avoiding her into an Olympic sport, Dana decided to avoid her right back for now. Instead, tomorrow she would take a different tack, and go and visit Ziggy's old guitar tech, Eli, who was, as Mr Two had said, in the 'ostible.

That decided, Dana felt another nap was in order before Evan brought her dinner through and then she would head off to bed for a proper sleep.

Monday dawned as Mondays often do: inevitable and remorseless. Much as Dana enjoyed running the Pick Me guitar shop, she still sometimes wished that Mondays would just take a break and chill out.

She deftly navigated the furry trip hazard that was Paws McCartney begging for his breakfast, topped up his biscuits and then stood well back as he face-planted into them. Ah, was there any more comforting sound than a cat simultaneously purring and crunching on treats? The whole house seemed to vibrate with Paws' happiness.

Dana had planned to leave Brody and Evan in charge of the shop again, but Brody had begged to be allowed to accompany her to the 'ostible… the hospital, she corrected herself. Goodness, another week or so of being exposed to Mr Two's vernacular and she'd be almost as incomprehensible as he was.

Anyway, she couldn't quite imagine what Brody found so exciting about visiting a hospital, but it turned out he was hoping for a bit of glamour by association. Maybe Eli the guitar tech would have some stories about famous musicians that Brody could dine out on later.

'He's in hospital with cancer, for goodness' sake, Brody,' she had remonstrated. 'It's not like we'll be chatting over a picnic with glasses of wine or whatever.'

'Yeah, but it might cheer him up, talking about the good old days,' Brody reasoned. 'Take his mind off things.'

Dana had eventually given in, partly to make up

for the way she had booted him out of the undercover work she was doing at the venue. At least this visit would be safe - Eli was hardly going to lever himself up out of a hospital bed and garrotte them with a guitar string, unlike the mysterious killer still on the loose at the Riffery.

She made Brody promise to hold any questions until after Dana had asked hers. And if they saw that Eli was not in a fit state for all of this, they would leave him be.

Eli had seemed happy enough to chat with her when she messaged him earlier, but she wasn't sure that he would be interested in talking about Ziggy's passing and all that old history.

Ziggy's ghost prodded her in the back.

'Okay, okay, I'm going,' she said to the empty room.

She went downstairs to get Brody, unlocked her old VW Beetle, made obeisance to the god of ancient starter motors, and eventually they were on their way.

They'd avoided the rush hour in Rockingham West, which was really more of a sluggish shuffle hour anyway. At this time of day there were hardly any vehicles on the road at all, and Dana enjoyed chugging along in the old Beetle, taking the scenic route through one of the local parks where some young people were playing football instead of going to school.

They exited the park and found themselves waiting at a set of traffic lights, Dana absently batting the gear stick while her foot held down the clutch.

A fragment of melody assembled itself in her head, unbidden.

'My heart in drive, my head in neutral', she sang softly.

'Nice', said Brody, 'what was that from?'

Dana's ears burned. She hadn't meant to sing that out loud.

'Oh, just a little part of a song that came to me.'

'It's good. You have any more parts?'

She shook her head. She hadn't written a song in ages. Now she thought about it, she hadn't written anything since… Ziggy.

She gave a wry huff. 'I don't think this is going anywhere, that's for sure. Nothing rhymes with neutral!'

She put the car in gear and took off as the lights turned green. Brody was quiet, looking out the passenger window. It was a tad unsettling. Dana wasn't used to him being contemplative.

After a couple of blocks, he blurted out: 'Gotta

find out if the feeling is mutual.'

'What?' said Dana, startled.

'The song. My heart in drive, my head in neutral. Gotta find out if the feeling is mutual.'

Several emotions were at war on his face. Pride, embarrassment, hope. This was the first time he'd ever suggested a lyric to Dana, let alone had the nerve to sing it to her. He couldn't meet her eye, which was a shame, as Dana was grinning from ear to ear.

'That's really good, Brodes!'

'Really?' He studied his sneakers, the ones that were held together with gaffer tape as he refused to spend money on anything that wasn't music-related.

Why waste money on clothes, he'd say. I have guitars to buy.

'It really is,' she reiterated. An awkward silence ensued, broken eventually by both of them going to speak at the same time.

'You think..?'

'Should we..?'

'Sorry, you go.'

'Okay,' said Dana. 'Do you want to have a go at finishing the song with me?'

Brody's face tried to play it cool but his knees didn't get the memo, and they started jiggling up and down, giving the game away.

'Oh, yeah, I guess we could do that,' he squeaked.

'Cool.'

'Yeah,' he sniffed. 'That would be okay.'

The rest of the drive passed in a silent companionable weird awkward loving friendship vibe because they were both introverts and that's how they rolled.

Eventually they arrived at what Dana simply could not stop thinking of as the 'ostible. It was scary how quickly Mr Two's speech patterns had wormed their way into her brain.

They found Eli on a reclining chair in his room. Though the chair looked dated, and the walls were bare institutional grey, and the bed looked about as comfortable as one she'd had when she was a student, Dana nonetheless found herself thinking how fortunate she was to live in a country with universal healthcare. As basic as this hospital room might be, the staff seemed attentive, and Dana knew that in many other less fortunate countries, someone like Eli simply wouldn't have been able to afford hospital care at all. It sent a chill down her spine, to think that people's lives could be lost because of money. And yet, even in Aotearoa there were politicians who campaigned on platforms of tax cuts for the rich. Taxes which paid for common-good things like healthcare.

Having spent most of her life thinking she wasn't interested in politics, Dana was finally having to admit to herself that many of the things she cared deeply about were actually political. She chuckled to herself internally. She wasn't so different from Aaron Swetters after all…maybe she should write a protest song?

Eli looked up as they entered, and shot them a cheery smile. People are rarely at the top of their game for receiving visitors when they're in hospital, but Eli looked like he'd mastered it. He wore his hospital gown with a certain elan, as if it were a fine pashmina draped over his body instead of flimsy cotton.

Dana hadn't seen him in a couple of years, but his short, bright-red hair hadn't changed. Nor his engaging smile. He still had enough facial piercings that he could have found work as a walking key fob.

Eli was one of the most positive, upbeat people Dana had ever met. He was also the guy who'd shown her how to loop her guitar cable around and through her strap so that it was less likely to be pulled out if she stepped on it by accident. These and other sacred guitar mysteries bound Dana to Eli, and she mentally kicked herself for falling out of touch with him since Ziggy's passing.

She'd been swallowed by her grief, but Eli surely must have been as well. She wouldn't make the mistake of withdrawing again, now that contact had been reestablished.

Dana took in Eli's happy visage and realised she hadn't expected him to look so… healthy, if she was honest.

'Hi,' she began. 'How are you?'

'Opinions vary,' said Eli, waggling a hand.

Curses. Dana wished the floor would open up and swallow her. What a stupid thing to say to someone in Eli's circumstances.

'I'm so sorry…'

'No, it's okay,' said Eli, winking. 'I'm pulling your leg, sorry. Gotta get my fun where I can, in this place. But as to my liver, they reckon they've caught it nice and early, so the oncologist is going to give it the ol' partial hepatectomy.'

Dana studiously did not look at Brody and she pretended not to hear him typing on his phone, presumably saving 'partial hepatectomy' as a potential song lyric.

'That's great news,' said Dana. 'From what Mr Two said, I thought we might find you in much worse condition. Not that I'm making light of your surgery either, mind you,' she hurriedly added. 'It's just very encouraging to hear that they're onto it so quick.'

'Cheers. Yeah, I'm hoping they'll cut just a tiny bit of me out and then I'll be right as rain. Like when you remove an extra verse from a song and the whole thing gets better. There are no guarantees with this shit, but the odds are looking good apparently, Little Zag.'

Little Zag. Dana had completely forgotten that some of Ziggy's old friends used to call her that. Zig and Zag, like they were twins almost. She felt a warmness in her chest and a tingling on her scalp as the memories resurfaced. Brody looked up from his phone and mouthed Little Zag? At her. She smiled.

'Wow, Eli, I haven't heard that name in a while. Thank you for reminding me. Actually, it leads me on to why we've come to visit you.'

'To talk about Ziggy?'

She nodded. 'Yeah.'

'Keen to hear a few old tour stories, maybe?'

'Well, not really. Um, but kind of. It's just one particular story that I need to check with you, in fact.'

He spread his arms. 'Ask away, Zag.' He pointed her towards the hospital bed. She perched on the edge of it, and Brody joined her.

'Right,' she said. 'So as I said, I visited Gerald Twomey recently – '

'Ha! How is the old geezer?'

Eli was one of those people who is quick to laugh. Like most of the roadies Dana had met, he seemed eager to enjoy life as much as possible, and wasn't going to wait around for some potential future good time that might not happen. These people knew how to suck the joyful marrow out of whatever funny bone life threw them. She admired them greatly for this.

'Gerald is…' she paused to compose her thoughts on this matter. 'I think he's what you might call incorrigible?'

Eli slapped his knee and laughed again. 'Damn right! So he should be too, at his age. What did he tell you?'

'I asked him about Ziggy's guitar, because it had recently turned up out of the blue, you see.'

'Yeah, yeah, I heard talk of that on the circuit. One of those rich guitar posers bought it, didn't they?'

Dana found herself defending Mikey Thunderbird again, just as she had when talking to Mr Two. 'I don't know if I'd call him that, in fairness. Mikey genuinely loves guitars. He looks after them well, and he plays them regularly. So it's in the best place it could be, all things considered.'

'Ha!' This time Eli's laugh carried a sharp edge. 'The best place for that guitar is with you, and Mikey Thunderbird knows that damn well. He should just give it to you. He can afford to.' Eli mirrored Mr Two's opinion on this matter exactly. But Dana stuck to her guns.

'Honestly, Eli, having Ziggy's guitar would be nice but it won't bring him back. I have my memories.' She cleared her throat. 'And that's why I'm here. There's a missing piece of the puzzle, and when the guitar turned up, I thought I'd finally get to find out what actually happened in Ziggy's last moments.'

'But you drew a blank?'

'It's worse than that.'

'How can it be worse than that?'

Dana took a deep breath before continuing. 'I went to Zander's Rare Guitars, because he's the one who brokered the sale. He said that the seller told him one of Ziggy's road crew took the guitar when he died.'

Eli suddenly seemed to be all out of laughs. He went dead quiet, locking eyes with Dana.

She was about to apologise and leave, when Eli spoke up.

'Well, that's gotta be bullshit. Not a single one of the road crew would have stolen Ziggy's guitar. I can tell you that for absolute certain. I know Zander, so I know he wouldn't make up something like that. But whoever told him that story is full of shit, frankly.'

'Are you sure?'

'You're damn right I'm sure. Every bloody one of the crew would have taken a bullet for Ziggy. No question.'

Dana knew she risked aggravating Eli further, but she persisted. 'None of the crew had, I don't know… money problems?'

'Haha!' Eli laughed long and hard at this.

Dana waved her question away. 'Sorry. Obviously not, then.'

'Oh, the opposite, Little Zag. Very much the opposite.' Eli chuckled. 'We were all of us on the bones of our arse. But I'm telling you. Nobody would have taken Ziggy's guitar. There are lines you don't cross.'

'The roadies' code?' Dana cocked her head.

'That's the very one. I mean, sure, Turpsy wasn't really on Planet Earth a lot of the time, and poor old Raisin Poop had so many electric shocks his brain was kinda rewired a little,' Dana made surreptitious notes on her phone as Eli carried on, 'but these were all good people. No, nobody touched Ziggy's guitar except me. And maybe…' He got a faraway look on his face.

'Maybe… who?'

'Oh, it's probably nothing. Not really my place…'

'Please, Eli, I need to know. Is there someone else who handled Ziggy's guitar?'

Eli looked very uncomfortable now. He coughed and mumbled and looked out the window.

'Is now really the time to be keeping secrets from me, Eli?' Dana's voice broke. 'With Ziggy long dead and me desperate to find out why?' She honestly couldn't help tearing up a bit as she said this. It seemed like she was forever getting just a little bit closer to the truth, only to be stonewalled by someone who had information but wouldn't share it.

Eli's shoulders slumped. 'Okay, okay, it's just… none of my business, you know? I'm just sharing gossip now.'

At Dana's imploring look, he made his decision, with a sigh. 'Right, well, Ziggy had started… getting close… with Cass.'

'Cass the drum tech?' Dana could feel her blood pressure rise. 'The one who's currently roadying at the Cranial Bypass reunion gig?'

Eli nodded at his lap, unable to make eye contact.

'Yeah.'

'How did I not know about this?'

'Well, it only really started when we headed off on tour, so you weren't around to see. And they were keeping it quiet. It was early days, you know. And Ziggy being Ziggy, he wasn't one to bang on about personal stuff. Unlike some of the older generation of rockers.' Eli finally looked up at Dana. 'For example, the guy I hear you're filling in for.'

This threw Dana off balance. The conversation had taken an unexpected turn. 'What do you mean - are you talking about Pox?'

She didn't want to get distracted, but couldn't help asking.

'Oh yes,' said Eli, raising his eyebrows. 'Mr BusLane was quite the one for… meeting new people, shall we say? He liked to make a new friend at every stop on a tour.'

'To be clear — you're saying he had sex with a lot of groupies, then?'

'Groupies, fans, cleaning staff,' Eli ticked them off on his fingers. Dana thought he might run out of fingers to tick off before he finished his list. 'The tour accountant, that guy who used to do the local news on that community TV show, do you remember him?'

Now it was Dana's turn for some eyebrow-raising. 'Wow. Okay, so his tastes were wide-ranging?'

'Oh yes, haha. There was even a rumour that at one point he'd enjoyed the reptilian embrace of Horgen's manager.'

'Trent Grainger?!' Dana physically recoiled at the thought of him. 'You must be joking.'

'I'm not saying it happened for sure, but hey, they did some long tours back in the day, and the boredom along with the self-medication would lead to some fairly unusual behaviours.'

'What goes on tour stays on tour, huh?' Brody interjected.

'Back in those days, anything went, at any time. Nowadays, of course, what goes on tour goes immediately on social media, and you wouldn't get away with half the stuff they used to. Ha! To be honest, it's a much healthier environment now, and people are looking after themselves better, which is a good thing as far as I'm concerned. In fact, who knows? Maybe Ziggy would still be with us if the touring life had been a bit more sensible back then.'

'Why?' Dana asked, 'what do you think happened to him?'

Eli took a deep breath and then let it all out in a puff. 'I mean, I don't know, for sure, I just think if things had been a bit less crazy on the road, someone might have been able to save him.'

'They tried to tell me he'd had a drug overdose, but I know Ziggy wasn't into that stuff. I'm sure of it.'

Eli went back to examining his lap. 'Listen, people can get sucked into bad things on the road, you know?'

'Not Ziggy.'

Eli cleared his throat. 'Okay, now, what I'm about to say has to stay between us, alright?'

Dana nodded, but wasn't sure she'd be able to keep that promise, depending on what Eli told them.

He sighed. 'Cass is a good person, right? But at the time, she was hanging around with some slightly unsavoury types, you see. I worry that they might have pulled Zig into some… bad habits.'

'No. Nope.' Dana waved this idea away. 'Absolutely not. Ziggy might have smoked a joint or two, but he would never have gotten into anything more serious than that. The official line that they pushed on us – that he died of a drug overdose – is just ridiculous.'

'Little Zag,' said Eli sadly, 'you don't know what it's like on the road.'

Dana's nostrils flared as she reined herself in from telling Eli to go screw himself. She knew he was only trying to be helpful, and wouldn't say something like this lightly.

'I'm not saying he became a habitual drug user overnight, Zags,' Eli clarified. 'I'm just saying, him and Cass were both good people who were sometimes surrounded by not good people. And if he happened to be persuaded to try something harmful when there wasn't anyone sensible around to look after him, then you can see how it might turn out the way it turned out, yeah?'

Dana wrestled with this idea, squeezing her hands into fists.

'I mean,' Eli continued, 'that's how Ziggy was. So trusting of other people.'

This was like a punch to Dana's gut. She couldn't deny the truth of it. Eli was right, Ziggy had had a carefree attitude and general kindness to everybody, and he'd assumed everybody else was kind too. Could this actually be what happened?

One thing was for sure: Dana would get Cass to talk even if she had to tackle her to the ground and put her in a headlock.

Dana let Brody take over the conversation, peppering Eli with questions about big tours he'd been involved with. Dana had a lot to chew over while they chatted.

No matter what Eli said, and no matter how

dodgy Cass was behaving, Dana realised she should still talk to the other two roadies whose names had come up. Having said that, there was no way she was going to ask around for people called Turps and Raisin Poop.

She waited for a lull in Brody's questions, and jumped in. 'Hey, Eli, can I get the real names of the rest of the road crew please?'

'Ha!' Eli's laugh had returned. 'I guess that would be helpful, right? Not everyone lives in our weird little world.'

It transpired that Turps' real name was Kurt Mangan, and Raisin Poop was Grayson Peters.

'Bit of let-down, isn't it?' said Eli. 'Finding out they have normal names, right?'

Dana nodded. 'It's like getting a glimpse behind the curtain, that's for sure.'

'Anyway, are you going to, uh...' Eli fidgeted with his hospital gown, 'tell Cass I was talking about her?'

Dana stood up. 'I won't mention your name, but I want answers. So yes, I will be talking to her. Unfortunately, she keeps running away from me. I guess I know why, now. Any suggestions on how I can persuade her to have a chat with me?'

Eli whistled. 'You're dragging me in deeper than I'd like to go, Little Zag.' He looked out the window for a minute before going on. 'But maybe try Gordon at Meltdown Music. He got on pretty well with most of the road crew, and I think he knew Cass from back in the day. Maybe he can broker a meeting for you.'

Armed with their new knowledge, Dana and Brody bade Eli all the best, and Dana promised to keep in contact from now on.

She couldn't wait to get all this stuff about Ziggy straight, and unearth Pox's murderer, so things could settle down and she could reestablish a slightly less strained friendship with Eli and Mr Two. Not to mention some of the local musicians. Treating them as suspects sure put a crimp in relationships.

Chapter 16: The Gordon angle

Dana and Brody piled into the Volkswagen Beetle again, and the tired old suspension springs sang them a creaky welcome song.

'Well, Brody,' said Dana, with a mischievous twinkle in her eye, 'shall I drop you back at the shop, or are you up for a visit to Meltdown Music?'

She already knew the answer. As if Brody would turn down the chance to visit Meltdown Music, the home of affordable music gear of all kinds. The place where even the uninformed came away with a decent instrument, but those in the know sometimes ended up with a unique treasure, and none of it at the inflated prices you'd see at a place like Zander's Rare Guitars.

Sometimes rarity didn't have to mean expensive. Of course, sometimes it just meant junk. But those with an eye – or an ear – for an oddball instrument with tons of character could emerge triumphantly from Meltdown Music if they were there on the right day. Gordon had a constant stream of items coming and going from the shop, as some people traded up, others of necessity traded down, and every so often someone left the music game completely and sold their gear. Some of these individuals ended up returning to Meltdown eventually, begging Gordon to find their old gear so they could buy it back. They realised they'd left a bit of their soul in the old guitar/bass/Farfisa organ, and they wanted it restored.

'Tis a truth sporadically acknowledged that any musician who's been in the game for more than a few years has a heartbreaking tale of an instrument they wish they'd never sold. Any gathering of musicians that gets onto that subject can be guaranteed to talk about nothing else for at least a few hours. Dana sometimes wondered how many songs of lost love were nothing more than thinly-disguised tributes to old flame-maple guitars rather than actual old flames.

'Does the Pope take a roll of toilet paper with him when he goes for a walk in the woods?' Brody replied.

'That's a convoluted way of saying yes, but I'll accept it,' said Dana, and she coerced the Beetle into first gear.

The flat landscape of Rockingham West spread out in front of them like a thin-crust pizza, if low-level housing was cheese, and the few tall buildings in the centre of town were poorly-distributed pieces of tomato. The residents, Dana mused, were the herbs and spices that gave the town its own flavour. No matter which way you sliced it, Rockingham West was a good, basic meal you could share with anybody, and Dana liked her towns the same way she liked her food: comforting and not too spicy.

The old Beetle puttered in between the metaphorical toppings. As they got closer to Meltdown Music, Brody's knee jiggled faster, so Dana could tell he was getting excited. Probably anticipating what cool old guitar or amp he might unearth at the shop this time.

The last time she'd taken him there, he'd walked out with a funky old valve amplifier. She hadn't seen him use it anywhere since then, but no doubt it was taking pride of place in his hoard – sorry, carefully curated collection.

They pulled up and it was as if Dana let Brody off the leash. He raced into the shop, almost toppling a display stand in his haste.

'Sorry about him, Gordon!' Dana called out as she entered.

'Dana!' he roared in answer. 'So lovely to see you again!' He held his arms open for a hug, and Dana obliged. Built like a bear prepping for hibernation, Gordon was a good hugger, and a pretty wonderful human being.

He stepped back and put his hands on his hips, surveying Dana and the scurrying form of Brody, who was sniffing through the stacks.

'What brings you to Meltdown today? Looking for something offbeat for your weird 'n' wacky wall perhaps?'

'Thank you, but no,' Dana replied. 'I actually just recently sold a bass/banjo hybrid thing and the other guitars are still recovering from having to share the shop with it.'

Gordon laughed a large mammal-sized laugh and Dana continued. 'No, today I'm actually here about Ziggy's road crew again, I'm sorry.' A cymbal crash came from the far corner of the shop, and a muffled apology from Brody followed.

Dana sighed. 'But it sounds like Brody will be buying something, so hopefully it's not too much of a waste of your time.'

'Please,' Gordon patted the air, 'it's never a waste of time, talking with you about Ziggy. What can I help you with today?'

He pulled up a performer's stool – complete with

guitar stand on the back – for Dana, and then scooted around behind the shop counter to take his own seat.

Dana was glad he hadn't offered her the stinky old drum throne that Brody had been lumbered with at their last visit. With any luck the offending item had been laid to rest, or better yet, set on a pyre and sent to the gods of rhythm as a burnt offering.

Dana fidgeted with her sleeve, not sure now how to broach the subject she'd come to discuss.

'Come on, Dana,' said Gordon, 'you can ask me anything. Out with it.'

Dana mustered up her courage and looked Gordon straight in the eye. 'Cassandra Trippel the roadie. She worked on Ziggy's last tour.'

Gordon nodded.

'I need to talk to her,' Dana continued, 'but she's avoiding me, and I think you might know why.'

Dana noticed that Gordon's left eye had developed a twitch, and his fingers were drumming on the shop counter, but he kept quiet, so Dana went on.

'Last time we spoke, you said you'd help me get in touch with the old road crew. You made it sound like you kept in touch with them. Eli just told me that Cass and Ziggy were together. Yet you neglected to mention that. Why?'

Gordon remained silent, but Dana raised her chin. This was something she'd learned from one of her old teachers at school, who was much shorter than the students, but still needed to be able to look down her nose at them to cow them into submission. It was surprisingly effective for something which really had no business working at all.

It was working today, thank goodness. Gordon's shoulders began to fidget along with his fingers, and soon he was drawing in a shaky breath and opening his mouth.

'Listen, Dana, I never meant to hurt you. In fact, when Cass asked me not to say anything to you, it was because we both wanted to not make it complicated.'

'You wanted to keep my brother's mysterious death uncomplicated?' Dana's tone would have frozen an active volcano.

Gordon gave an exasperated wave of his hand. 'Dana, that's not what I meant. We just thought that you already had enough on your plate at that time. Cass and Ziggy had only just started seeing each other, it hadn't turned into anything serious yet, so she didn't want to, you know...' he shrugged, 'steal focus, and make it all about her, when you were grieving so bad.'

Dana softened a little. She could certainly imagine Gordon wanting to spare her feelings, but Cass was an unknown quantity.

'You don't think she was just feeling guilty?'

'Guilty?' Gordon was taken aback. 'About what? Getting close to your brother?'

'No. Guilty about having something to do with his death.'

'Whoah there!' Colour was creeping into Gordon's face now. 'What are you saying? You think Cass killed Ziggy? That's bloody crazy.'

Now it was Dana's turn to fidget. She tucked her hands between her legs to stop herself from pulling on the drawstrings of her hoodie.

'Hey, I'm not saying she killed him herself, okay? Just that E...' she caught herself just in time and managed not to drop Eli in the deep end. 'It's just that everybody seems to think she was hanging out with some dodgy people.'

'Name me one musician who hasn't hung out with someone dodgy at some point,' Gordon railed. He calmed himself with a visible effort. 'You know very well there are a lot of dodgy people who make a habit of hanging around musicians. That doesn't mean you endorse their behaviour, does it? And it certainly doesn't mean that Cass did anything wrong. In fact…' He looked up at the ceiling, shaking his head as if struggling with saying anything more.

'In fact what?' Dana asked. 'I'm sorry, Gordon, I don't mean to be offensive, but you know that I need to have answers. I can't go on like this.'

Gordon let out a long breath. 'Okay. Listen, a few weeks before Ziggy passed away, Cass told me that yes, she had been running with a bad crowd, but she had just recently cut them off. Told them she wanted nothing more to do with them. It isn't any of my business, and I didn't think it was any of yours either, since she hadn't even told you she was with Ziggy. So it's not for me to pass that on, really. But I want you to know that she's not a bad person, okay?'

Dana took a minute to process this. 'Thank you, Gordon. I believe you. Now, given all that, do you think you could get her to sit down and talk to me?'

Dana thought she'd seen and catalogued all of Gordon's facial expressions over the years of their friendship, but her inner librarian was able to add a couple of new ones to the database today.

Gordon's eyes bugged out and his jaw dropped. He looked as though someone had just brought in a vintage Martin acoustic guitar and told him it probably wasn't worth much because the name

Martin was so common in the general population.

'Gee, Dana, you sure know how to blindside a guy, don't you?' He ran a pudgy hand over his face. 'Let me get this straight: you accuse Cass of being involved in Ziggy's death, you accuse me of knowing about it and covering it up, and now you're asking me nicely if I can invite Cass for a cup of tea while you accuse her to her face?'

'Of course not, Gordon! I mean, I won't accuse her of anything. If you vouch for her, then I trust your judgement. And I'm sorry I was mad at you before, I wasn't thinking straight. But still, Cass knows more about Zig's last days than anyone else alive, so I need to talk to her. You can see that, right?'

'Yeah, yeah, I get it. Phew. Okay, I'll do my best, but if she's set on avoiding you I can't guarantee it'll work.'

'Thank you so much, Gordon. You're an absolute gem.'

Gordon went to open his mouth to reply, but was interrupted by the sound of several angry ghosts wailing, or maybe five cats having a fight.

'What the hell was that?' Dana gasped.

'Sorry!' came Brody's voice from the back of the shop. 'Looks like I'm buying this harmonium I just stepped on.'

Chapter 17: Cornering Cass, and more bloody musos

While she waited for Gordon to come through with a meeting with Cass, Dana still had work to do with the Cranial Bypass band. It might be a little awkward turning up to the venue while Cass was still studiously avoiding her, but hopefully that wouldn't be the case for too much longer.

Dana's heart was a bit lighter knowing that she was getting closer to finally extinguishing the burning coal that sat in her chest - the mystery of Ziggy's death.

So she put that aside for now and turned her thoughts back to learning her guitar parts for playing with Horgen and the boys. Oh, and uncovering Pox's killer too, of course. And whoever the hell wanted to kill the poor young roadie Andrew. She made a mental note to ask Wade if he'd had any news from the hospital about

Andrew's condition. Hopefully he was recovering well and would soon be ready to talk.

She dropped Brody back at the shop with his broken harmonium. Brody had felt so bad about stepping on it that he felt he should take it off Gordon's hands. With a bit of work, the pump-driven organ would live to wheeze another day, so it wasn't a complete write-off. For his part, Gordon had given him a very good deal on it. And then shooed them out the door.

Dana knew it hadn't been the most convivial visit, and she resolved to make it up to Gordon at a later date. He was a good friend and deserved better than being hassled about withholding information. Well, he actually had withheld information, but not in a nasty way. Even though Dana was still upset about it, she also appreciated that Gordon had only been looking out for her, as best he could.

While Brody lugged his new purchase into the back office under Evan's bemused gaze, Dana went and grabbed her guitar from her flat.

By the time she got back downstairs, Brody must have finished explaining what had happened, leaving Evan mournfully shaking his head.

'It's bad enough you keep buying funky old instruments, but now you've taken to buying broken old funky instruments? Not only that, you're the one who broke it in the first place!'

Brody's face went red. 'I'm sorry, Evan. I guess I'm just clumsy.' He shrugged.

Evan melted, and enveloped Brody in a hug. 'Awwww, it's okay Brodes. Of course you're clumsy. It's one of your endearing qualities. And hey, now we get to find out how to repair a harmonium, so that's cool, right?'

Dana patted Brody on the back as she walked past. 'You live and learn, Brody. And you never know, once it's fixed up you might find someone to sell it on to.'

'Ooh, that's right,' said Brody, breaking from the hug. 'I might even make a little money on the deal.'

Dana laughed. 'I guess it's possible, sure. Hey, Evan, has everything been okay here at the shop while we were out?'

'Yes, boss,' said Evan, with a crisp salute. 'We've done a good trade on strings today, and thanks to the publicity around you and Cranial Bypass, a couple of people have bought guitars like the one Pox used to play. Bit of a nostalgia thing, I guess. Maybe they just want to hang the guitar on the wall… although one of the buyers took your number for guitar lessons too, so you never know.'

'Oh that's great! Thanks, Evan. I guess I'll leave

you and Brody to it then. I have to pop back to the Riffery for another practice session with Horgen and the others.'

'Be safe, boss,' said Brody.

'Will do. And, Brody?'

'Yeah?'

'Try not to stand on any of the instruments in this shop please, okay?'

'Hey!' Brody protested. But Dana just gave him a wink, and zipped out the door.

She arrived at the carpark of The Riffery a bit too early for practice, and was just pondering whether to go for a walk when she spotted another car pull up, and out jumped Miriama, from the band Giant Penguins. Since Dana had recently found out that Miriama had been involved in a big argument with Pox a few months ago, she really wanted to talk to her about it.

Even though Dana couldn't imagine such a tiny person strangling Pox to death – Miriama only came up to Dana's shoulder, and Dana wasn't exactly Tall-y McTallerson herself – Miriama carried herself with a grounded swagger which exuded energy. Dana couldn't precisely put her finger on it. Miriama wasn't overtly muscle-bound, but she looked like someone you wouldn't want to mess with.

Nonetheless, Dana decided to go and mess with her anyway. It was what she was there for, after all.

She was halfway across the parking lot, guitar case in hand, when a word that Hinemoa had used came to mind. Feistiness. That's what she could sense pouring off Miriama in waves. She looked like the kind of best friend who'd make you do things you wouldn't usually do, encouraging you to grow out of your shell. And also the kind of friend who'd punch a guy in the face if he looked at you wrong.

The kind of person, it seemed, who would threaten bodily harm to a singer if she suspected him of being involved in white supremacy.

Dana hoped she could cross Miriama off her list of suspects because she liked her already and she hadn't even met her yet.

'Excuse me! Hi!' Miriama's head whipped around as Dana called out to her. 'Sorry to bother you. Hi, I'm Dana.'

Miriama looked her up and down with a steely gaze, and then spotted her guitar, and softened. 'Oh, are you the one who's playing with Cranial Bypass now? Hinemoa mentioned you.'

'Yes, that's me!' Dana stuck out her free hand. 'Nice to meet you.'

Miriama shook Dana's hand. She looked much

more friendly now. Nobody likes being accosted by a stranger in a parking lot, so Dana was thankful for Hinemoa's introduction.

Dana considered herself culturally aware, so was disappointed with herself when she realised she was staring at Miriama's moko kauae. Facial tattoos were quite common among Māori people in Aotearoa, but Dana was forced to admit that she wasn't really used to seeing a moko kauae up close. It looked so cool, it was hard to stop staring. Dana wondered what it must have felt like, having it done with traditional tools, and all your family around you.

Snap out of it, Dana, she scolded herself. Focus.

'Did you want to ask me something?' said Miriama, who no doubt had people staring at her chin every day.

So at least Dana wasn't going to ask her about that.

Dana decided to just jump right in.

'Ah, yeah, when I was talking to Hinemoa, she mentioned that you'd had a bit of a run-in with Apocalypse BusLane before he passed away.'

'Oh.' Miriama was startled by this unexpected angle, but quickly recovered. 'Well, yeah, of course it was before he passed away. What did you expect me to do? Wait till he was dead and then have an argument with his corpse?'

'Heh heh… right. What I meant was, why were you arguing with him?'

Miriama leaned back and narrowed her eyes. 'Why are you asking about that? What are you, writing a book about him or something?'

Shit, that would have been a great cover story, Dana realised. Pity it was too late to switch it up now. She should have set the scene earlier on with Horgs and the others.

'Well, not really. I suppose I'm just wondering what I'm getting into. Stepping into his shoes, you know, with the band. Is there anything I need to be careful about? Are you and me going to be okay working the same gig?'

Miriama nodded slowly. 'You and me don't have a problem, I don't even know you. Whereas Pox… well, I'd been reading a lot about the rise of social media posts by these right-wing fascist arseholes, and there's this one Cranial Bypass song where Horgen let Pox write the lyrics, and I thought it sounded like they might be referencing that stuff. So I had a go at him about it.' Her eyes bored holes into Dana. 'I don't work with anyone who's into that scene, and I don't hold back telling them about it, either. You got an issue with that?'

'Heck, no,' Dana replied. 'Good on you.'

Miriama lifted her chin in approval. 'Sweet. Well, anyway, Pox sat me down with him and Horgs, and they told me I'd got the wrong end of the stick. Pox apologised. You could see that the accusation really hurt him. He said he hated to think that anyone might mistake his pagan references for white supremacy.'

'There can be some overlap, I gather, especially with metal bands.' Dana had heard some pretty depressing stuff about this over the years, and while she could forgive people for inadvertently using imagery they didn't fully understand, what mattered was what they did when they found out about it. As for Cranial Bypass, Dana knew their catalogue back to front, and she knew they weren't tainted by any of that horrible stuff. She'd even tried playing some of their songs back to front – no racism that way either.

'True,' said Miriama, 'I was fifty-fifty on believing him, but Horgs spoke up for him. Told me all the good stuff Pox had done over the years for minorities. Told me some of the stupid crap he'd done too, just to keep it real, so I'd know he wasn't pulling my leg. In the end, we shook hands and were just starting to become friends over the next few weeks. In fact, just before he died, he asked me to play on a new track he was working on. Damn shame he passed away before that could happen. It would have been awesome. I heard a demo of the song, and it was a whole new direction for Pox. Even had that hippy guy on it, Sweatstains or whatever.'

'Aaron Swetters,' Dana corrected her automatically. 'Yeah, he told me he was working on some stuff with Pox. Wow, I didn't realise he was getting you involved too.'

'Well, why would you know about it? It was a solo project, not something with Cranial Bypass.' Her eyes flicked up above Dana's head, as she consulted her memory. 'In fact, I'm not even sure if Horgen knew about it. He certainly wasn't on the demo, anyway. Pox was singing, and there was someone else doing harmonies. The harmony singer had a real similar sound to Pox's voice, just a little smoother, you know?'

'But you don't know who it was?' Dana told herself she should have another listen to the songs on the flash drive that Aaron Swetters had given her once she got home.

Miriama shrugged. 'No idea. Maybe the Swetters guy? Although I've heard him sing a few times now, and he's more of a high lonesome type, if you know what I mean.'

'Old-time country kind of thing?'

'Exactly, that kind of voice, but leaning more into the folk side of country.'

Miriama looked towards the venue's back door. 'Anyway, that's enough gabbing about poor old Pox. Were you on your way in?'

'Yes!' Dana hefted her guitar case. 'Time for another practice with the guys. Hey, thanks for the chat. Good to know that you and me can work together with nothing hanging over us.'

'Sure,' said Miriama, opening the door and waving Dana through. 'I mean, you seem a bit nosy, but apart from that I'm sure you're okay.'

Oof. Dana knew she deserved that.

Inside, it was the usual cheerful chaos. Now that Dana had been chosen as Pox's stand-in, and the actual gig was only a couple of weeks away, everything went into overdrive – not just Dana's guitar overdrive pedal, but everybody involved with the show. There was a lot riding on this, not least the fact they were trying to do something worthy of the mighty Apocalypse BusLane.

This included everyone in the support acts too, not just Cranial Bypass. It also affected the venue staff, the roadies, the merch people. Everyone was amped up, quite literally in many cases.

It seemed to Dana that more new people

appeared every time she turned up. There were so many people involved in making a big show happen. It was a far cry from a DIY punk gig.

She raised enquiring eyebrows to Sione, who was busy directing the installation of a crowd barrier in front of the stage. He waved her in the direction of the green room out the back, where she found Ollie the bass player and Marty the drummer. Ollie was doing back stretches and Marty was wrapping something around his wrists and elbows. It was like watching boxers getting ready for a fight. Or perhaps a couple of old folks preparing for a long bus trip to the shops.

Dana decided not to share that observation with anyone present.

Friendly greetings were exchanged, and Dana was looking forward to hanging out with the rhythm section and getting to know them better. Sadly, the next person to walk through the door was none other than Greasy Grainger (as Dana had started to think of him). He was about as welcome as a bad case of the runs, and Dana noticed it wasn't just her who felt that way.

Ollie's smile fell, and he retreated into a corner to tune his bass. Marty greeted Grainger, but there was no warmth in the exchange, and he soon went back to fussing with his elbow support, rather pointedly not making eye contact.

Dana went to open her guitar case, but Grainger called out to her.

'Hey, did you bring that contract today?'

'Not yet, sorry. I haven't had time to go over it properly.'

'Pffft. Haven't had time? It's been, what? Two days since I gave it to you.'

'Half of which time I spent either immersed in the river, or recovering in bed,' Dana protested.

'Ahhh, there it is,' said Grainger.

'There what is?' Dana knew she should just shrug off the creep's prodding but she couldn't help herself.

Grainger nodded slowly to himself. 'I knew that a woman wouldn't be up to the job. If you're just going to keep coming up with excuses, maybe you should throw in the towel now, and let someone else have a go.'

Dana's mouth fell open.

Before she could explode, and kick the odious manager in his deductibles, Ollie called out from where he sat with his bass on his lap.

'Come on, Trent, don't be a prick all your life, will ya?'

'Yeah,' Marty joined in. 'She saved the life of one of the crew, and you're giving her shit about it?

Don't be a dick, mate.'

'Hey, hey, calm down,' said Grainger, 'the kid in the river was a ring-in, not a permanent crew member. What are you getting so upset for?'

'Are you actually telling me,' Dana growled, 'that you measure the worth of a person's life based on their economic attachment to your organisation?'

'Of course not! That would make me…' Grainger paused, trying to think of the right word, then quickly looked it up on his phone, '…a psychopath?' He frowned, then muttered to himself. 'Crap. Really?'

Dana glanced at the other band members. Was this conversation actually happening? From their bemused expressions, she had to assume this was real, and not a nightmare she was trapped in.

'Anyway,' Grainger continued, 'have you considered the idea that it was that young roadie kid who killed Pox? I saw him talking with Pox when he first came onboard, and Pox looked real upset afterwards. So maybe someone was getting him back for that.'

'Are you saying that you threw Andrew in the river?' Ollie stood up, still holding his bass.

'No! I wouldn't do something like that. Do you think so little of me?'

Ollie avoided answering the question by

becoming instantly absorbed in tuning his bass.

Marty whistled and suddenly found a spot on the ceiling very interesting.

Dana wasn't quick enough, and Grainger caught her eye.

'Seriously? Far out, you people think I could just murder someone in cold blood?'

'It's how you do everything else,' Ollie murmured.

'Oh, wow, thanks very much. Perhaps you need to consider that, if this kid is the one who killed Pox, maybe he was overcome with…' Grainger was at a loss for the correct word again. Once more he consulted his phone with a quickly-tapped query. 'Remorse? Huh.'

'Makes sense,' said Dana. 'Young guy kills a famous rock star, then feels so bad about it he binds his own hands and feet and somehow throws himself in the river.'

Grainger, seemingly impervious to sarcasm, spread his hands wide. 'Exactly! Thank you. Maybe I'll keep you on after all, guitar girl. You're nicer to look at than these goons, anyway.'

Two wolves materialised inside Dana. One wanted to run as far away from Grainger as possible, the other wanted to tear his throat out.

Lucky for Grainger, Dana was more of a cat

person, so she just sniffed with disdain and ignored the creep.

Sensing he'd lost his audience, Grainger threw his hands in the air, turned and left the room. 'Honestly, you try to compliment someone…'

The atmosphere immediately became more relaxed once the human greaseball was gone.

'I'd apologise for him,' Ollie offered, 'except he's nothing to do with me. But still, I am sorry you had to suffer through that.'

'How did he even get involved with all this?' Dana asked.

'Oh, he's been with Horgs for years, nobody really knows how Horgs can stand him though.'

'True,' Marty interjected. 'I heard once that Grainger was a distant family member of Horgen's, and he felt he couldn't fire him.'

Ollie shrugged. 'It might also be just that Grainger makes Horgen a lot of money. I mean a *lot* of money. Pox had his own personal manager, and I heard that he ended up with less in the bank than Horgs.'

Dana had her own thoughts about this, now that she knew Pox had been financing a new album, and recording with other musicians. He might have ended up with less money than Horgen simply because he was using his share to further his art.

She was musing on this when Ollie spoke again. 'I wouldn't be surprised if it was Trent who tried to kill Andrew, actually. I mean, the man literally had to look up the word remorse. I've met bass amps with more emotional intelligence.'

'Pffft, I don't think he'd do that,' said Marty. 'There's no monetary gain in it for him.'

'Maybe Andrew asked for a raise?'

Marty paused. 'Oh yeah, that might do it.'

Dana was tuning up her guitar with a headstock clip-on tuner (free with every bulk pack of strings at Pick Me Guitar Store this month) but she looked up to see if the guys were having her on. 'He wouldn't really have it in him to kill someone would he? You guys have known him for a long time. What do you think, honestly?'

Ollie and Marty exchanged a look. There was a pause, and then they both spoke at once. 'Of course not, he wouldn't do that.' 'No, not really.'

They strode out to the stage, leaving Dana absently turning the tuning peg for the B string until it finally snapped.

Dana growled. What horrible timing – she was supposed to be onstage with Cranial Bypass in a few minutes.

Even though she was very well-practiced at changing guitar strings, she had a sudden brainwave. Somewhere not far from here there'd be a certain roadie who was so proud of their string-changing abilities they'd given themselves a nickname based on it: Mr Two.

Two minutes to change a whole set of strings? Then one string by itself should be a doddle. And, since Dana still had to talk through some arrangements with the rhythm section, Mr Two should have her string all sorted by the time that was done.

She grabbed a fresh set of strings from her gig bag, hefted her guitar, and rushed along the corridor to where she'd found Mr Two last time, relaxing in his ostentatious rocking chair. Please let him be there, please let him be there…

Aha! She was in luck.

'Dana, my girl! My wee pocket watch. My heart's —'

'Sorry to interrupt, Mr. Two, but do you have time to do a quick string change for me, please?'

'Oh my giddy stars!' roared the rusty old roadie. 'Do I have time? Is my name Mr Two or isn't it?'

Dana beamed. 'You're a gem! I'm supposed to be onstage right now, so I really appreciate this.'

She thrust the guitar and the packet of new strings into the grizzled yet trustworthy hands of Mr Two.

'Actually my dear, I need to ask a favour of you too, if I may?'

'Anything! Yes, fine.' Dana was already halfway out the door.

'Sione needs this room so I have to put my rocking chair somewhere. Can I leave it at your shop?'

'Of course! Love you. Bye!'

Dana raced through the labyrinth of corridors to the stage, almost stopping for a heart attack along the way as she belatedly realised she'd called out 'love you!' instead of 'thank you!' to Mr Two. That was embarrassing. Although, Mr Two probably thought it was fine, so why should she worry?

No time to worry about that now, anyway.

She zipped up the stage stairs and found Horgen and the others deep in discussion about exactly how much fog could be allowed onstage before it got too hard to see where your microphone stand was located.

'Hi, Dana!' Horgen called out. 'How are you doing?'

'Good, thanks, Mr Greymantle.' He rolled his eyes, so Dana tried again. 'Good, thank you, Horgen.' This elicited a smile.

'No guitar today?' he asked.

'Oh, Mr Two is just restringing it for me. Had a

little string incident backstage.'

The tips of Horgen's ears went red. Was it just Dana's imagination or did he seem a bit flustered?

'String incidents can, ahh… happen to anyone.' He clapped Ollie on the shoulder. 'Am I right, mate?'

Ollie shook his head. 'Nope, not me. I haven't changed my bass strings since I bought it. Reckon they'll bury me with those strings.'

If anything, Horgen looked even more unnerved now.

Marty noticed, and took the reins. 'Hey, can we run through the middle eight of Brain Drain by Aeroplane? I think we need to get tighter on the section where we switch from four-four to five-four.'

Horgen shook off whatever was on his mind. 'Sure, good idea, Marty.'

Dana panicked, but then felt a tap on her shoulder and turned to find Mr Two holding out her guitar.

'Perfect timing! Thank you so much for this!'

'Not a scubbins, your honour,' Mr Two declaimed, waving away her thanks. 'Now, get out there and knock their socks sideways.'

'I'll certainly try,' Dana promised with a smile.

The practice went well, and Dana really enjoyed playing with Cranial Bypass. The material was exactly the right kind of challenge, and the band was beginning to gel even though they'd only just started playing together.

'That was great, Dana,' said Horgs after they finished up. 'Honestly we might sound better than we used to, with you on board.'

Dana blushed. 'I doubt that, but thank you for the vote of confidence.'

'No, I mean it.' Horgen paused, tapping a finger on his lips. 'Maybe we should look at booking some more gigs after this, yeah? We could plan out a tour, and maybe even some recording? I actually have a lot of songs ready to go, full demos, guitar parts and everything.'

'Oh,' said Dana. 'I didn't know you wrote all that, I always thought Pox wrote the music and you did the words.'

'Yeah, well, a lot of people don't realise I can do that, and maybe it's about bloody time they found out.' Horgen seemed to realise his voice was rising, and he calmed himself. 'Sorry, it's just that it's hard being in the shadow of someone like Pox. We had a good run, and I'll always be grateful to him for the part he played, but maybe it's now time for me to show everyone what I can do, you know?'

'Sure,' said Dana warily. 'I mean, after all, wasn't Pox already working on some new material by himself too?'

Horgen took a step forward. 'How did you know about that?'

Dana gulped. 'Um, I talked to Aaron Swetters and Miriama Tipene-Dawes. Aaron had been working on songs with Pox, and Miriama had been talking about doing something just before he passed away.'

Horgen was nodding. 'Right. Swetters, and Miriama. But they hadn't recorded anything yet. Pox told me that himself.'

'Not officially, no. But Aaron showed me some demo tracks they'd done.' Dana smiled at the memory. 'They sounded great. There was – '

'What do you mean, you've heard the demos?' Horgen broke in. 'Pox said there weren't any copies of those recordings.'

'Well…' Dana didn't know how much she should say, but surely Horgen had a right to know. 'All I can tell you is that Aaron has half a dozen song demos, just him and Pox. Oh, and someone on backing vocals.'

Horgen's gaze hardened. 'That bloody backing vocalist.' He turned and slammed his fists onto his hips. 'And now I need to have a chat with Swetters too. Listen, don't tell Trent about these demos, will you? He got pretty upset when he heard about Pox's side project. Reckoned it would steal focus from the main act, rob our momentum and so on. If he found out that Swetters has recordings of Pox... I don't know what he'd do.' Horgen stood there for a second, then suddenly seemed to remember himself. 'Uh, and good work today. See you tomorrow.' And then he took off down the corridor, leaving a puzzled and shaken guitar store owner in his wake.

Chapter 18: It must be Grainger

Dana suddenly wanted nothing more than to be back home, chatting about inconsequential rubbish with Brody. She grabbed her guitar and started off down the corridor, but noticed there was someone at the other end. Damn, she just could not catch a break these days. She really didn't feel like talking to anyone else right now.

As she walked along, the shadowy figure resolved itself into the shape of a burly police officer she knew well. To her surprise, she was actually glad to see DCI Shaw.

'Hi, are you here with Hinemoa again?' Dana asked as they got closer.

'Hi, Dana. Yep, just checking in. Everything okay with you?' She leaned in close. 'You look like you've seen a ghost. And I just saw that Greyskull guy striding away. Did he do anything to you?' She cracked her knuckles.

'No!' said Dana hurriedly. 'No, everything's fine. But thank you for asking. I'm just looking forward to going home now, that's all. Oh!' Dana slapped her forehead. 'How rude of me to forget! I need to thank you.'

'What for?'

'The other night. I'm told you're the one who pulled me out of the river. Probably saved my life.'

Shaw propped a shoulder against the wall and shook her head 'You pulled yourself out of the river, remember? And you saved that kid's life. I just happened to be walking past, and called the ambulance.'

'Well, anyway, I want to thank you for that.'

'All part of the job, Ms. Osborne. But honestly, you seem pretty good at saving yourself.' She pushed away from the wall, and gave Dana a wink as she walked off. 'Maybe you should think about becoming a police officer?'

'I thought you banned me from ever going near a station again?' Dana called after her.

Shaw just laughed.

By the time Dana got home the shop was closed, and Brody and Evan were gone. She went straight up the back steps to her flat and put on an album by

The Bad Plus while she cooked dinner. The discordant notes floating out of the speakers helped her think, distracting her from the obvious, and helping her make random connections between neurons.

Paws McCartney demanded attention, cuddles and food, definitely not in that order.

When the cat was finally settled and food ready, she sat at her table with a contented sigh. Just as she brought a fork to her lips, the doorbell rang.

'Oh, come on!' She slammed the fork down as she rose from her chair, and spilled pasta on her jeans. 'Dammit!' Her noise scared Paws McCartney, who jumped off his perch on the sofa and ran under her feet, almost toppling her.

'Look out, Pawsy! Grrr!'

The doorbell rang again, and she grumped her way down the stairs. 'I'm coming!'

When she opened the door, she came face to face with Mr Two's rocking chair. A couple of men lurked behind it, looking like they were just about to take off and leave the chair where it was.

'Wait!' Dana called out. 'Could you help me get this upstairs please?'

Reluctantly, they did, only scraping paint in a few places as they manoeuvred the ridiculous piece of furniture up the stairwell and into Dana's flat.

Wordlessly, they plonked it in the kitchen and retreated back down the stairs.

Dana stood there looking at the rocking chair, wondering what on earth she was going to do with it. Paws McCartney reappeared, gave the chair a sniff, then promptly jumped up into it. It wobbled underneath him, and he growled and leaped off it, running into a corner, looking at Dana accusingly as if she'd just tricked him.

'Don't blame me, Pawsy. You'll have to address any rocking chair complaints to Mr Two.'

She dragged the offending item into her lounge area. 'It's just going to have to go there until Mr Two comes to take it back, okay Mr McCartney? You'll get used to it.'

And indeed, when Dana got up the next morning she found Paws firmly ensconced in the rocker, swaying slightly and purring contentedly.

'I'm glad you slept well, Paws. I certainly didn't.'

Overnight she'd been plagued with nightmares about Horgen's strange behaviour, about being trapped underwater, and also one particularly scary one where she was playing in front of a huge crowd with Cranial Bypass, but when she looked down she had Aaron Swetters' bass-banjo in her hands instead of her guitar. She woke herself trying to scream.

So she found herself relieved when Brody turned up for work, with Evan in tow. Nice to have someone to share yesterday's weirdness with. Extra nice that Evan had thoughtfully brought along croissants.

While she made coffee, she told them all about her interaction with Greasy Grainger, and then with Horgen acting weird.

'I don't know, guys, something is definitely off there. Horgen went strange whenever I mentioned demo recordings. And strings, for that matter.'

'Wait, are you saying what I think you're saying?' Brody asked.

'Depends on what you think I'm saying.'

'Well, it kinda sounds like you're saying that Horgen killed Pox.'

'No!' Dana almost scalded herself with the coffee. 'Horgen would never do anything to hurt Pox. They were partners in music for decades. They dragged themselves up by their shoelaces.' She shook her head. 'No way Horgen would do that. Grainger, however… I reckon Horgen told Grainger about the demos, and Grainger didn't like the idea of Pox going solo. Taking focus, and money, from the main act.'

'So, you think Grainger killed Pox?' said Evan.

'I think that's the more likely option.' She shivered. 'Urgh. The guy gives me the absolute creeps. And he seems completely devoid of empathy or emotion. Classic psycho killer, yeah?'

Evan nodded slowly. 'I guess so. But then, he would have known he'd be leaving Cranial Bypass without their famous guitar player co-founder. So he'd be ruining his own business.'

'Would he though?' Dana plunked herself down on the sofa. 'Because from where I'm sitting it looks like Cranial Bypass are getting more press than ever. Which means they're probably selling a truckload of albums and getting a shedload of streams. And now that Pox is gone, all the songwriting money probably goes to Horgen, since Pox didn't have any family to bequeath his royalties to. Not only that, I've had a closer look at my contract, and I'm being offered a pittance. Yep, I'd say Horgen is suddenly making a lot more money, which means Grainger is too, by taking his cut as manager. Paws, stop that!'

This last comment was directed at the wilful ball of fur that was currently using the arm of Mr Two's rocking chair as a scratching post. Dana couldn't imagine how upset the old roadie would be if a cat ruined his prized rocker.

'We'd better tell Wade, then, right?' said Brody. 'See what he thinks?'

Dana nodded, inhaling the steam from her coffee. While she was very much hoping she'd get to see Grainger carted off in cuffs, she wasn't looking forward to being in the middle of the circus he'd leave behind as the big gig approached.

She left Brody and Evan in charge of the shop again, and Beetled into town to meet Wade.

True to form, Wade suggested they meet at a kebab place. 'I get to bill it back to the station, since I'm meeting an informant,' he told her, stuffing the receipt into a pocket.

Dana wasn't complaining. A free kebab was surely the least the Police could do for her, since she was doing all their work for them.

'So what's the story – did you find the killer?'

'I think so, Wade.' She filled him in on everything she'd learned.

'Sounds plausible,' he said, wiping sauce off his chin, 'but do you have any evidence?'

'I was rather hoping you and your lot could find some of that,' Dana replied. 'Can't you get a warrant to search his office? CSI his laptop, and all that jazz?'

Wade snorted. 'On our budget, the IT forensic department consists of a guy called Ian, who does twenty hours a week for the Police, keeping our PCs going, and another twenty hours a week tagging items online so that an Artificial Intelligence can learn enough to take his job in a couple of years. And, I tell you what, the AI job pays better too.'

Dana sighed. 'Alright, but even so, what do you expect me to do? Wear a wire, and get him to confess?'

Wade went to reply but Dana shot him down. 'I will not be doing that, are we clear? Suggest something else.' Although, now she thought about it, Grainger was just the kind of guy who would probably casually confess to a murder. Still, while Dana would happily keep her phone handy for recording, she was not willing to go into a room alone with Grainger and try to sweet-talk him into saying he did it. Hell, she wasn't willing to be alone in a room with him full stop.

'Okay, it's fine,' said Wade. 'No wire. We just need anything that can tie Grainger to Pox's murder. Something more firm than just a bad feeling.'

Dana took a bite of her kebab and chewed thoughtfully as she planned a way to get into Grainger's office without him being there.

Chapter 19: Distraction infraction

Mr Two answered the phone with a completely true-to-form greeting.

'Tell me something groovy!' he yelled.

Dana hastily moved the phone away from her ear, belatedly realising it might be best to do this on the speaker.

'Hi, Gerald,' she called out.

'Who? How dare you? What's a Gerald when it's at home?'

'Sorry! Hello Mr Two!'

'Ah, that sounds like me ol' peahen Dana. Is that you, dear?'

'It is.'

'Oh no, I 'ope that chair en't given yer no trouble, 'as it?'

'Not at all! In fact, Paws McCartney has adopted it as his permanent residence, it seems. But I just wondered, since I'm looking after the chair, would you do me a wee favour in return?'

'By Satan's corduroy trousers, of course I'll 'elp yer. You don't need to call in no favours with me, Dana. What do yer need?'

Dana felt terrible about feeding Mr Two a made-up story, but she didn't have much choice. Even though she trusted the rocking chair roadie's heart implicitly, she was less confident in his mind and mouth keeping things private. The only filter between his brain and his lips was the butt of a cigarette. She was very fond of him, but definitely wouldn't drag him into this whole undercover operation.

'I appear to have left my notes on the song arrangements at the venue, and I really need them for practicing at home. You've got keys for all the rooms at The Riffery, right? It's just that I'm not one hundred percent sure where I left them.'

'Notes? On paper, Dana? I fought you'd be one of them electronic doodad people.'

'Call me old-fashioned, but I don't trust that kind of technology. I knew a guitarist who had his whole set's worth of arrangement notes loaded on an iPad, but it accidentally synced with the bass player's notes, and he kept skipping forward to look at the next song while they were playing!'

'Oof! That's tough.'

'I'll say. The guitarist played a few bars in the completely wrong key before he figured out what was happening. You'll never see that happen with a piece of paper. Anyway, can I borrow your keys please? I'll get them back to you by dinner time.'

Dana knew the venue was empty during the day, musicians and crew being nocturnal creatures by nature. She could zip in, look through Grainger's office area, and be out before anyone else turned up.

'Okay my little podocarp, come round and grab 'em when you're ready.'

Dana thanked Mr Two and grabbed her car keys. She went downstairs and found Brody waiting by her Beetle.

'Need a lift somewhere, Brodes?'

'I'm coming with you to The Riffery.'

'No you're not.'

'I am.' Brody crossed his arms. 'You'll need a lookout. And remember, I helped with that last case. I found that secret room, and recorded a confession, and everything.'

'Yes, but you did most of that by accident, while falling on your head.'

'I can fall on my head again if I have to.' Brody jutted his chin out. 'I want to help, and I think you need it. What if you get caught in there by yourself?'

Dana shrugged. 'What if we get caught in there together?'

'Well, I'll…'

'Fall on your head?'

'That was uncalled for, boss.'

'I'm sorry, Brody, you're right.' Dana sighed. It actually would be nice to have some backup for this little escapade. And a clumsy lookout was better than no lookout at all, she supposed.

'Alright,' she said, and Brody raised his arms in victory.

'Yes!'

'But listen, you have to do exactly what I say. And don't touch anything, Brody.'

'Gotcha, boss.' Brody yanked open the car door and jumped in, clonking his head on the doorframe in the process. 'Ouch! Dammit, has your car shrunk or something?'

Dana took a moment to send a hopeful prayer to the gods of musical mayhem, before getting into the car herself.

They picked up the keys from Mr Two, who looked bewildered about it, and Dana had to run through the whole story again. But he cheerfully agreed a second time, and then they were on their way to the venue.

'Hey,' said Brody, 'are we going to have to disable the security cameras? I brought a gun.'

'What?!' shrieked Dana. 'Why? Where did you get a gun?'

'Fly-killing gun. See?' Brody brandished a small plastic gun with a disc at the end of the barrel. 'I can shoot this at the cameras and…'

'Tap them gently with a piece of plastic?' Dana's heart rate slowly went down as she looked at the – thankfully – flimsy toy in Brody's hand.

'Well, then I thought I could put gaffer tape on the disc, and it would stick on – '

'Leave it, Brody, we won't need that.'

'But what about the cameras?'

'If anyone goes to look at the recording, they'll just see people who have a legitimate reason to be there, using keys provided by the head of the road crew.'

'But what about if we take evidence from Grainger's office? Won't he be able to find out it was us?'

'I'm only going to photograph things, not take them. So nobody will ever need to check the cameras, because nothing went missing. Listen, it's probably best if you stay outside in the carpark anyway. Keep a lookout from there, where you can see both the front and rear entrances.'

'Oh. Right. Cool.' Brody looked down sadly at his fly-gun. 'So I don't need this then.'

'No. Sorry, Brody. Maybe next time.' She smiled.

They parked at the venue, and Dana took a second to brief Brody before they got out of the car.

'Okay, now listen up. I'm going to head straight to the room where Grainger has set up his office space. It's at the back of the venue, upstairs, looking out over the river. You'll stay here in the car, where you'll be able to see people approaching from any direction, whether they're coming from the back door or the front entrance. Got it?'

Brody nodded. 'Yep. And when do I come upstairs?'

'Never,' said Dana emphatically. 'You do not go upstairs. The lookout stays here, looking out for people. You see?'

'Oh, right. So you don't want me inside, helping you?'

'You will be helping me, Brody. By keeping both entrances in view and texting me if anyone turns up.'

'Hmmmph. Sounds boring.'

Dana patted his arm. 'Boring is good, Brody. Boring is safe. Let's try to keep it boring, shall we?'

'Yeah, yeah, I get it.' Brody threw the fly-gun into the back seat, crossed his arms, and glared out the windscreen. 'Go on then, MacGyver. I'll be out here being bored.'

'Thanks, Brodes. Keep your phone handy, okay? And just text front or back if you see anyone. You don't have to write a whole big message, I'll know what you mean.'

'Sure. I can handle that.'

Dana could see he was upset with her, but she was just going to have to deal with that later. For now, she needed to get this thing done, and quickly.

She walked to the back door as if she was a regular, authorised person on regular, authorised business. She tried to put on a facial expression that said 'silly me, I left my notes behind', but wasn't sure she was altogether pulling it off. Probably should have practiced in the mirror first.

Once inside, she stopped for a second, listening to make sure nobody else was about. Just because there were no other cars in the carpark, didn't mean someone might have come in by bicycle or bus. But no, thankfully, it seemed like the place was deserted.

She proceeded up the stairs, and after a couple of attempts, located the correct key to open Grainger's office door.

Oh boy – the place stank of cheap bourbon, and something else she wasn't sure she wanted to identify. There were clothes scattered all about the place. What a messy creature this guy was.

Dana held her nose and started scanning the room in detail.

She opened filing cabinet drawers and riffled through papers. Most seemed to pertain to expenses for putting on the reunion gig. She raised her eyes at the amount he was paying Sione for hiring The Riffery. Dana knew that Sione would normally be asking double that price. Grainger was obviously very good at his job. She hoped it all worked out for Sione and he didn't lose any money out of this enterprise.

In the next drawer were a lot of stubs from horse races, and a half-eaten packet of fries, congealing sadly in the back corner.

Dana gagged, and hurriedly shut that drawer.

In the last drawer were some more official documents. She checked her phone. No messages from Brody. Good. Nobody was about. Or else, she supposed, he might have fallen asleep. Oh well, nothing she could do about that…

She skimmed the documents. Lots of deals Grainger had done with local bands. He'd obviously been checking out the local scene, and signing up anyone he thought he could make a dollar off.

Seriously, these contracts were rubbish. Dana knew some of these acts. She would try to talk to them later and see if they could get out of these terrible terms.

Wait… here was a will, in the name of Archie Evans.

That probably wouldn't mean much to a lot of people, but to a Cranial Bypass fan like Dana, it was a huge deal. Archie Evans was the real name of none other than Apocalypse BusLane. Her heart fluttered. This could be big.

Her eyes flew over the document, looking for – aha! There it was, a section dealing with his songwriting royalties. And boom – just like that, Dana knew she had the evidence she needed.

She took a few photos, then popped the will back in the drawer. Wait till she showed Wade!

Her phone vibrated in her hand. Bringing up her messages, she saw one from Brody: 'Front. Get out!'

Shit.

She turned for the door, and froze. There was a stack of small boxes in behind the door. That's why she hadn't seen them on the way in. Tiny boxes she knew very well from her work at the guitar shop. All those boxes held guitar strings. And these particular strings were… phosphor bronze, just like the one that Pox had been murdered with.

She fumbled her phone into camera mode again, just as she heard footsteps downstairs. Come on, come on!

Two quick clicks, and she was done. She raced downstairs, taking them two at a time.

Thank goodness for Brody's warning - she knew that she had to avoid the front door. She might still be in time to get out of the building without being seen.

She charged into the labyrinth of corridors that led to the back door. Great, she should be out of the line of sight from the front door now. That meant she could slow down, and quiet her footfalls in case the person heard her. She was only a few steps from freedom.

Dana tip-toed around a corner, and smacked right into Trent Grainger.

Chapter 20: Grainger grumps

'Oof! What the hell is this? Get off me. Help! Thief!' Grainger pushed Dana away and contorted himself into some kind of pseudo-Bruce Lee martial arts pose.

Despite the situation, Dana couldn't help but laugh. 'Put your hands down, Grainger, you'll do yourself a mischief.'

'Osborne?! What are you doing here, you stupid tart? I could have killed you!'

Numerous comebacks flooded Dana's mind. Not like that, you couldn't. Or: Did you seriously just call me a tart? But the one that actually came out her mouth was more pressing.

'Why don't you have any trousers on?' Grainger's lily-white legs were on full display, and Dana was also being treated to the sight of some extremely tight black underwear. She started looking around for something to throw up in.

Grainger glanced down at himself. 'What are you talking about? These are Speedos. I've been swimming in the river. I've just come back to get changed.'

'Right,' said Dana. 'Sure. That's a perfectly normal answer. You're the manager of a huge rock band. Don't you have a pool at home?'

Grainger's face went red. 'It's none of your damn business, but I'm living here at the moment.'

Ahhh, the clothes strewn around his office made sense now.

'Why are you living in a pub?' Dana hoped that she could keep control of the conversation, and then get out of there before Grainger came back to the question of what was she doing there.

'As I've already said, none of your damn business. But if you must know, I actually have an offer on a mansion out of town. I'm just waiting on some... investments to mature.'

Dana's mind flashed to the gambling ticket stubs in Grainger's filing cabinet. He might be waiting a while for those investments to mature.

'Okay, well, it's been nice chatting with you Trent, but I have to be off now.'

She circled past the sodden manager, and the venue's back door was in sight.

'Hold up,' he called out. 'Why the hell are you wandering around here when there's nobody else around?'

'Oh, I left some of my notes here and needed them for practicing at home.'

'So you found them?'

'Yes, all good thanks. Right, see you later.' Dana edged closer to the door.

'Where are they?'

'Sorry?'

'The notes you came here to get. You don't seem to be carrying any notes.'

Curses! 'Oh, I… ummm…' Dana stammered.

'There you are, boss!' Brody came rushing from the direction of the front of the venue. 'You dropped these.' He waved a sheaf of paper in front of him. 'Hey, nice undies mate.' He winked at Grainger, whose face quickly went from red to purple as he tried to deal with this comment.

'You… that's… get out! Both of you, get out of here now!'

'Will do,' said Dana. She grabbed Brody by the hand and dragged him past the discombobulated manager, out into the sunlight, and freedom.

Back in the car, Dana tried to do some slow breathing to calm herself down.

'Oh my god, Brody, you saved my arse in there – thank you!'

'You're welcome, boss.'

Then she gave him a whack on the arm. 'But why the hell did your text say he was coming through the front door, when he was at the back?'

'I meant you should go *out* the front door, because he's coming through the back. I thought that was pretty clear. You just told me to text front or back, and I thought you wanted to know which way to leave.'

Dana went back to her breathing. Yes, in retrospect, they should have gone over the plan in a little more detail. Still, it had worked. They had what they needed.

'Fine. Thank you, Brody. Now, let's go and see Wade. I think he's going to be very pleased with what I found.'

Chapter 21: An arrest

The next day, Grainger was "invited" down to the Police station to help them with their inquiries.

Wade texted Dana the good news, and she felt like she could finally relax properly for the first time in at least a week. She still didn't know why Grainger would have wanted to kill the young roadie Andrew, but at least now she could leave all that to the Police to uncover. Her job was done: she'd found Pox's killer. Hallelujah!

She called Brody and asked him and Evan to come over and celebrate. Hopefully by lunchtime Wade would come over too, and they could all raise a glass to successful operation.

Dana got some cheap bubbly from the supermarket, along with breads and dips, and sprawled on the sofa awaiting her visitors.

'Stop that, Paws!' She waved a hand at the cat in

a feeble attempt to dissuade him from scratching Mr Two's rocking chair arm. He seemed to have settled on one particular side as his favourite scratching area, and Dana was worried that if Mr Two didn't take the thing back soon, there might only be one arm left.

The boys turned up and attacked the provisions, but had only just got settled in when Wade appeared.

'Wade! Hi! Is Grainger in jail now?'

'No he is not.' Wade grabbed a serving plate and sat down with the whole thing. 'In fact, Mr. Grainger is back on the streets right now. And frankly, if I were you, I would stay well away from him for a while. He is not very happy with you.'

Dana's mouth fell open. 'What? How is that creep free right now? What happened?'

Wade seemed to wrestle with himself for a minute, then finally he decided, and tossed a flash drive to Dana. 'For privacy reasons, this never happened, and I was never here, and also, do you have any more of that hummus? It's delicious.'

Dana looked at Evan, confused. Evan shrugged, but spotted Dana's laptop on the kitchen bench. He went and got it and Dana plugged in the flash drive. A video clip opened – it looked like it was from a camera in a high-up corner of a very bare room. In the room was a table. From the cheap look of it, and the multiple chips and scrapes, Dana knew they were looking at a Police interrogation room.

On one side of the table were Grainger and a woman in a swanky suit. The woman had very expensive-looking nails and TV-star hair, and Dana found herself unconsciously sitting up straighter as she mirrored the woman's confident posture. There were two people on the other side, and even though Dana could only see the back of their heads, she knew one of them was Wade and the other was DCI Shaw.

The woman in the swanky suit was talking.

'I would like to revisit the question of how you came to be in possession of such detailed knowledge of the contents of my client's personal office area, which caused you to execute a search warrant, but for now, let us address your concerns one at a time.'

The back of Wade's head nodded.

'Go on then. Explain yourself.'

'Of course.' The woman who was obviously Grainger's lawyer continued. 'You found the last will and testament of one Archie Evans.'

'Correct,' said Wade.

'And from this, you inferred that my client had

motive to kill Mr. Evans?'

'That's right. The will says that in the event of Mr Evans' death, control of all his songwriting royalties goes to his management. And, ever since the reunion gig idea was mooted, Mr Grainger has been the manager for the whole band. Seems like a pretty strong motive to me.'

'That isn't exactly what the will says, though, is it?' She tapped a manicured fingernail on the document in front of her. 'To be clear, it says here that control of the songwriting royalties go, in the first instance, to any living relative of Mr. Evans. If none can be found, only then do they revert to management.'

'I think it's common knowledge that Mr. Pox... sorry, Mr. Evans didn't have any living relatives. Isn't that right?' Wade opened his arms out, palms up, as if waiting for a previously undiscovered relative to fall from the ceiling.

The lawyer leaned back in her rickety chair. 'Well, that's not for me to investigate, officer. That's probably more in your wheelhouse. You might want to check into that before accusing my client on this flimsy pretext.'

'Nonetheless,' Wade said on the video. 'He had motive, he had opportunity – he was living right there at the venue, for goodness sake – and he had the means.'

The lawyer smiled. 'From this I assume you refer to the guitar strings in my client's office?'

'I do refer to those very things, in fact,' said Wade, sounding very confident. Almost cocky. 'Our independent expert has confirmed they are the very same kind of strings used in Mr. Evans' murder. Let's hear your client explain his way out of that.'

'Alright then,' said the lawyer. 'My client keeps those strings close at hand for whenever Mr. Green needs a new set.'

Brody, watching over Dana's shoulder, whispered: 'Mr. Green? Is this Reservoir Dogs or something?'

'She means Horgen,' said Dana. 'Hush now.'

'Mr. Green does not buy his own strings,' the lawyer was saying. 'He relies on my client to take care of all the small details like that. My client buys the strings in bulk, both to save money and also to ensure there's always a ready supply on hand for Mr. Green, for maximum convenience all round. In addition, my client tells me that it is well-known that one of the local folk musicians hands these same kind of guitar strings out for free, on the same premises even! Now, in light of the fact that anybody can walk into the venue and put their hands on a set of those strings, do you have any further questions?'

Brody was now leaning so close that when he swore under his breath Dana felt it on the back of her neck.

'She's good, this one,' said Dana.

'Horgen plays guitar?' said Evan. 'I didn't know that.'

Dana sighed. 'Yes. He plays acoustic on a couple of songs in the middle. There's a bit of a mellow part there before they ramp up again towards the end of the show.'

'So it appears,' the lawyer went on, clearly enunciating each word and imbuing each with a dollop of scorn, 'that none of your so-called evidence points to my client. Or certainly not to any stronger degree than it does anyone else who frequented the venue recently.'

'But we found all that stuff in his office.' Wade pressed on, but the back of Shaw's ears were turning red now. Dana was very glad she'd not been in that room with them.

'By that logic,' said the lawyer, 'if I were to kill someone with a gun and then place that gun in your kitchen, you would be guilty of the crime, is that correct?'

'Ah, well, no, not in that situation.'

'I think we're done here, don't you?'

'Hold on,' said Wade.

Shaw finally spoke up. 'Yes, we're done, Miss Heatley. Thank you for your time, and we're sorry to have inconvenienced your client today.'

Suddenly the lawyer was all smiles. 'Not at all, DCI Shaw. So nice to make your acquaintance.' She turned to Wade, and her smile dropped like a sack of wet sand. 'Mr. McNeish. Good day to you.'

The video clip cut off. Dana looked up from her laptop to see that Wade had finished off pretty much all the food while the others were busy watching it.

'Oi! You could have saved some of that for us.'

'And you,' he pointed a hummus-laden finger, 'could have saved me from looking like a fool in front of DCI Shaw.'

'Me? I just showed you the will and the guitar strings. I didn't make you arrest him. In fact, I remember asking you whether it was good enough evidence. You're the one who went ahead with it.'

'Yeah, but you said he was really dodgy. You wanted him locked up.'

'Both those things are still true,' Dana replied.

There was a pause while everyone mulled over the ruinous turn of events.

Eventually, Dana spoke up. 'So, what do we do

now?'

'Get more evidence?' suggested Evan.

Wade shook his head sadly. 'We can't have another crack at him now. The only way we're getting him is if he walks into the station and voluntarily confesses. Or if we unearth something that absolutely positively links Pox's murder with Andrew's attempted murder. And, frankly, I don't think it's likely at this stage.'

There was a scritching sound from the corner of the room, and Dana turned to scold Paws McCartney for the hundredth time for demolishing Mr Two's rocking chair.

'Oh my goodness, Paws, you've ripped this bit right off!' she exclaimed.

She rushed over to haul him off the chair, but as she did she finally noticed what he'd been scratching at. There was a tiny compartment on one of the arms of the chair. She flashed back to the time she'd seen Mr. Two picking at that part of the chair when she spoke to him just before her pre-hire chat with Horgen. She'd thought he was just distracted, but why? What had they been talking about? Dana was pretty sure she'd been telling him about bumping into the kid, Andrew.

Hmmm… to be fair, with Mr. Two he could just as well have been distracted by an interesting air current, or some birdsong.

Anyway. The cunning old larrikin had a secret compartment in his chair! And since Paws McCartney had been trying to break into it for the last twenty-four hours or so, she wondered what kind of… herbs and spices she might find in there.

There were some small pieces of paper or something sticking out. Right, this must be where he kept his roll-your-own supplies, she thought.

She went to close the little wooden top back up, but Paws raced up from under her, grabbed a piece of paper in his teeth, and raced off into the kitchen.

'Naughty cat! Come back here with that.'

She cornered Paws, and distracted him with fancy cat food long enough to safely rescue the piece of paper. Only, it wasn't just a random piece of paper. It was a small photograph.

'Uhhh… guys? You're going to want to see this. I think Paws might have solved the case.'

'Again?' said Brody. 'What's up with that cat?'

An hour later, they were gathered around Dana's kitchen table, with the full contents of the chair's secret compartment spread out in between them.

'Shiiiiiit,' breathed Brody.

'Yup,' said Dana.

'Andrew the roadie is Pox's son.'

'Sure looks like it.'

There were photos from about twenty years ago, showing a young mum with her baby. On the back someone had written 'Harmony and Andrew'.

A series of photos showed the baby growing up. Some of them had notes from Harmony on the back: 'He'd like to meet his father.' Or: 'I'm sorry to be a pain, but Andy needs braces and I can't afford them.'

None of the photos featured Apocalypse BusLane.

'What are we actually looking at here, you guys?' Dana asked. 'Are we thinking that Mr. Two kept this as blackmail over Pox? Or that maybe he was the go-between, sending messages on Pox's behalf?'

'It's impossible to know,' said Wade. 'But I think it's time we had a chat with your gregarious roadie. Oops, wait up.' He plucked his phone out of a pocket. 'Oh, actually, you know what? Apparently Andrew is now well-recovered at the hospital, and ready to talk. Maybe we should go and get his side of the story first?'

Chapter 22: 'Ostible redux

'Thank you, Ms. Osborne, for saving my life,' Andrew croaked. His throat and lungs still hadn't completely recovered from his near-drowning then. But Dana was very pleased to see him looking alive and well.

Dana and Wade stood on either side of the young man's bed. Wade tried not to loom. In general, he wasn't much of a loomer, but the police uniform gave off a certain aura of loomage all by itself that a sensitive officer had to work hard to dispel.

Dana gave the kid an awkward hospital-bed hug. 'You're very welcome, Andrew. How are you feeling?'

He waggled a hand. 'Well, I'm breathing air, which is much better than trying to breathe water, I can tell you.'

Dana shivered as she flashed back to when she

was deep in the river, trying desperately to save the young man. Things could so easily have turned out so much worse, for both of them.

'Hey, listen, we have an officer stationed outside your door, twenty-four hours a day,' said Wade, 'so don't worry about anyone having a crack at you again. I'm pretty sure we'll have the perpetrator in custody very soon, in fact.'

'Really?'

'Yep. Actually, we have something to ask you which might help us track them down.' Wade fished out a plastic bag with the old photographs in it. He took out one or two and showed them to Andrew.

'Oh wow,' he chuckled. 'I see you've been talking to grandad.'

'I'm sorry?' said Wade, 'We don't know who your grandad is.'

'You found these in his rocking chair, am I right?'

'You what?' cried Dana, her jaw almost hitting the floor. 'Mr. Two is your grandfather?'

'Sure. You didn't know?' He waved a photo at them. 'I thought this must mean you figured it out.'

'No. I mean,' Dana floundered for words. 'Gosh, I had no idea. Yes, we found these in Mr Two's rocking chair, but we kind of thought…'

'What? That he'd kept random photos of some young woman and a baby?'

'No!' Dana cried. 'Well, yes, but not like that. We wondered if maybe Pox had fathered a child and then taken off, and Mr Two was helping them – you – out.'

'That's exactly what happened, actually. Didn't grandad Gerry tell you this himself? Wait, is he okay? Has something happened to him?' Andrew started to get visibly agitated, and began coughing terrible, hacking coughs.

'He's fine!' said Dana, still getting her head round the concept of grandad Gerry. 'It's all good, we just came here first because we heard you were ready to talk. We'll catch up with him next, actually.'

Wade cleared his throat. 'Hey, Andrew? Any chance you could tell us who the woman in the photo is?'

'It's my mum, obviously.' Andrew looked at Wade as if he was assessing the policeman's mental capacity.

Wade rolled his eyes. 'Yes, I had gleaned that from the context.' Andrew looked reassured as Wade deployed his fancy words. 'It's just,' Wade went on, 'we were wondering how Mr. um… hey, can we just call him Gerald Twomey from now on? Would you mind? This Mr Two business doesn't really work for me.'

Dana smiled. 'Sure. Okay with you, Andrew?'

'Of course.' Andrew nodded. 'It'll be a relief to just go back to calling him grandad. I had to work hard not to call him that while I was working at the gig.'

Andrew sighed heavily, and that started him off coughing again.

'It's just that… I mean, we wanted to keep it quiet. My dad wasn't…' he teared up a bit, and had to take a drink of water before continuing. 'Sorry. My dad wasn't quite ready to tell everyone about me just yet…'

'I'd like to talk more about that,' said Wade, 'but first, how is Mr. Twomey related to you?' He pointed at the photo. 'Just to be clear. Either this young lady is his daughter, or else, the late Mr BusDepot is his son.'

'BusLane,' Dana hissed.

'My mum is… was… grandad's girl.'

'Was?'

'Yeah, she – 'Andrew was wracked with a coughing fit once again, and this time it finally brought a nurse into the room. They looked Andrew over, clucked their tongue and then shooed Wade and Dana out of the room.

'We'll be back to chat again later,' Wade called out as they were ever so politely given the boot.

Their next stop was Mr Two's house. They didn't call ahead, as he probably wouldn't remember any appointment made anyway.

Dana rang the doorbell, and they waited. And waited.

'Do you think he'll be at the venue?' Wade asked.

'No, I doubt it,' Dana replied. 'There's nothing happening there till later this evening. I wonder where he is. I hope he's okay.'

'You don't think Grainger came around to tie up some more loose ends, do you?'

Dana swore. 'The bastard. If he's done anything to Mr. Two I'll tear his legs off.'

'Sounds like we have probable cause to smash the door in, then.'

'I'll say. Do it, Wade.' Dana stood off to the side as Wade lined himself up for a hefty kick. He hauled back, winding up his leg for a powerful blow near the door's handle. With a bang, the door sprang open easily, as if it hadn't even been latched, let alone locked. Wade wasn't expecting that, and almost lost his balance. The door slammed into the wall behind, then bounced back and caught Wade just as he was righting himself. He went tumbling back into a small, neglected flower garden.

Dana absolutely did not laugh at the policeman

as he picked himself up, dusted himself off, and removed some bedraggled nasturtiums from his ear.

'Okay, ' he grumped, 'I should have maybe tried the handle first, in retrospect.'

'I couldn't possibly comment, officer.'

'You alright there, my son?' came a hoarse voice from the hallway. There stood Mr. Two, wearing nothing but a towel. 'You interrupted me bathing time, young 'uns. But that's all good, all good. Come inter me parlour, said the arachnid to the… buzzy thing… muscoidea, maybe?'

As they followed the mostly naked man into his house, Dana was sure that Wade was thinking the same thing as her: if only Mr. Two had used the towel to cover his waist rather than his shoulders…

Thankfully, he soon muscoidea'd off and quickly returned wearing more normal attire. More normal for him, anyway. A pair of boxer shorts, some woolly socks, and a silky bathrobe covered the principal objectionable areas, rendering the overall display less of a… what would Mr. Two call it? An 'elf and safety hazard.

They settled into his rickety sofa, while Mr. Two offered them an eclectic selection of drinks, not all of which were alcoholic, thank goodness.

Wade accepted a Fanta ('haven't had one of these since I was a kid!'), while Dana took a punt on something that promised healthy gut bacteria and vivid dreams. It was a risk, but she was quietly confident that Mr. Two wouldn't let her ingest anything actively harmful.

'Mr. Twomey,' Wade kicked off. 'We've just been to visit your grandson.'

Emotions warred on Mr. Two's face. Surprise, hope, suspicion, pride and some others that Dana couldn't identify by sight. After a brief skirmish, most of them surrendered the field, and pride won out.

'You mean Andrew, yeah? They called not long ago to tell me he's doing okay.' Mr. Two sighed, and seemed to relax. 'Well, I don't need to keep me gums shut on that particular secret any more, do I? How'd yer find out?'

Dana outlined the superior sleuthing skills of her cat Paws McCartney. Mr. Two nodded in approval. 'Got a mystery needs solving, give it to a cat, I always say.'

'I'm sure,' said Dana, handing the photos back to their rightful owner. The old roadie received them gratefully, rubbing a thumb over them with a fond gaze.

'So, the woman in the photos is your daughter?' Dana prompted.

As soon as she said it, she remembered the first

time she'd visited this house. She'd seen an old photo of a young girl sitting on a guitar amplifier. Mr. Two had clammed up about it back then, but now he no longer had a reason to hide anything.

He was silent for a minute, lost in reverie, nodding.

Eventually he spoke up, voice scratchy with emotion. 'Light o' my lamp, she were. Thump o' me heart. Any fool'd see you could swap a dozen of me for just the one of her, any old day. The very idea that a worn-out old boot like me should still be 'ere breathin', while my darling girl…' He choked up.

Dana shared a glance with Wade. Mr. Two's grief was palpable, and she didn't want to scrape open old wounds, but they needed to know the whole picture. Information about Andrew's mother could be relevant to the case. Of course, it might be completely unrelated, but they wouldn't know till they asked.

Wade pointed a subtle thumb at Dana. Right, she was taking the lead, then. Okay.

'Ah, so, Mr. Two… Gerry. I'm terribly sorry to ask you this, but can you tell us more about your daughter, and Andrew, and why Pox was keeping his relationship with them secret?'

Gerald Twomey, Mr. Two, roadie raconteur, larger-than-life legend, seemed to shrink in on himself before their eyes.

He exhaled so heavily that Wade and Dana, sitting in front of him, would have failed a breathalyser test for the next hour.

Eventually he pulled himself together enough to tell them the story.

It seemed that, in his youth, Apocalypse BusLane had been quite the one for sowing his wild oats, having his cake and eating it too. He wanted all the good times and none of the responsibilities. He partied like it was 1999, and it was pure coincidence that it actually happened to be 1999 at the time. He wanted to live the life of a rock'n'roll star like the ones in the magazines, but the magazines rarely showed any of the hard work, reliability and teamwork that went with becoming a global superstar.

So he just didn't do any of that stuff.

He was dedicated, for sure. And fiercely loyal to his bandmates. They all knew they had something special, and they wouldn't let anything come between them.

This was partly why, when Pox fathered a child, he did what he thought was the right thing, and buggered off, leaving the mother in the lurch.

Or rather, that's what he would've done, had he

not had a visit from an aggrieved Gerald Twomey, who'd just been hired as part of Cranial Bypass' road crew. Mr. Two conveyed his unhappiness with Pox's intransigence in short, sharp words, and the use of some very graphic imagery.

Mr. BusLane had a sudden change of heart on the matter, and agreed he would stand by the young lady and his progeny. But, in the way of rockers in the old days, Pox didn't want any visible ties to the mundane world. He wasn't looking for a relationship. All he wanted was everything that was on offer, all the time.

So, the arrangement between them was thus: Pox would funnel money to the young lady, Harmony, via her dad, Mr. Two. The child would grow up without a chaotic, unreliable, unruly father, but with a loving mother and grandfather, and with some financial security.

None of them would speak of Andrew's paternity, leaving Pox free to live out his wild, ladies' man fantasies.

And that's exactly what happened.

Until…

Mr. Two wiped his nose on his sleeve. Tears fell heavily from his chin as he continued.

'My darling Harmony called me one day, about

six months ago. Said she'd been feeling a bit off for a while. Went and had some tests. They told her she only had a couple o' months to live.

'She wanted to meet with Pox one time before she passed away. Get him in a room with Andrew so they were all together at least once before...' he sniffed. 'You know... Anyway, I didn't hold much 'ope that Pox would say yes, but some little piece of conscience must have stirred in his breastplate, because blow me down he said yes. He didn't look happy about it, but I fink he knew he owed them both that much, at least.

'So he turns up on the day, at a discreet motel unit. He's all ready to hand over some cash and say cheery-bye to them, and then waltz off into the sunset and carry on with his carrying-on ways. I knows this, cos I saw the wad of cash he'd prepared. He showed it to me and asked if it were enough. I told him only he could say that for sure.

Mr. Two wiped his nose again. 'The plonker.' But he said it with affection. After all, Dana knew that he'd worked with Pox for decades, so they must have got on alright for the most part.

'You must have seen some good in him,' she chanced an observation. 'What was he like to work for?'

'Oh, like the knees of a thousand bees, he was!'

said Mr. Two in a most Mr. Two-ish way. 'Good fun, great camaraderie, and he looked after the crew well. He were just a useless dad, is all. Well, he was until that day.'

'What happened?'

'Well, once 'e popped his head inter the motel room, the gravity of the wotsit seemed to hit him. 'E never pulled the cash out his pocket in the end, he just sat down, gave them both an 'ug, and talked. Properly talked to them, like 'e'd never bovvered to before. And, blow me gasket, next fing I know, he's putting Harmony up in a la-de-da 'ospice, only the best will do, and cetera. Then he finds out that Andrew's into music as well, and suddenly they're working on an album together, and all this palaver. Pox is suddenly planning to leave Cranial Bypass, change his ways, make up with all those he's wronged over the years. He promises to set Andrew up properly, but first he's got to arrange a few things, business-wise. He needs to square it with Horgs and his manager, needs to talk to the boys and make sure nobody's left hanging.

'So, he sets Andy up with a road crew job, but asks Andy – and me – to keep shtum about the whole family thing, until he finds the right time to 'ave a conversation with Horgen, Grainger, Ollie and Marty. I mean, 'Pox weren't planning on leaving Cranial Bypass in the lurch, right? He was gonna do the reunion gig. But he'd changed. I could see it was for real. He'd changed. Two decades too late, but he'd become a dad finally. Harmony passed away not long after they met in the motel room. So it was very much too late for me darling girl, but not altogether up the clanger for Andy to 'ave a proper relationship with Pox.

'Along with that,' Mr Two continued, 'Pox had seen the error of his angles in so many fings 'e'd done over the years. Suddenly he was finking about what kind of world he wanted to leave behind when it finally came time for him to sashay over the ol' rainbow bridge. He wanted to leave somefink good for Andy, and try to make the world a better place for 'im to live on in.'

As Mr. Two told it, the only way that Apocalypse BusLane knew how to do that was via the medium of music. Really, what else could he offer? The band hadn't made any serious money for a while. They were literally banking on the reunion show to fix that. But he'd spent decades living a fairytale life where thousands of people hung on his words and the notes from his guitar. If he was going to build something better, those were the tools he could use.

Lucky for Pox, he'd met other people who were trying to use music to move hearts and minds. He recruited Aaron Swetters, folk music activist extraordinaire, and Miriama Tipene-Dawes, with her deep spiritual connection to the land.

'It were all coming togevver nicely, in fact,' said Mr. Two. 'But then…blammo! Pox gets offed just before he makes his big move. And then, someone 'as a go at my Andy.'

He turned his watery eyes to Wade. 'So I very much 'ope you're getting closer to catching the son of a warthog who's responsible.'

Wade shifted uncomfortably on the tattered sofa. 'Actually, Mr. Twomey, there has been a development in that area, in truth.'

Mr. Two clapped his hands together. 'Brilliant! And lemme guess: you've come to offer me five minutes alone in a room with the toe-rag before you arrest 'him?'

Wade rubbed his chin. 'That's not a service the Police provide. But no, I'm wondering if you can provide us with some more information.'

Mr. Two threw his hands up. 'Pffft! Ent I give yer enough already? Criggins, I feel like I just explained me 'ole life to yer, and you want more?'

'What you've told us today goes a long way to establishing motive for the killer,' said Wade in a soothing tone, 'but what I'm looking for now is specifics. Their timetable, usual movements and routines, and specifically, anything out of that routine. Then we can really tie them to the crimes. Both the killing of Pox, and the attempt to kill young Andrew.'

Mr. Two sat a moment, the cogs in his brain trundling along this new track, as he slowly realised the ramifications of what he was being asked.

'You fink it's someone I know?' he growled.

'It's possible,' said Wade. 'We'd like to have more evidence, but we very strongly believe that Trent Grainger is the man behind these crimes.'

Mr. Two sucked in air between his teeth, as if he'd been scalded. He sounded like a vexed tea kettle.

'That's one 'ell of an accusation to level, my amigo.'

'You don't think it was him?' said Dana.

'Ach,' Mr. Two's head bobbed left and right like a dashboard ornament. 'I din't say that now, did I? Phwoah, Trent's a slippery eel and no mistake. And about as empafetic as a rusty bucket. I suppose, if he'd seen some monetary increment in the scene, he could be induced to a spot of light savagery. I'd not 'ave thought he'd stoop so low, so it'd have to be a significant angle to force his 'and in that direction. But what good would it do him to attack my Andy? He's as poor as a church mouse's uncle wiv a gambling problem.'

Dana looked at Wade, who paused, then signalled her to go on.

'We found Pox's will, you see.'

'Did yer now? Just lying about, was it?' He held out his hand and snapped his fingers.

Dana blushed. 'In a manner of speaking.' She handed Mr. Two's keys back to him. 'Ahem. But listen, it said that in the event of Pox's death, all his royalties go to his manager.'

'He hasn't had a manager in donkeys,' Mr. Two broke in. 'Didn't need one, once the band stopped bein' so popular.'

'But now, with the reunion gig on the way, management responsibilities were assumed by Grainger.'

'Hmm… okay, I can see where you're going with that. I 'eard they were selling a goodly amount o' merch and albums online in the lead-up to the gig. But surely Grainger would've wanted to wait till after the gig before he made his killing, so to speak?'

'He probably would've, all things considered, except there's one more clause in the will.' Dana steadied herself before continuing. 'The royalties don't go to Grainger if there's another living relative of Pox.'

'Ahhhh…'

'That's right. And since Pox was about to embark on a whole new musical journey with a different band, he'd have a whole new set of songs with royalties that would never go to Grainger.' Dana shrugged. 'I can only guess that he was thinking that, by killing Pox now, he'd stop him siphoning off interest in Cranial Bypass with his new band, and also there'd be a big spike in interest in the old material. It often happens when an old rocker passes away, doesn't it? Suddenly everyone and their cat is professing to be a fan from way back.'

'You're right about that, my little Labradoodle. Seen it a million times. Never 'eard of it being suggested as an actual career opportunity, but, well, with Grainger I could imagine it.' He scrunched up his face. 'Wait a second, though. We kept quiet about Andy being Pox's son. How would Grainger know about that?'

'I can only assume that Pox finally decided to tell Horgen and the others what he was planning on doing. You said yourself he was going to say something. And with other musicians at the reunion gig already in the know, he could hardly keep it secret for much longer, could he?'

'Too true. It's often been said that a band and its crew runs on cold beer and hot gossip, and the way those guys drink, we were starting to run low on beer.'

'With all that in mind,' said Wade, bringing everyone back to the business at hand, 'can you think of anything that will help us pin down Grainger as the person who killed Pox? If we can get him on that, then nailing him for the attempt on Andrew's life will be much easier.'

'You told me you saw Pox just after he'd been killed, isn't that right?' Dana reminded him. 'Well, Pox's body, I guess I should say.' She shivered. 'You told me you were all ushered out of the venue but nobody was saying why. Did you see Grainger doing anything funny just before that?'

Mr. Two leaned back in his chair, closed his eyes, and took a big breath. 'Let me cogitate on that fer a minute, will you, friends? My old brain cells aren't quite the wotsit they used ter be, you understand?'

'Sure,' said Wade. 'Can I get you anything while you're thinking? A glass of water maybe?'

'I know one thing that'll help me relax, but people wearing uniforms like yours tend not to approve of it.'

'I'm not sure it'd be a great help with your memory, either, quite frankly,' Wade replied, heading out to the kitchen anyway. He popped his head back into the living room two seconds later.

'You were talking about drugs, right?'

Mr. Two, eyes still closed, just smiled.

Dana had time for a glass of water and a walk round the block, and then Mr. Two's eyes snapped open.

'Aha!' he waved a finger triumphantly. 'Yes. I fink I did see the tricksy manager going into Pox's dressing room before all the shit went down. I remember now. I was showing Andy where the spare microphone stands were kept, and we went past Pox's room, and there was Grainger, coming towards us down the corridor.'

'You saw him go into Pox's dressing room?' asked Wade.

'Ahhh… I fink so, yeah. He had some bit o' paper in his hand, and he looked all wound up, like.'

'So Andrew should be able to corroborate this, then?' said Dana.

Wade leaned over and nudged her shoulder with his own. 'Corroborate. Good one. You've been doing your police homework.'

'Yeah,' said Mr. Two. 'Definitely.'

'Right then. This is very helpful, Mr. Twomey,' said Wade, rising from the sofa. 'We'll just need you to come down to the station and make a statement, please.'

'Oh, I can't do that, officer.'

'What?' said Wade, stopping mid-rise. 'Why not?'

Mr. Two jerked a thumb at Dana. 'We got a final dress rehearsal to do, don't we?'

Dana froze. With all the events of the last couple of days, she'd completely forgotten about the impending gig.

'But...' she stammered. 'I mean, that won't be going ahead now, will it? If we arrest Grainger, the whole thing falls apart, doesn't it? Who'll run everything?'

'It's all set up now, my dear,' replied Mr. Two. 'And maybe you haven't 'eard, but the show always goes on.' He stood up and clapped his hands. 'Always. So I'll see you at the venue.' He pointed at Wade. 'And I'll see you at the station afterwards. Right-o?'

Chapter 23: The last practice

Mightily bemused, Dana found herself back at the venue half an hour later. Head in a whirl, she set herself up onstage, and was soon enveloped by the sights and sounds she was becoming very familiar with as part of Cranial Bypass.

Horgen was doing vocal warmups out front. Ollie was searching for that elusive mid-range frequency that would make his bass amp capable of punching down walls. Marty's drum kit seemed to have grown a few extra parts since their last practice. Dana wouldn't have thought it possible, as it already encircled the drummer to the extent that he was in danger of being lost in its labyrinth forever.

Roadies were bustling about, and the lighting tech was testing out the system by, it seemed, blasting a spotlight into Dana's face every two seconds.

In other words, everything was proceeding as normal.

The only difference was, Dana knew that their manager was being arrested for the murder of the late, great Apocalypse BusLane, and nobody else did. Well, except Mr. Two, of course. But no amount of erratic behaviour from him would raise an eyebrow. In fact, it was impossible to define 'erratic' when it came to Mr. Two.

Dana caught the eye of Cass, the drum tech, as she brought in a bracket for some inscrutable piece of percussion. Now it seemed there was at least one other person acting differently tonight.

Because Cass didn't run away from Dana this time. Instead, she approached her once she'd offloaded the drum paraphernalia to Marty. She looked uncomfortable. Maybe guilty? Maybe contrite?

The object of Dana's quest for information about Ziggy now stood right in front of her. After all the times she'd wanted this conversation, Dana suddenly didn't know how to start it.

'Umm... hi,' said Cass, looking at the ground, apparently feeling the same way. 'Listen, I know we're both busy right now, but maybe we can talk later?'

Dana nodded dumbly, speechless.

'Gordon called me,' Cass continued. 'He explained some stuff.' Finally she looked at Dana. 'I owe you an explanation.'

'Right,' said Dana, just as Marty began pounding a beat on his kick drum, and any further discussion was firmly off the table. Cass scurried offstage, and Horgen signalled the start of their first number.

The juggernaut that was Cranial Bypass fell straight into place, and all systems were go. It was a testament to Dana's musicianship that she slotted right in, to the extent that Horgen only seemed to notice her when it was time for her to take a solo in the spotlight.

'Step up, my girl,' he yelled in between numbers. 'You're a bombastic rock star now – act like one!' She moved to the front of the stage and put a foot onto a monitor, at which Horgen gave her a smile and a thumbs-up. 'That's the spirit!'

The set blew by so quickly, Dana felt like she could have played on for another hour easily. Buoyed by the adrenaline of performing, she noodled a wee riff out while the others were starting to pack down.

Ollie looked over, a smile of appreciation spreading on his face. He grabbed his bass back out of its case, plugged back into his amp, and started jamming along. Marty, twigging to what was happening, jumped back behind his kit, and suddenly they were soaring.

The riff she'd been working on to potentially go with the lyrics she and Brody had come up with now felt like a real song. Like one you'd hear on the radio, by a real artist. No longer just a silly little project between friends, once the professional, road-tested musicians joined in, they brought proper authority to it.

Dana was so emboldened by this that, before she could stop to think about it and get all nervous, she stepped up to a microphone and sang.

'My heart in drive, my head in neutral.'

She switched chords, and Ollie followed her seamlessly.

'Gotta find out if the feeling is mutual.'

She didn't have a proper chorus for the song yet, so she just sang the verse lyrics again. By the end of the second line, someone had joined in with a harmony. Dana turned to see Horgen Greymantle, famous rock god, singing along with her song! Well, her and Brody's song, but still. Wow!

Harmony vocals by Horgen – this was too much.

That made her think of Mr. Two's daughter, whose name had been Harmony. That made her think of Harmony's son Andrew being chucked in the river to drown, which made her think of Andrew's father being strangled with a guitar string, and the next thing she knew, the song had fallen to ragged pieces under her fingers.

What was she doing? This couldn't go on. Once the other band members found out she'd snooped around behind their backs, she'd be out on her ear.

Flushed, she hurriedly unplugged her guitar.

'That was great!' Ollie yelled out. 'We should chuck it on the setlist, Horgs!'

Horgen's smile stiffened. 'Well, I mean it was fun, but it needs a bit of work. Let's not get carried away, huh?'

'What's the matter, mate? Worried about having a song on the setlist that you don't own the copyright to?' Ollie laughed.

Marty joined in. 'Yeah, come on Horgs. Throw the newbie a bit of love. If she's that good a songwriter we could have a new album ready in a couple of weeks.'

'It takes more than a clever riff to make a good song,' Horgen grumped. 'You guys don't know what you're talking about. I've worked my arse off on the setlist for Cranial Bypass over the years. If you're looking for new stuff, we should try that song I brought along a couple of months ago.'

'The one in A?' said Ollie. 'Yeah, that had potential.'

'Potential?' roared Horgen. 'It had number one written all over it. Let's give it a bash while we're all here.'

'Okay, sure.'

Ollie and Marty were now looking at Dana expectantly, so she plugged her guitar back in again and waited to see what would unfold.

Marty counted them in, and Ollie began playing a loping bass-line that was crying out for some muted single-note guitar accompaniment, so that's exactly what Dana supplied.

Ollie's face immediately lit up with a grin, and Horgen gave her an approving nod. He sang a verse and Dana listened and watched keenly as Ollie traversed the song's pathways. She followed close on his heels, adding what she thought was needed. She eventually came up with a guitar line that was simple but catchy, and didn't sound like something she'd ripped off from anybody else. Sure, it had traces of her influences in it, but she was fairly sure she'd invented something original, something that sounded cool. Something that sounded like her and nobody else.

Marty's eyes went wide, and he pointed a drumstick at her and then saluted her. It felt good.

Far out, she was writing a song with Cranial flipping Bypass! She was literally writing a song with them right now, in real time.

Once they'd been through it a few times, Horgen wound it down.

'Now that's what I'm talking about!' he yelled. 'Number one hit, you mark my words.'

'Well, it will be, now that Dana's parts are in there,' said Marty.

'You lucky bastard,' Ollie chimed in. 'You went looking for a guitar player and found yourself a gold-star writing partner to boot.'

'Writing partner? Bullshit. That's my song,' Horgen protested.

'I don't think so,' Ollie laughed. 'It's yours and Dana's song now, and it's way better for it too. Take the win, mate. Don't get upset because someone improved your work.'

'You guys don't know shit,' said Horgen, and Dana finally realised he wasn't joking around – he was properly annoyed about this.

Horgen stalked off the stage in a huff, leaving Dana feeling like a naughty kid who'd just upset dad.

Oh well, none of this would matter in a few days anyway. The whole thing was doomed to end, and all because of her. She felt bad about not being honest with the other band members. She felt upset that they would probably kick her out of this world-class band, just as she was hitting her stride. But at least she felt good about having helped catch Pox's killer, and that was absolutely the main thing.

She packed up, lifted her chin to Ollie and Marty, who were babbling excitedly and pointing at her, and then she disappeared into the labyrinth of corridors backstage.

Dana was really no longer in the mood to talk to Cass, but she wasn't about to pass up this opportunity, having waited so long. She planned to put her guitar in the artists' green room out the back, walk outside for some fresh air for a few minutes, and then head back to wait at the side of the stage until Cass had finished doing whatever drum techs did when their drummer employers have finished playing.

Dana knew that drum kits were complex beasts, having sold quite a few herself. Tonight, all the bands were practicing in reverse order, so Cass was now having to tear down most of Marty's kit and set up a new one for Hinemoa and Miriama's band Giant Penguins. Their drummer had some rather unusual percussion items, so that could take a while.

That was fine by Dana. It had been an emotional

rollercoaster of a day, and she welcomed the idea of a few minutes to herself to decompress.

She pushed open the door of the green room, and someone grabbed her by the throat.

Chapter 24: Rocking revelation

Dana's fight/flight/freeze response kicked in, but unfortunately for her it went with freeze.

This couldn't be happening to her, surely? Said an incredibly obtuse, yet obstinate, part of her brain. Grainger wouldn't attack us here, would he? Therefore, let's wait and collect more data before reacting.

Her assailant used their free hand to grab her arm, and then threw her onto the couch, face first.

Her guitar case went clattering off into a corner, as she pushed herself up to see if she could find an escape route past... wait. What the hell?

It wasn't Grainger.

Her attacker was none other than Horgen Greymantle himself.

And by crikey, did he look angry.

'How fucking dare you?' he growled, low and

dangerous like a vicious dog.

'How dare I what?' she wheezed through a rapidly-bruising throat. 'I don't understand what's happening here, Horgen. Is this about Grainger?'

'Grainger?' He kicked the door closed behind him without even looking, and cracked his knuckles. 'What the hell has he got to do with… oh, wait, don't tell me you slept with him?'

'Piss off!' said Dana, getting angry herself now. 'You went straight to "she must have slept with him" did you? Come on, that's pathetic.'

'Well, what are you talking about then? Actually, I don't give a shit. I'm not here about Grainger. You know what you did.' He stalked closer.

Dana's anger asked to be excused, and went and hid behind her fear. This was not good. She was shut in a room with a man who looked angry enough to… oh. She realised that he actually looked angry enough to kill. The picture that she and Wade had so carefully been building up over the last couple of days started to fall apart before her eyes. Could it be they'd been looking at the wrong man?

But how could that be? Why would Horgen murder his long-standing bandmate, and ruin the good thing they had going?

Horgen began to pace in front of her, spitting out his rage. 'You think you can just swan on in here and start writing songs, do you? Songs for my band?' He jabbed a finger at her. 'You were hired to do one thing. Play the fucking guitar and look good.'

Dana swallowed a retort about that being two things. It didn't seem like a great time to bring it up. Also, she'd been told that she'd been hired purely for her guitar skills, and now he had the cheek to say it was because of her looks? What a dick.

Still, this was a conversation she'd prefer to have at a later time, and preferably on a video call rather than in person. She would never relax again until there was at least a kilometre between herself and this enraged version of Horgen Greymantle. If she could just get out of this room alive…

Horgen took her silence for acquiescence.

'That's right, now you look all sorry about it. Trying to take a cut on my song! The bloody nerve. I wrote the damn thing, you just put a pretty little flourish on top, got it, you daft slag?'

Dana's mouth hung open. Was this really the same guy who'd been so amenable when he hired her? She scanned the room for a weapon. If this really went south she knew she wouldn't be able to overpower Horgen – he was much bigger than her.

Horgen paced closer, and her heart pounded in her chest. Her eyes flashed around the room. Damn!

Nothing useful was within her reach, just some cushions, a guitar magazine, and… oh dear! A musician had foolishly left their cherished double-neck instrument in the room. It was lucky for her, of course, but it was an instrument she knew all too well, sadly. Could she…? *Should* she use it in self-defence?

'I won't let you get away with it,' Horgen ranted on. 'I didn't let Pox take his songs to another band, why would I let you?'

Dana's blood ran cold. There it was, the reason why Horgen had killed his oldest friend. She tried to keep him talking while she scooched slowly over to the side of the couch towards her intended makeshift musical weapon.

'Did you really kill him because of that?' she asked. 'Just for money?'

'Just for money?' Horgen spat. 'It wasn't just for the money. What about the disrespect? He had to start a new band to write those songs, did he? Taking up with those hippie freaks. Trying something new, he said. But we've always been the most progressive band around. He could have done anything with Cranial Bypass, and we all would have gone along with it. Okay, yes, I was annoyed that he wanted us to sell our publishing rights too, that was a step too far. The idealistic prick.'

'What?' Dana gasped. 'Why would he want to sell your publishing rights? Isn't that the biggest part of your income?' She scooted a little further along. Almost there…

'I know, right!' Horgen was apoplectic. 'After touring and merch, of course, but yeah. He'd gone all fucking la-di-da, save the world kind of bullshit. Wanted to sell the rights for a big sum and give it all to an environmental charity. I told him he was fucking enviro-mental if he thought I'd go along with that. And all for what? Because some kid had turned up and called him daddy? What a load of crap. I wasn't going to sit by and let him sign away our hard work for that. No way. So I…' Horgen faltered, his nostrils flaring. 'I had to do it, you see, don't you?'

Just a little further and Dana would be there. She kept slowly scooting her butt across the couch. 'And then you tried to kill Andrew too?'

'Bastard!' Horgen growled. 'I thought that getting rid of Pox would be the end of it, but then the next day Trent tells me about his will. How everything would go to that little shit, when everybody knows it should rightfully be mine. I've been doing this for decades, me and Pox did it all, and now this little prick turns up and thinks he can just take it?' His voice had risen and risen until now the veins were standing out in his neck. He shook his head. 'No. Enough. And enough of this blabbing too. I'm sick of it. I'm sick of people turning up and thinking they can take what's mine. I've had it.'

He rushed at Dana, and she dodged to the side. Her fingers made contact with the bulky instrument she'd spied, just as Horgen reached out and put his hands around her neck.

She wasn't going to freeze again, that's for sure.

Dana got a good grip on one neck of the double-necked instrument, swung with all her might at Horgen's head, and smash! There was an almighty twang, and pieces of wood went flying everywhere as Aaron Swetters' beloved bass-banjo gave its life that Dana might live. She hoped.

Horgen had taken some of the blow on his shoulder, but it was enough to make him loosen his grip. Dana wriggled away from him, then ran for the door. But just before she got there, a hand grabbed her ankle, and she went down.

She sprang back up again, but Horgen was upon her straight away. He aimed a punch at her kidneys that she managed to mostly dodge. She'd feel that later. If there was a later.

The next bit happened in slow motion. She could see him step forward again for another punch, and just before his foot touched down, she channelled her inner Johnny Lawrence. Turning her body just a little was all it took to bring her own foot around, tap his ankle and sweep his leg to the side. This left him perfectly off-balance, as suddenly he had nothing to plant his weight on. Now that she had control of his centre, and she was already turning her waist slightly to the right, it was so easy to bring up her palm and smack it under his chin.

He went backwards in a heap, falling onto the couch that she'd only recently vacated.

Dana turned and yanked the door handle, screaming for help. Horgen was already getting up and shaking off her attack. A low growl came from his throat. The vicious dog was back.

The hairs on the back of Dana's neck stood up. She didn't know if the door was locked or just stuck, but she didn't have the bandwidth to deal with that right now, so she simply kept frantically tugging at the door handle as Horgen advanced, dripping with anger.

He took a swing at her head, which she ducked away from, but it meant she had to abandon the door. Skirting the outside of the room, Dana tried to keep one eye on Horgen while she looked for anything else she could use as a weapon.

There was nothing, damn it! She resorted to throwing cushions at him to keep him occupied while she attempted to edge back towards the door.

His focus entirely on Dana, Horgen didn't notice when the door opened behind him, and DCI Shaw stepped through.

She took one look at the situation, then calmly walked over, picked up one of the broken-off necks from the bass-banjo, and clocked Horgen so hard he went down like a detuned guitar.

'Hi, Dana,' she deadpanned, chucking the instrument neck onto a pile of other broken pieces. 'I hope you know a good instrument repair shop.'

Chapter 25: Debrief, and Cass

'Tell me again,' Brody begged. 'Pleeeeease?'

Dana was recovering – or at least, attempting to – back at her flat. Lying on the couch being pampered by Evan, and pestered by Brody, who was incensed at missing out on all the "fun stuff" as he called it.

It certainly hadn't felt much like fun to Dana at the time, being assaulted by an enraged rock star, even if he had been one of her childhood heroes. Urgh, she might never be able to listen to a Cranial Bypass song again as long as she lived. Well, maybe just the guitar solo parts – she was still a big fan of Apocalypse BusLane after all, may he rest in the realm of rock'n'roll perpetuity.

Anyway, Shaw had arrested Horgen as he was trundled out of the venue on a hospital stretcher, barely conscious, and then Wade turned up and took Dana to hospital for her own checkup. When he dropped her home, he'd insisted on staying over, sleeping on her couch. But, since he'd already called Brody and Evan to tell them she was okay, they'd turned up too, and once they were assured she was fine, it had morphed into a bit of a party. They celebrated the successful conclusion of the case by staying up late and arguing over the playlist on Dana's stereo. At least, the guys had – Dana took herself off to bed early, and planned to spend the whole of the next day there too if she could manage it.

Wade had toddled off to work the following morning, leaving her in this current situation. With Evan making her some rather fabulous soup, and Brody constantly asking for detailed action replays.

Dana sighed. 'I've already told you, Brodes. Shaw came in and smacked him on the head with one of the necks from the bass-banjo I'd already broken.'

'Yeah, yeah, I got that bit, but rewind a bit and tell me again about what Ollie and Marty said about our song.'

Dana laughed. 'Right. Well, it doesn't matter how much they liked it now, does it? I think that ship has sailed. There won't be much in the way of a Cranial Bypass reunion gig now that one of the founding members is dead and the other's in jail.'

Brody frowned. 'I know. Still, they said they liked the song, though, right? That's pretty awesome.'

'Yes, Brody.' Dana smiled. 'It really is.' She felt a warm glow spread through her body as she reflected on how it had felt to stand on a stage, however briefly, with such talented musicians, and to be accepted as their equal. It must be how Ziggy felt when he got picked up to tour with his first big act. Well, Dana would never set foot on any of the big stages that Ziggy had. She wasn't the type to tour the world, she preferred her wee shop and her cosy flat. But it definitely was a nice feeling to have been part of that world for a little while, and to know that she was good enough to do that if she wanted to.

There was a knock at the door, and Evan went down to see who it was.

'Ah, I'm sorry, mate.' His voice came up the stairs. 'She's not seeing anyone today'

'She'll bloody well see me,' another voice reverberated through the stairwell.

Dana sighed. She knew that annoying voice, and she also knew that the annoying person it belonged to would probably stay there being annoying until she relented. Might as well get it over with.

'Let him up, Evan,' she called out.

There was some grumbling, and then Evan

appeared at the top of the stairs.

'There's someone here to see you, Dana,' he announced, his voice dripping with disapproval. 'And he's promised he won't stay long.' He glared at the visitor.

Grainger bowed his head in acknowledgement. 'Yeah, I got the message, kid.' He looked around Dana's wee apartment with disdain. 'Nice place you got here, Osborne. Kind of…small. Suits you.'

'Beats living in your office at the back of a pub, I'd say,' she retorted.

'I told you, that's just temporary. Especially now.' He flashed her a completely fake smile, and handed her a bouquet of wilting petrol-station flowers. 'My stocks are on the up, darl… Dana.' She noticed that he'd caught himself mid-darling, and begrudgingly admitted that at least he was learning. Slowly. A leopard might not change its spots, but could perhaps rearrange them in a more pleasing manner if necessary.

'Your stocks are up?' she asked. 'Or Horgen's? I'm guessing that you have a controlling interest in his share of the songwriting royalties now.'

'Could be, guitar girl, could be indeed. Anyway, I just wanted to pop in and say no hard feelings for trying to get me sent to jail for a crime I didn't commit. Water under the bridge and all that.'

Dana got the impression he was quite used to being accused of crimes, as he really didn't seem bothered at all. The money probably helped, and let's face it, most of that was thanks to Dana. She'd put Horgen in jail, and increased the publicity around Cranial Bypass in the process. That had to be good for Grainger's wallet.

'Well, that's kind of you,' she allowed. 'I just hope that Ollie and Marty aren't too put out by all this. I'd like to speak to them personally and try to explain myself. Try to make it up to them if I can.'

'Make it up to them?' Grainger shrugged. 'Tell them whatever you like, as long as you're at the gig.'

'What do you mean, at the gig?'

'Whoah, you didn't think I was gonna cancel the gig, did you? You can't back out now. The boys are looking forward to playing with you.'

'They are?'

'Damn right they are. Now that young Armageddon BusLane's been brought in as lead vocalist, it's all coming up roses, isn't it?'

'Armageddon BusLane?'

'Pox's boy, Andrew.'

Dana threw her head back and laughed at the sheer audacity and persistence of Greasy Grainger. Give him a pile of muck and he'd sift gold out of it.

You just can't keep a bad man down, it seemed. He'd really managed to turn this whole sorry mess into a marketable spectacle.

And, Dana had to admit, the thought of playing the gig after all was very satisfying.

'You're a terrible man, Mr. Grainger,' she said. 'It's a pleasure doing business with you.'

'Speaking of which,' he replied. 'I've taken the liberty of drafting an updated version of our contract.'

'No!'

'Just look it over, will you?'

'Get out, now, please.'

He held up his hands in surrender, and started to back out of the room.

'Alright, alright. See you at the next practice. I've even assigned Pox's dressing room to you.'

'Wait a minute.' She'd just remembered what Mr. Two had said, about seeing Grainger on his way to Pox's dressing room with a piece of paper in his hand. 'Did you go and talk to Pox, just before he was murdered?'

Grainger turned back to her and grinned. 'Yeah, I did. What of it?'

'Why were you there? We thought maybe you were angry at him, and went to confront him about his will.'

'Ha! Far from it. No, I went to discuss a new business opportunity. After he told me he was going to start a new band with his kid and the other lunatics – I mean, musicians – I thought I'd better get in quick and sign them to my record label. Before some scumbag got in there and ripped them off, you know.'

He winked, and left.

'Huh,' said Brody. 'I don't think I like that guy.'

'I don't think he cares, Brody.'

They'd barely had two minutes to digest Grainger's news when another knock came at the door.

'No,' said Dana, and sent Evan down to get rid of whoever it was.

It didn't work. He soon reappeared, with a bulky shape looming behind him. Dana sat up straight and adjusted her slightly soup-stained top. She always felt like a schoolgirl when DCI Shaw appeared, for some reason.

'I couldn't tell the police to bugger off,' Evan apologised, sotto voce.

'That's fine, Ev,' said Dana. 'I'm quite happy to see my rescuer.' She pitched her voice so that Shaw would hear. Hopefully she was only here to check up on Dana, not to tell her off for interfering in another investigation. Even though Wade had asked her to, Dana was certain that Shaw wouldn't be happy about it.

'How are you feeling today?' Shaw asked.

'I'm good, thanks.' Dana realised it was true. She was feeling good. She'd helped solve another case, and she had a very cool gig lined up. The shop was doing well under Brody and Evan's care, and Mr. Two had left his rocking chair for Paws McCartney, as he seemed to have claimed it as his reward for helping uncover Pox's killer.

All things considered, things had turned out better than she could have hoped.

Evan offered Shaw a cup of tea, which she took, and sat opposite Dana, watching her intently.

'You appear to be making a habit of this, Ms Osborne,' said Shaw.

'Like a nun with a sewing machine,' Brody observed.

Shaw gave him a look, and he suddenly found something interesting to look at out the window.

'So,' Shaw continued, 'you decided to go undercover, putting yourself in danger, dragging my Detective Constable into your hare-brained scheme and potentially ruining his career. Is that pretty much the size of things?'

'Hey, now,' Dana protested. 'Wade asked me to

do it.' Oops. It hadn't taken long for her to drop poor Wade right in it.

Shaw chuckled, and took a sip of her tea.

'I know, Dana.'

'What?'

'I knew all along. Why do you think I was there all the time? I was keeping an eye on you.'

'Oh.' Dana felt foolish for not spotting that Shaw had gone undercover to watch over Dana while she went undercover to watch the musicians. Poetic justice, she supposed.

'Surely you didn't think Wade would throw you in the deep end like that without backup?'

'Well, I kind of… you know… handled myself fine the last time,' Dana mumbled.

'Sure, that sounds about right,' said Shaw with a healthy dollop of sarcasm. 'In fact, didn't I save you that time as well? I seem to recall turning up just as you and wee Brody here were about to get your heads caved in by Devon Stevens.'

Dana blushed. 'Okay, yes, that's true.'

'I know.' Shaw shook her head ruefully. 'So that's why, even though I agreed with Wade that we needed you to go undercover for this case, there was no way I was going to leave you on your own.'

'Well, it's nice to know you care. Thank you, DCI Shaw.' Dana felt glad to have a friend like her.

'No indeed, we'd have been in all kinds of trouble with the boss if something went wrong. Plus the paperwork! My goodness, the damn paperwork would've been debilitating.' She sipped her tea, but Dana could swear she caught a cheeky smile edging onto the corners of Shaw's mouth all the same.

A lightbulb went on in Dana's head. 'Wait, is that why you were there so quickly when I dragged Andrew out of the river?'

Shaw grimaced. 'Yes, I'm sorry I wasn't there to help you sooner. I just didn't have a good excuse to follow you along the river path at night, without tipping my hand, so I had to hang around at the venue. When I noticed that your car had been sitting there for a while, I finally went out to have a look for you. I truly am sorry about that, Dana. I thought you would only be in danger at the venue itself. You acquitted yourself very well, but we could have lost you then, and that would have been a shame.'

'Wow, now you're really starting to sound like a recruitment officer. Where do I sign?'

'Haha and no,' said Shaw in a voice like a brick hitting concrete. 'This was a one-time thing, and I definitely do not want to see you anywhere near any police business again, are we clear?'

Dana had heard this before, but was quite happy

to give her assent again. She had quite enough on her plate now without all this undercover business. Maybe someone else could have a go next time. Actually…

'Hang on, how come Wade asked me to go undercover, when your Hinemoa was already there?'

Shaw snorted. 'Ask her to investigate her own band members? I don't think so. Imagine how well that would have gone down if word got out. Also, technically she was a suspect herself, so I wanted to keep her hands squeaky clean.'

The corner of Dana's mouth quirked up. 'But you didn't mind a bit of muck on my hands, huh?'

'Hey,' Shaw demurred, 'you're the one who keeps saying you're good at this investigation stuff, right?'

'Well, yeah I guess I am good at it, actually,' said Dana, mollified. Though she'd been through some twists and turns, she'd come up with the results. Again.

'Was that Trent Grainger I spotted on my way in?' Shaw changed tack. 'He of the refrigerated mouth.'

'Pardon?'

'Butter wouldn't melt.'

'Oh. Gotcha. Haha.'

'That guy narrowly avoided being arrested yesterday. In fact, I'd still be keen to arrest him anyway. He definitely looks like he's been up to something.'

'You're not wrong, he is always up to something,' Dana agreed. 'It's just hard to figure out exactly which dodgy thing to arrest him for. It's like trying to fish for a single whitebait with your bare hands. There's too many of them, and they all slip past.'

Shaw took her leave, and eventually even Brody's interrogations petered out, leaving Dana in blissful repose for the remainder of the day.

Until her phone rang.

She answered it with a cheery, 'I'm not here'.

'That's good,' came the voice of Mr. Two, 'you must be on your way to The Riffery then?'

'I don't think so,' said a bemused Dana. 'Why would I be doing that?'

'You left your guitar 'ere in all the palaver last night.'

Dana laughed. 'I'm not worried about that, I'll pick it up tomorrow.'

'You wanna come down 'ere, trust me, my dear.'

Something in his voice made her take note.

Vexed, and curious, she reluctantly bade farewell to her cosy flat once more.

On arrival, she was greeted with the sound of an off-key police siren wailing. Or perhaps it was a whale, somehow stranded several kilometres from the shore?

Dana, ever a slave to her curiosity (a trait she must have picked up from Paws McCartney, she mused), followed the soul-tearing sound through the warren of corridors at the back of The Riffery, till she found herself at the door of the green room. The very same room where, the night before, Horgen Greymantle had attempted to wring the songwriting royalties out of her by force.

What kind of horrible thing was going on in there today? Well, she couldn't just turn on her heel now – she had to know.

She used her toe to nudge the door open a tiny crack.

To her surprise, it looked like there were two men in there, kneeling down in front of a small mound of sticks and… maybe praying? No, that couldn't be right, one of them had their arm around the other.

Abruptly, she realised she was watching Mr. Two attempting to console Aaron Swetters over the ruins of his beloved bass/banjo. The instrument which Dana had smashed to smithereens on Horgen when he attacked her.

Mr. Two must have heard something because he

looked up and spotted her. With a pat on Aaron's shoulder, he got up and reverently backed his way to the door where Dana stood.

'I should probably go and say something to him,' she whispered.

'Aye, 'e might appreciate a wee eulogy from yerself, it's true.'

'I wish I hadn't had to break it. I know how attached you can get to an instrument, especially a unique one like that.'

Mr. Two shrugged. 'Well, don't punch yerself in the guts too hard about it.' He leaned in to whisper in Dana's ear. 'Everyone else in the building is mighty relieved that the damn thing has become kindling.'

Dana stifled a snorting giggle at that.

'I am going to get it restored,' Dana said. 'I'm not a complete monster.'

'Well, again,' Mr. Two retorted, 'there's some 'ere who'll think you're a monster if you do make it playable again, so don't go rushing into it, alright?'

He winked.

'Oi, 'ere's your guitar,' he went on, grabbing it from where it sat next to the door and handing it to her.

'Thanks,' said Dana. 'Ummm… so, is that it? Can I go home now?'

Mr. Two solemnly shook his head. 'Follow me, duckling.'

He took off deeper into the bowels of the building. Past even the areas that Dana knew, and she knew most of them. But Mr. Two led her down in the deep dark to where the road crew dwell. Nobody else would dare set foot in these places without being accompanied by an initiate, a monk of musical machinery. If Dana hadn't been following Mr. Two, she'd have fled.

She wondered what he was up to.

As they walked, Mr. Two ruminated aloud on the fallout of Dana's investigation.

'Broke me 'eart when it turned out to be Horgs what did for Pox, after all.' Dana translated that in her head to I was terribly sad to learn that Horgen killed Pox.

'I know,' she replied. 'I'd have thought they were like brothers.'

'Wot, like Cain and Abel, you mean?'

Dana gave a sad chuckle. 'Alright, you got me there. Maybe found family was more the vibe I was looking for.'

Mr. Two sighed a heavy sigh. 'They were that, for sure. And I guess that were it, in the final wotsit. Horgs loved being Pox's equal but couldn't stand the thought of not being needed. If Pox took off and wrote songs without 'im, and brought my dear Andrew into the fold instead, ol' Horgsy must have felt it like a stiletto to the ventricles.

He said darkly, "E should never have messed with my Andrew though. That were purely about the moolah, no matter what he said otherwise. Turning a body into a corpse just for a few dollars…' he shivered. 'That's arctic cold, that is.'

Dana wholeheartedly agreed. Personally, she thought that it was the break with Pox had tipped Horgen over the edge. He couldn't handle the thought of Pox going off and making music without him, and it broke his mind. She preferred to think so, rather than struggle with the idea that Horgen could have done what he did while completely rational. Now it was Dana's turn to shiver.

Eventually they arrived at what Dana assumed was the interior of a lean-to at the very back of the building. Corrugated iron plinked discordant notes as the sun warmed the roof. The smell of fretboard oil and kick drum grease hung heavy in the air, seasoning the humans within the room by seeping into their pores.

It was gloomy in there, so it took Dana a second to spot Cass in the corner, sitting on a drum stool, fidgeting with a hi-hat clutch.

'I'll leave you to it,' said Mr. Two softly, and he left the room.

Dana gently put her guitar down, not wanting to spook the other woman with fast movements, still worried that she'd race out of the room rather than talk to her.

But Cass stayed on her stool, and indicated another one for Dana to sit on.

'Did Gordon talk to you?' Dana ventured.

Cass nodded.

'So he told you why I wanted to talk to you? I'm not here to make your life difficult, I only want to find out what happened to Ziggy.'

Cass took a breath and looked up to the ceiling. Dana thought she looked like she was trying not to cry.

'Hey, Gordon told me that you and Ziggy were… together,' said Dana. 'I'm fine with that, if that's what you're worried about.'

'It's not that,' Cass finally spoke. 'It's…'

'It's what?'

Cass broke down and sobbed. 'I killed him!' she wailed. 'It's all my fault.'

Dana's jaw dropped. 'What are you talking about?'

Cass thumped a fist on her thigh, a look of immense frustration and self-recrimination on her face. 'I introduced him to these guys I knew. They were bastards, one and all, and I didn't like them hanging around, but I'd gotten to know them from working on some other gigs over the years, so when they turned up at the motel room and demanded to meet Ziggy, I thought it better to let them in than start a fight. Ziggy had no idea, he thought they were just some run of the mill crazy roadies, and you know what he was like, he thought everyone was nice like him.'

'Anyway, they all started drinking, and then this guy Boris threw me his car keys and sent me out to get more beer. I didn't want to go, but they weren't the kind of guys you argued with. I took Ziggy's guitar with me because I had a suspicion they would steal it if I let it out of my sight for more than two seconds.'

'I came up with a plan that, when I got back, I'd ask Ziggy to come out and help me bring the beer in from the car, but then actually we'd just take off together. But…'

Cass bit her lip, and looked down at the floor. 'When I went to drive back to the motel, the car wouldn't start,' she wailed. 'The guy from the liquor store said he'd give me a jump start, but customers kept turning up. And by the time I eventually got going, it had been about an hour since I left. I raced back, hoping they hadn't convinced Ziggy to go off somewhere else with them, but when I opened the door, they'd all gone, and left him…' she sobbed, 'by himself, on the sofa.' Her voice broke as she continued. 'He wasn't breathing, and I could see a bottle of pills on the floor and…Boris and his friends had obviously started giving Ziggy the pills, since I hadn't come back with the beer, and he'd passed out, and they'd just left him.'

Dana's heart stuttered. She had to remind herself to breathe.

Cass raised her eyes. 'I panicked, Dana. I lost my mind. I'm so sorry. I just took off. I felt so guilty, but if I told the police what had happened, well… Boris knew people who could make you disappear.'

She sniffed. 'After a while, I couldn't bear to have Ziggy's guitar in the house, reminding me of him every day. Reminding me of what I'd done. So I sold it to a collector. I should have brought it to you, I know, but I… I just couldn't face you, Dana. Couldn't face telling you what I'd done.'

Once Cass finished, Dana was quiet for a long time. There was a world of hurt to take in, and only one small heart to hold it. She was furious with Cass. She felt sorry for Cass too. She wanted to punch her and hug her and have a good cry with her. They were both in pain, and Dana didn't know how they'd both feel about everything tomorrow, and she didn't know if she'd ever be able to speak to Cass again, but there was one thing she did know: at very long last, she finally knew the truth about her brother's death, and that was just going to have to be enough for now.

She stood up, and Cass watched her with trepidation, perhaps expecting an outburst. But Dana had so many things to say that they were blocking up her throat. In the end, all she could do was give Cass a nod in farewell.

She picked up her guitar and left.

Chapter 26: At home at last

When she got back to her car, there was an envelope tucked under the wiper. Tearing it open, she discovered a photo. On the back of which Mr. Two had written: *To Dana. Many thanks for saving my grand-boy. You'll always be road crew to me, my duckling.*

Dana flipped it over, and a warm smile spread across her face.

She arrived home in a swirl of emotions, which Paws McCartney completely ignored, instead choosing to weave between her feet and demand food.

'Fair enough, Pawsy, you deserve it,' she told him as she filled his dish. 'You helped me find the killer. Again. Who's a clever kitty?'

Paws didn't bother answering, because they both

knew it was him.

Dana found a frame, popped the photo in it, and set it on her table, next to a photo of her and Ziggy when they were kids.

Paws jumped up on the table, in the manner of a cat who is strictly forbidden to do so, and rubbed his cheek on the photo frame.

Dana gathered him into her lap, and patted him as she sat gazing at the new photo.

In the centre, Apocalypse BusLane beamed at the camera, looking much older and more weather-beaten than in any of his official publicity photos, but one hundred times more genuinely happy. On one side, his arm was around the shoulder of his son Andrew, who stood awkwardly, looking much more self-conscious than Pox but no less pleased. On his other side was Harmony, pale and thin, and, if not overjoyed, then at least satisfied, and maybe even a little hopeful.

Paws kneaded Dana's thighs for a minute, digging his claws painfully into her legs. Then finally, with a bone-shaking purr, he settled down for some quality sleeping time.

Dana pondered the ups and downs of human existence. Life was like a prog-rock song, as far as she could tell. There were loud bits and quiet bits. Fast and slow. Many different tempo changes. And you could never really tell from the start how it would end. All you could do was press play, and hope.

Darn it, she should have made a cup of tea before Paws settled in. Now she was stuck there. Oh well.

Paws twitched. Perhaps in a dream he was chasing something, or maybe solving another case. Dana smiled and stroked him some more.

'Nice work, Paws McCartney. Nice work.'

About the Author

Bing Turkby lives in Aotearoa with his wife and an assortment of feline landlords.

He makes music with Heavy Blarney and The Bing Turkby Ensemble

Find more books by Bing at turkby.co.nz

Sign up to the mailing list to hear about new releases and special offers.